PENGUIN BOOKS
BBC BOOKS

This Life

Sam Colman is a pen-name for William Sutcliffe, whose two novels, *New Boy* and *Are You Experienced?*, have been described by the press as 'both very modern and timeless', 'fresh and wonderful' and 'very funny indeed'. He lives in London.

This Life
A Novelization

Sam Colman

PENGUIN BOOKS
BBC BOOKS

PENGUIN BOOKS
BBC BOOKS

Published by the Penguin Group and BBC Worldwide Ltd
Penguin Books Ltd, 27 Wrights Lane, London W8 5TZ, England
Penguin Putnam Inc., 375 Hudson Street, New York, New York 10014, USA
Penguin Books Australia Ltd, Ringwood, Victoria, Australia
Penguin Books Canada Ltd, 10 Alcorn Avenue, Toronto, Ontario,
Canada M4V 3B2
Penguin Books (NZ) Ltd, 182–190 Wairau Road, Auckland 10, New Zealand

Penguin Books Ltd, Registered Offices: Harmondsworth, Middlesex, England

First published by Penguin Books and
BBC Books, a division of BBC Worldwide Ltd, 1997
10 9 8 7 6 5 4 3 2 1

Based on the television series
produced by World Productions Ltd
for the BBC

BBC™ used under licence

Set in 10/13.5pt Monotype Galliard
Typeset by Rowland Phototypesetting Ltd, Bury St Edmunds, Suffolk
Printed in Great Britain by Clays Ltd, St Ives plc

Contents

Part One

Chapter 1

Reunions

The light, chopped up by a venetian blind, slices into the boardroom, falling on to the faces of six dark-suited men. One of them, sitting in the centre, is on a chair slightly higher and plusher than the others: Hooperman – the boss. Overweight, his face radiates the complacent but slightly forced *bonhomie* of a man who loves being in charge, but who wishes he was ten years younger. Hooperman is trying to read the one-page CV on the table in front of him, but his thoughts are wandering – to a veranda in Tuscany, and a glass of chilled white wine.

On his left sits Graham, dourly examining another copy of the same CV for the third time. His eyes scan up and down the page, checking the dates for potential inconsistencies, picking out and mentally underlining exaggerations and distortions in the applicant's account of her life.

On Graham's left sits Miles – more than twenty years younger than the other two. He hasn't got past the heading at the top of the CV. ANNA FORBES, it says, in large type. He knows that name from somewhere. He has definitely met someone with that name before. He doesn't know who she is, or where they might have encountered each other, but for some reason his groin is quietly stirring under the boardroom table.

On Hooperman's right are three more Suits – the kind of blank-faced men you find in City law firms – smartly dressed, but utterly forgettable. Just Suits.

The door opens, and Anna enters, legs first. Before her torso has even entered the room, Anna has made a favourable impression.

Slightly thrown by the beauty – and sheer scope – of leg on view, Hooperman somehow forgets to ask Anna to sit down.

'Anna – we'd like you to tell us who you are.'

'What do you mean?'

'Take a seat,' says Graham.

Anna sits, noticing that the chair is still warm from the previous interviewee.

'Something about your childhood. Was it a happy one?'

'I'd say no,' she replies. 'Definitely not a happy childhood.'

'Why was that?'

'My father left when I was eleven, and my mother went to bed with a pack of Temazepam. She's still there.'

Anna scans the faces of the panel for a reaction. Nothing. Stony faces all round. Except – she notices one face at the end of the table. It's smirking. She does a double take and finds herself blushing. *Shit! Miles! The official Public-School Dream Boy from college. What the hell is he doing on an interview panel? And when was it they'd shagged?*

She drags her attention back to the rest of the interview panel and, desperately trying to salvage the interview, says, 'Is this the kind of thing you want?'

'Do you take drugs yourself?' says Graham.

'There have been nights when I've lost it. I've always found it again in the morning, though.'

She grins.

Graham stares back.

Hooperman's eyes are slightly glassy. He's still in Tuscany, and hasn't really heard anything Anna has said. 'Tell us, Anna,' he says, 'why do you want to be a barrister?'

'For the money,' she replies, confidently.

The entire interview panel suddenly stop stroking their chins and their arms fall in shock on to the table. The room reverberates to the sound of five Rolex watches thumping on to mahogany, slightly muffled by a layer of Yves Saint Laurent shirt cuff. This is *not* the thing to say. One doesn't go into law for the money. One enters the legal profession for . . . for . . . just, not for the money.

* * *

A few hundred metres away, separated by millions of pounds' worth of real estate and thousands of unfeasibly wealthy lawyers, Egg, an old friend of Anna's, is entering a large building: the offices of Moore Spencer Wright Solicitors. He, too, has a job interview.

He hovers outside the interview room, pacing up and down. *I will get this job. I will get this job.* Then he catches sight of himself in a mirror. *Why do I look such a twat in a suit?* He remembers back at college, the first time he ever saw Miles put on a suit – and it looked like Miles had just arrived home after a long journey – like he had just put on his real skin for the first time. When Egg puts on a suit, he immediately looks shorter, poorer and younger. Miles in a suit looks taller, richer and older.

Egg checks the mirror again. *Shit. I'm never going to get this job.*

Egg's interview is held by O'Donnell, the head of the firm. The questions turn out to be the usual tedious stuff Egg was expecting but, somehow, he can't muster any decent responses. Boring questions – boring answers. Although he doesn't want to admit it to himself, he also took an instant dislike to O'Donnell from the moment he walked into the room. There was something slimy about him – a false friendliness – a greasy charm that somehow didn't even seem to be making a pretence at sincerity. This dislike, Egg reflects, was bound to have been mutual. These things never travel on a one-way ticket. Antipathy always buys a return.

There is one glimmer of hope, however. When they had got on to the subject of football in general, and Manchester United in particular, a flash of interest had sparked across O'Donnell's face, and they had both suddenly been at enormous pains to clarify that they weren't just fair-weather supporters, and had been even bigger fans when the team was crap. In fact, they had gone on to spend almost half the interview debating the Cantona-temperament issue, and whether further discipline problems would leave a potentially fatal midfield vacuum.

As Egg closes the door behind him, he reflects that maybe there is a tiny chance O'Donnell might take him on. It had been a bad interview, but at least they'd connected over something. Then he catches sight of himself in the mirror. *Shit*, he thinks, *I'll never be a sodding lawyer*.

Egg is on his way to the exit, when he sees Milly – a slim, attractive Pakistani girl, walking towards him, her arms full of papers. He glances around – no one is coming. Bounding towards her, he goes down on one knee at her feet and takes her hand. 'Madam,' he says, 'I simply must know your name. I think I love you.' Then he leaps to his feet, presses her against the wall, and kisses her full on the lips.

Milly drops her papers, and spits out his tongue.

'Egg,' she says, 'don't be such a knob. Someone'll see.'

'Don't care.'

'How did it go?'

'Terrible.'

'Why?'

'I dunno – I just . . . didn't really get on with him. He's a bit of a slimy git really, isn't he?'

'He's not. He's nice.'

'Maybe he is. We just – didn't hit it off. And he's got hairy knuckles.'

'What's that got to do with anything?'

'Look – believe me. I just cocked it up. It's probably not such a great idea, anyway – us two working in the same office.'

They hear footsteps approaching, and instantly step apart – but too late. They've been seen touching.

'Hi,' says the owner of the footsteps, warmly.

Milly doesn't recognize him, and responds with a cool 'Hi.'

'Warren Jones,' he says. 'I was at college with you. You probably don't remember me. I remember you. You're still together. That's nice.'

'Isn't it,' says Egg.

'Must dash. Interview,' says Warren.

'Right,' says Milly. 'Good luck.'

'D'you remember him?' says Egg, as soon as Warren is out of earshot.

'Vaguely. He's changed.'

'I thought he was a poof.'

'Maybe he's found poof love,' says Milly, casually registering that every month she spends with Egg, she gets less and less PC. When she started going out with him, she'd assumed that casual pressure over time would turn him into a New Man. Five years on, and she finds herself using the word 'poof' without even noticing, and regularly reads Egg's copies of *Loaded*.

'Bet he gets the job,' says Egg.

'Naa.'

'He will. You only need to look at him. He looks . . . kind of . . . he just looks a natural in that suit.'

Milly laughs. 'You're paranoid. If you're so worried about how you look, maybe you shouldn't buy your suits at Top Man. Anyway – there are two jobs. You might both get in.'

*　　*　　*

Outside chambers, Anna is leaning against a wall, unable to move while she recovers from her grilling. She needs a serious nicotine hit to bring back her powers of auto-locomotion. Her knees went half-way through the Interview From Hell, and she almost didn't make it out of the office without falling flat on her face.

Miles emerges from the building and crosses the road towards her.

'Hello, Miles,' she says.

'Hi. We've um . . .'

'Met before?' she pouts.

'Yeah.'

'Had sex?'

'Yeah. That too,' he mumbles.

'You never called me. Arsehole.'

'Well . . . it was one of those nights. End of term and all that. You know how it is.'

'Sure I do. It wasn't my real phone number, anyway.'

'Really?'

Anna smirks. Same old Miles. Still sexy. Still utterly gullible.

'What are you doing on an interview panel, anyway?'

'They sometimes bung me on. Voice of youth and all that.'

'So do they like me?'

'Think so.'

'Am I in?'

'Dunno.'

'Did you put in a good word for me?'

'Yeah – I told them you give great head.'

'Funny guy.'

'I said what I could. Honest. I did my best for you.'

'Why don't I believe a single thing you say?'

Miles shrugs, smiling broadly. For some reason, he takes this as flattery.

* * *

Although Egg brings her breakfast in bed, Milly can't get anything down. She's too nervous. It's her first day in court as a qualified lawyer. The harder Egg tries to calm her down, the more he succeeds in getting on her nerves. Fortunately, she's arranged to meet up at the courts with Anna. Although Milly loves Egg, at times of stress he does have the tendency to turn into a spaniel.

Anna, on the other hand, can be guaranteed to say the right thing. She'll take the piss – say something cutting that hits the spot and somehow catches Milly's mood. She's the only person in the world who can do that for Milly. Not that she's a misanthrope. There *are* other people she likes. Somewhere. Probably.

She kisses Egg goodbye, reluctantly accepting his tongue for a second or two, and steps out of the house, feeling guiltily relieved to be on her own. She's still nervous, but less so now that she's out of Egg's flapping zone – and is reassured by the fact that she'll have a good few minutes with Anna before she has to step into the courtroom.

The courts are swarming with people – barristers, policemen, solicitors, secretaries – all dashing around at first-thing-in-the-morning speed, blinking their way to the day's first cup of coffee. Milly spots Anna the second she enters the building, grabs her by the arm, smiling tightly, and drags her into the Ladies.

The door closes behind them, and Milly's professional veneer shatters. 'Jesus! I'm crapping myself.'

'Oh, shut up. You always say that, and you're always brilliant.'

'You think so?'

'Stop fishing for compliments, you dozy cow. You're fantastic.'

Milly smiles – for the first time that day.

'Christ,' says Anna, catching sight of herself in the mirror. 'I look like shit.'

'You look fine.'

'Nothing that a bit of Dulux emulsion can't fix.' Anna fishes out her lipstick, and applies it thickly. 'I thought I'd never do this.'

'What, lipstick?'

'No – CPS. Here I am, the long arm of the law – prosecuting some poor sod who just needs a break.'

'You're prosecuting?'

'Yeah.'

'What's the case?'

'Oh, it's crap. I need that job so badly.'

'You'll get it.'

'Don't think so.'

'You will.'

'There is one way I could improve my chances, though,' Anna muses.

'What?'

'There's some guy on the panel –'

'Stop now. I don't even want to hear it.'

'He's an old friend. An old boyfriend. Sort of.'

'Forget it, Anna. Just forget it.'

Anna, however, doesn't forget it. And before long, she finds herself in a wine bar, with Miles, tipping the dregs of their second bottle down her throat. Miles is swaying on his stool slightly, and blinking in slow motion. Anna, strangely, feels completely sober. She calculates that with a guy like Miles, sexual promises get you a lot further than sexual favours, and before he has quite figured out what is going on, she has pecked him on the cheek and disappeared into the night, wiggling her arse for all she's worth.

Miles, feeling too pissed and confused to handle the tube, takes a taxi home. It's a grotty house in Southwark, but despite the poor state of repair, it is built to generous Georgian proportions, and always feels spacious. Although he's been there only a couple of weeks, it already feels like home. Sharing with his old mate Egg is working well, too. The girlfriend's a bit uptight, but still – she's reasonably fit, and keeps Egg occupied.

The door sticks, and Miles gives it a frustrated shove which slams it open, the interior door handle chipping the plaster inside.

'Ooops,' says Miles, pushing the door shut with his foot, and fingering the tiny hole he has made in the wall.

He briefly contemplates a bit of late-night telly, but

changes his mind and lumbers noisily upstairs. He flops on to the bed to rest for a second before getting undressed, and the next thing he knows it's daylight, and there's a madman screaming in the downstairs hallway.

'WEHEEEE! I GOT IT! I GOT THE JOB! I GOT THE JOB! ZIP-A-DEE-DOO-DAH ZIP-A-DEE-DAY – MY OH MY WHAT A WONDERFUL DAY! ZIP . . .'

It's Egg's voice.

So he got the job – big deal.

Miles crawls to the shower.

*　　*　　*

Warren marches to work. He has a whole new posture and gait now that he's in full City uniform, with suit and briefcase. After a specially arranged pep-up session with his therapist, positive thoughts are ringing in his ears. He's going to be the toughest, hardest, meanest, richest, (gayest) solicitor the firm has ever had.

On arriving at work, he's amazed to see that the other place went to Egg – and rather dismayed to find that they have to sit opposite one another. How can they have given *him* the job? He's so obviously . . . a dissolute character. You only need to talk to him for two minutes to realize that he doesn't take law seriously and has a generally negative attitude to the office environment.

I'm going to have to talk to my therapist about this, he thinks. *The last thing I want is to have to share my personal space with a poor worker. Low concentration breeds.*

'What's the briefcase for?' says Egg.

'Carrying things.' Warren smiles thinly.

'What do you have to carry on your first day at work?'

The briefcase – brand-new – pigskin – contains two Biros. They rattle slightly when he walks.

'Just things,' says Warren, tetchily.

'Tampons, you mean?'

Warren stares at Egg, stony-faced, wondering if in some obscure way this is a homophobic comment. He doesn't know whether or not Egg knows.

'Joke? Humour? Funny haha?' says Egg.

No. He probably doesn't know. Just a bad joke – not a bullying one.

'Next time, tell me in advance, and I'll know I'm supposed to laugh.'

Egg rolls his eyes.

Shit, thinks Warren. *If only I was good at being witty. I'd better talk to my therapist about that, as well.*

* * *

Jo is wide. Not fat. Wide. A barrow boy. As junior clerk in Hooperman's chambers, it's his job to distribute briefs to the barristers. As such, he's a little guy with a lot of power. It's not a difficult job – it's not a glamorous job – but he's at the nerve centre. He knows everything that's going on in the company, he chooses who much of the work goes to, and as a result, everyone – *everyone* – is nice to him.

Jo is a happy man.

Anna prepares a smile, straightens her shirt, and enters Jo's office.

'Have you got a letter for me?'

'Sure.'

He flips through a pile of mail, and hands her an ominously thin envelope. He already knows what's in it, and tries to prepare her for the bad news by handing it over with a frown.

She tears it open.

'Shit! Bastards! Did Miles fuck this up for me? Is this Miles's fault?'

'Anna. Wait here. Don't move.'

Jo grabs the letter out of her hands and charges out of the room.

Anna opens the window and has a cigarette sitting on the window-sill, blowing her smoke out into the street.

She's stubbing it out in the window-box, when Jo returns, smiling.

'I had a word with Hoopie – 'cos we got bits and pieces lying around you could do. If you want. He says it's OK.'

'I can squat?'

'Yeah.'

'And you'd give me work? Really?'

'Sure. No sweat.'

Anna yelps with glee, stretches her arms out wide, and is about to give Jo a hug when she thinks better of it. He's a nice guy, Jo, but physical contact isn't his bag. She restrains herself – punching the air a few times – then gives him a peck on the cheek.

'Jo – you're my hero. I love you.'

'I do my best,' he chuckles.

He's still chuckling while she charges out of the office

and down into the street. That's the secret of being a successful clerk. Do people favours. Put people in your debt. It all comes round in the end. Besides, she's fit.

Anna is so out of breath that she can hardly get the words out. 'Message . . . for . . . Milly Nassim . . . must come down to reception at once . . . urgent.'

The receptionist mumbles into the phone and, after a while, Milly appears in reception, an anxious look on her face. The minute she sees Anna, though, Milly knows what has happened.

'You got it!' says Milly, just getting the words out before Anna sweeps her off the ground in a bear-hug.

'Sort of,' replies Anna, eventually. 'As good as. They're letting me squat. And there's enough work to keep me going.'

'That's brilliant. I'm so pleased.'

'Lunch. Now,' Anna insists.

Milly glances at her watch. 'All right.'

Within five minutes, the pair of them are sitting on their favourite bench in Lincoln's Inn Fields, munching on tuna baguettes. Two cans of Diet Coke and a pair of apples are perched unevenly on the wooden slats between them.

'I'll have money. For the first time, *ever*, I'll have real money. To spend.'

'You can pay off your debts.'

'Thanks, Milly.'

'Sorry.'

'I can move out of that godforsaken bedsit.'

'Really?'

'Yeah. Fuck the debts. I want a decent bedroom.'

'What about my house?' Milly says.

'What about it?'

'It's got two free rooms. We've just moved in. We've been painting it and stuff – and we were just about to start looking for people.'

'You never told me that.'

'I told you I'd moved house.'

'You didn't say there were spare rooms.'

'I didn't want to hurt your feelings. It's eighty quid a week. I thought it might be a bit much.'

'Eighty quid? I'm in.'

'Really?'

'Yeah. Is it just you and Egg so far?'

'And one other bloke. Old friend of Egg's. Lawyer – surprise surprise.'

'What's he like?'

'Bit pompous. Fancies himself. Toff pretending to be a lad. But he's basically OK. Objectively, he's a bit of a dish – but I can't see it myself.'

'Do you need to ask Egg?'

'Technically. But the word "no" isn't in his vocabulary, so it won't be a problem.'

By ten o'clock that evening, the spare top-floor bedroom is piled floor to ceiling with Anna's stuff – hastily transported in an array of plastic bags and cardboard boxes with the aid of one extremely pissed-off taxi-driver.

When everything is done to her satisfaction, Anna settles

17

down on the sofa in front of the TV. She forces her way between Milly and Egg, putting one arm round each of them.

'This is so cool,' she says. 'My two favourite people. I'm so happy.'

'Can you turn it up a bit?' says Egg.

A key rattles in the front door so, instead of turning the volume up, Milly hits the off switch on the remote.

'What are you doing?' shrieks Egg.

'Introductions,' says Milly, with a glare.

'Oh, right.'

Miles slouches into the room, and freezes when he sees Anna.

'Oh my God! What are *you* doing here?' says Miles.

'I live here.'

'You live here? Since when?'

'About an hour ago.'

'But –'

'I was about to tell you,' says Milly. 'We rented one of the rooms.'

'To *her*?'

'Do you two know each other, or something?' says Egg.

Chapter 2

Delilah

Jo gives Anna a desk (half a desk, in fact – a laser printer has the better spot), and her first 'mode of trial' at court. She tears the ribbon off her brief and rushes to court to meet her clients: Delilah Sumner, the witness, and a defendant called . . . Truelove?

Delilah stands out a mile – dressed not so much for the court-house as for a how-much-flesh-can-you-expose-without-being-completely-naked party. Despite the warm weather, Truelove is dressed in Siberian Gangsta Chic – a four-seasons down coat up around his ears, with a hood almost entirely masking his face.

Delilah greets Anna noisily, and Truelove doesn't even look up.

'Is that his real name?' says Anna.

'Yeah. Wicked innit.'

'It's his real name?'

'Truelove? Yeah. He's a graphic designer.'

'Right. Is he asleep?'

Delilah doesn't even hear the question. She's spotted Miles, striding across the other side of the atrium, looking rather fine in a new cashmere coat. Delilah's pheromones instantly go into overdrive, causing Miles, ever alert to promising scents, to look round. Delilah winks at him.

Anna, rendered mildly nauseous by this display, decides to give up on Delilah and to explain the situation to her comatose client. She sits down next to him, and aims her words into the small gap between the top of his zip and the bottom of his hood.

'Listen. The prosecution allege a fraudulent claim for housing benefit based on the fact that you represented yourself to your local authority as Miss Sumner's tenant when in fact you were cohabiting. Boyfriend and girl-friend.'

'Never laid a finger on me,' interjected Delilah, temporarily distracted from her long-distance flirtation.

'And you two want to go up?' says Anna.

'Wot?' shrieks Delilah.

'He's electing to go up to Crown Court for trial by jury. It's my duty to ask you if you've thought this through properly. The judge at Crown Court's got stronger sentencing powers. It's possible that, if found guilty, he will penalize you for wasting the court's time and the taxpayers' money when you could have pleaded guilty down here. It's possible that he'll sentence you to a short term of imprisonment.'

'Prison! But he's innocent!'

'Then he should go up for trial and plead not guilty.'

'Yeah – and we're going to prove he's innocent,' says Delilah. 'I mean, I'm his witness.'

Anna lifts Truelove's hood with one finger and peers in. 'He's dribbling,' she says.

'Hi,' says a male voice behind her. She looks up. It's Miles.

'Hi. You've come to meet my new friends?' says Anna, sarcastically.

'Are you the bloke I fucked in Ibiza?' Delilah asks.

'I don't *think* so,' replies Miles, with a faintly perceptible pout.

'You look like him.'

'Well, I've never been to Ibiza. Unfortunately.'

*　　*　　*

'What do you think of this?' says Milly, reading from a small notepad. 'It's for the *Standard*. "Room in large friendly house, near City, cheapish rent, no mod cons."'

Miles, Egg and Anna look up from their breakfast.

'Fine,' says Miles. The other two nod.

'Thanks for your exuberance, guys,' says Milly.

'It's great,' says Anna. 'We love you. Now pass the milk.'

Miles, despite himself, chuckles. He almost tells Anna that she's extremely witty for a girl, but pulls away at the last minute, deciding that a little self-censorship is probably in order.

'Isn't this nice?' says Egg. 'One big family, all having breakfast together.'

'I think we should work out some rules,' says Milly. 'Rotas and stuff – for washing up, hoovering and the rubbish.'

Within a matter of seconds, Milly finds herself alone at the breakfast table.

'It needs to be done!' she shouts in the vague direction of the staircase. She hears three doors slam, shortly followed by what sounds like a tussle for the bathroom.

*　　*　　*

Egg, staring out of the window, is depressed to notice that the sun is setting, and he's *still* at work. *This is no kind of life*, he thinks. *Every daylight hour spent under strip lighting in a huge open-plan office. What a waste!*

'What do you think of this?' says Warren. Egg looks round, to see that Warren has an early edition of the *Evening Standard* open on his desk. '"Room in large friendly house, near City, cheapish rent, no mod cons."'

Egg's face drops. Realizing that he's being rude, he summons a smile which sits on his face so falsely that even an air-hostess would be impressed. 'Err – sounds um . . . OK. You can probably get better, though. Maybe.'

Lying his way out of tight corners has never been Egg's strong point.

'Do you reckon we can go home yet?' he says, desperately trying to change the subject.

'I wouldn't if I were you,' says Warren, frowning.

'But we haven't got anything to do.'

'There's always something to do.'

'Jesus,' says Egg. 'You're unbelievable. I'm stuck sharing a desk with fucking RoboLawyer.'

From Warren's face, Egg sees that he's gone too far. Warren stares at the floor, takes a few deep breaths, then looks up. *Thank God for that anger-management course.*

'Listen,' he says, eyeballing Egg for the first time. 'My father works in a factory, my mother works in a department store. I come from a small town – a very boring small town. And I'm sorry about this but I'm actually grateful to be here . . . not there. I want this job, and I want to do it well. That's nothing to be ashamed of.'

Egg, embarrassed, looks away. 'Sorry,' he says. 'You're right. I'm a middle-class tosser.'

Warren smiles. 'Forget it.'

*   *   *

The minute Anna spots her opposing solicitor, she recognizes the type. Cheap suit, spots, gangly walk and no hairstyle. This can only be a council solicitor.

'You're for the council,' she says, before he introduces himself.

'How did you guess?'

'Female intuition.'

He smiles, uncertain of whether she's being flirtatious or taking the piss.

'Listen,' says Anna, 'these cohabitation cases are notoriously difficult to prove. You've got an informant, am I right?'

'Er . . . well . . .'

'It's OK. I don't want to know. I've unexpectedly acquired a very juicy witness. We're going to adjourn for a witness statement.'

'Oh dear. Er . . . who?'

'The flatmate,' says Anna, indicating Delilah with a nod.

'Oh dear. That can't ... I mean ... She's our informant.'

'You serious?' says Anna.

'Afraid so. I've had these before.'

'Had what before?'

'Girlfriend shops boyfriend to the council in secret, then casts herself as heroic defence witness and gets him off the hook.'

'What for?'

He shrugs. 'Search me. It passes the time, I suppose.'

Back in chambers, Anna pokes her head into Hooperman's office.

'Anna?' he says, smiling.

'Sorry to disturb. I just wanted to say – you know – it's great to be here.'

'Enjoying it?'

'Yeah – I'm having a brilliant time. Thanks for letting me squat. I appreciate it.'

'You've got an edge. I like that. I like to be able to give people a chance – people who can bring something a bit special to the job. And Miles underlined it for us.'

'Miles?'

'He told us you were a very remarkable, very intelligent young woman. And I think he was right.'

*   *   *

That night, the house is alive with sexual excitement. The buzz of flirtation between Miles and Anna is so intense, so palpable, that by nine o'clock Milly and Egg have sneaked upstairs for a mid-evening shag in the hope that it would relieve the tension. Twenty minutes later, they're back on the living-room sofa, in their dressing-gowns, watching TV. Miles and Anna, however, are still wandering all over the house, striking sparks off one another.

Something, Milly notices, seems strange. From her vantage point on the sofa, she detects that while Anna is flirting with Miles, Miles is just generally flirting. Even Milly's getting it. In fact, Egg doesn't actually seem to be excluded. And although Miles came home from work with a bottle of champagne, he *still* hasn't opened it.

The doorbell rings, and Miles – uniquely – goes to answer it. He almost runs. Milly instantly understands. Miles has been walking around with an erection all evening because he's expecting a visitor. Oh dear. Poor Anna.

Miles yanks the door open, his grin falling away as soon as he establishes the gender of the visitor.

'I'm Warren. I've come about the room.'

'Oh. Right. You'd better go in.'

Warren steps into the living room. Egg decides that he would rather die than face the embarrassment of the conversation that is about to occur.

'Hi, Egg. Hi, Milly,' says Warren, seemingly unsurprised to see them.

'Warren!' says Egg. 'Good to see you. Good to see you. That advert. I was about to say that . . . you know . . . to mention that it was my house . . . when you read it out . . . but . . . er . . . you changed the subject. I mean . . . the subject got changed. And I forgot to mention it.'

'I knew it was your house, anyway. Milly showed me the ad, and told me to come round and see if I liked the room.'

'Oh, right. That's OK, then.'

'I was about to ask you if you'd mind me coming to take a look, when you went bright red and told me that it sounded nice but that I could probably find somewhere better.'

'Did I?'

'Yes.'

'Um . . . accidental comment. Accidental. Off-the-ball incident. Yellow card. Indirect free kick. What can I say?'

Due to this near-lethal cocktail of guilt and embarrassment, it isn't long before Egg is metaphorically on hands and knees, begging Warren to take the spare room. Which he does. Miles grunts his approval, Anna sighs hers, and Warren is in.

The doorbell rings, and Miles sprints down the stairs. Anna follows, and watches from the first-floor landing. On the porch is Delilah, clutching a handbag. Without a word, Miles steps over the threshold and snogs her. Then, still wordlessly, he takes her by the hand and drags her up the stairs. She skips excitedly behind him, brushing past Anna, who is frozen to the spot on the landing.

''Allo, luv,' says Delilah, giving Anna a wink. 'I like your flatmate.'

Sexual frustration and insomnia are a bad combination at the best of times, but when your insomnia is caused by orgasmic shrieks reverberating through a partition wall, it is particularly galling.

It is one in the morning before Anna remembers that she has both her briefcase and the cordless phone in her bedroom. She slips out from under the duvet, and steps over to her desk.

Inside her briefcase, she finds what she's looking for: witness notes.

'Name: Delilah Sumner. Address: 39c Ambleton Road, SE11. Tel. No.: 0378-148029.'

Yup. Just as she thought. A mobile number.

Anna picks up the phone and dials.

Through the wall, a muffled ringing starts, and the moaning stops.

The telephone earpiece clicks. ' 'Allo?'

'Will you do me a favour, and SHUT THE FUCK UP!'

Chapter 3

The Trojan Wait

There is a word – three syllables – that on its own has the power to give Warren cold sweats. Family. Fa-mi-ly. That's all you need to say if you want to watch him display all the symptoms of advanced malaria.

He has convinced himself that when he left Wales, not only did he leave behind small-town life, but he also severed the bonds of duty, guilt and embarrassment that bound him to his parents. All he has to be now is Warren, the successful youngest son who went to London and became a lawyer. The rest is for him. He's paid off his debt to his parents – he's 'a success' – and they're happy for him. So his private life can be private.

Given that his parents rank homosexuality somewhere between prostitution and paedophilia on the moral scale – yes, they're *Daily Mail* readers – Warren knows that the rest of his life has to be spent with his mother and father at arm's length. Several arms' length. In fact, two hundred miles would seem to be the bare minimum.

As a result, when he hears the voice of his cousin Kira

on the end of a phone line, his first response is to panic. *A spy!*

He tries to get rid of her by playing Warren The Successful Lawyer and acting like a bit of a tosser, but she isn't put off. Warren slowly recalls that from the moment she popped out of Auntie Rita, Kira has had one defining feature: persistence.

First, Warren takes her out for a drink – determined that this will fulfil his sense of family duty for the year, and he won't have to see her again until Christmas. Unfortunately, two nights later, he finds that he's somehow been talked into taking her out for a meal.

Then, without even noticing how it happens, he's gone clubbing with her, invited her over to the house for a few meals, asked around at work about temping placements, found her a spot, and – suddenly – she's working in his office. Kira – Cousin Kira – messenger with a hotline to Satan – is working in his sodding office.

As Warren watches her flitting around the office, dropping off mail, passing round messages, winking and giggling her way into everyone's affections, it dawns on him that the more confidently he behaves, the more people seem to get the better of him. He makes a mental note. *I must talk to my therapist about self-assertion.*

*   *   *

The house has lived through a brief 'happy families' phase – brief, as in a few hours – and mutiny is now in the air. Delilah, without a word of approval from anyone other than Miles, has become a fixture. She's installed not just a TV set, but also herself – permanently – on the sofa. Her tendency to act as a conversational juggernaut has also failed to endear her to her housemates. If Delilah is in the room, it's only a matter of time before the topic under discussion will swerve into one of two grooves: the progress of Delilah's modelling career, or the book that Delilah is writing about – you guessed it – Delilah.

It also hasn't escaped the notice of Milly, Anna and Warren that the coughing and flushing noises that fill the house after most mealtimes seem to have something to do with this permanent guest, who eats like a horse, yet has the figure of a piece of string.

Egg, however, thinks she's 'interesting', and respects her for trying to write a book.

Miles, meanwhile, is in love. As a result, he barely notices that a lot of his loose change seems to be going missing.

*　　*　　*

It's a sunny day outside and the house is empty, but for Delilah, who is lying on Miles's bed, tussling with a packet of chocolate Hob Nobs. Although she is swimming in a blissful calorie trance, it slowly dawns on her after several minutes of irritation at the noise in the street that the disturbance consists of a man calling her name.

She hides the biscuits under the bed, walks to the window and wrestles it open. Sash-windows may look nice, but they're a pisser to open – particularly for emaciated bulimics.

Oh well, thinks Delilah as she pokes her head out into the street, *that's my exercise done for the week.*

'Delilah! Delilah!'

Shit. It's Truelove.

'Go away.'

'Delilah – they're after me for the money.'

'Well – give it to them.'

'They're after you too. You owe half! It's half each!'

Delilah disappears from the window, and a minute later appears at the door, laden with a camera, a Discman and a couple of Gameboys.

'Give them my stuff.'

'It's my stuff 'n' all. We bought it together.'

'Fuck off – it's mine. Look – this pays my part of the debt, right?'

'Yeah, but he said he's gonna kill us.'

'He's not killing me. I've paid.'

*　　*　　*

The Sheringham case has made Hooperman's year. There's nothing he enjoys more than large-scale industrial fraud, laced with intrigue and back-stabbing. Miles was initially flattered to be assigned the case, but five minutes alone with Hooperman is enough to convince Miles that he's in the shit. Hoopie The Blob suddenly thinks he's in the cast of *L.A. Law* – pacing up and down, plucking reference books off the shelves, and generally acting like a D-list TV actor making a bid for stardom.

'OK,' says Hooperman, 'here's the set-up. Our man – Sheringham – he's got a great new job, and he's going along in his chauffeur-driven Merc when, all of a sudden, he's told to buy, buy – his own shares – Magnitech shares.

He does it through dummy companies – all perfectly legal – and this inflates the Magnitech share price so that it's big and fat and ready for a take-over. But then it turns out Sheringham's shopping spree hasn't been reported to the Stock Exchange.'

'Let me guess,' says Miles. 'Sheringham then says, "It wasn't my job to report it." And the other directors go, "We knew nothing about it."'

'Thereby dropping him in the shit. It's fascinating what they do to each other, businessmen. He's innocent. He's done nothing wrong, but the whole City want him to take the fall.'

'And we're going to get him off?' says Miles, sceptically.

'Less of the cynicism, Miles. This is a big opportunity for you. And me. We're not going to cock this up – and we're not going to take any short cuts. I want you to read that by Monday.'

Hooperman points at a giant heap of papers on the floor next to his desk. *Read it?* thinks Miles. *I couldn't even lift it.*

By the time Miles has looked up and recovered from the shock of his confiscated weekend, Hooperman's head is down, and he's already working on something else.

Miles crouches to pick up the mountain of papers. The second it's off the ground, the pile slumps to one side and spreads over the floor.

'Two journeys would be easier,' says Hooperman, without looking up.

*

Back in his office, Miles rings home and tells Delilah that he has to work late. To his surprise, Delilah doesn't seem to give a toss. This causes Miles a moment of temporary insecurity, during which he finds himself agreeing to meet her at midnight, in Bagley's nightclub.

Miles hates clubbing. He's into the *idea* of clubbing, and he goes at least once a month, hoping to convince himself that he does get some pleasure out of it, but it never works. He always has a miserable time, worsened by secret fears that his failure to enjoy himself makes him a middle-aged git. In fact, there's only one thing he hates more than a night clubbing with mates – and that's a night clubbing on his own – which is the situation he finds himself in on Friday night, stood up by Delilah.

Back home, only Anna is still awake. Miles tries to explain to her that he's worried about Delilah – that she's disappeared. Anna doesn't seem too concerned.

'You know what?' she says.

'What?' says Miles, anticipating a pearl of feminine wisdom that will unravel Delilah's complex psychological make-up.

'You're probably homosexual.'

'WHAT?'

'In the closet.'

'What?'

'I just thought that you display all the symptoms of having problems with your sexual orientation.'

'What are you talking about?'

'You know – they say that if you fancy extremely thin women it's because of suppressed homosexuality. What you're really hankering after is a little boy.'

Miles opens and closes his mouth a few times, then storms out of the room.

'What's wrong with a few womanly curves?' Anna calls after him. 'Breasts and stuff! You should try it. They're fun to play with. You can suck them, too. Might help with your Oedipus complex.'

*   *   *

'Delilah! Delilah! Delilah!'

This time she doesn't bother with the window, and goes straight to the front door.

'What is it now?'

'We still owe them over three hundred. They're on my back, man. We're in big shit.'

'I've got nothing left to sell. What about your car?'

'My car?'

'Yeah.'

'I'd have to pay someone to take it away. It's a piece of crap.'

'We could leave the country.'

'I've got a better idea,' he says.

'What?'

'This is a nice house, yeah?'

'Yeah.'

'They give you a key?'

Delilah smiles, holds still for a while, then reaches into her pocket.

*

It's Saturday night, and Miles doesn't get home from the office until nine o'clock. He goes straight to his room to change out of his suit, not even bothering to wonder where Delilah might be. There she is, though. In his room. Putting lipstick on with the aid of his shaving mirror, dressed in clothes somewhere between provocative and pornographic.

'Come on,' she says, 'we're going out.'

'I'm knackered.'

'Come *on*. Get changed.'

She unzips his trousers and pulls them down.

Half a minute later, Miles is standing in the middle of the room, wearing nothing but an erection. He can hear Delilah fumbling around behind him, and is waiting for her to toss him on to the bed.

Suddenly, he feels a T-shirt sliding over his head. He turns round. Delilah passes him a pair of jeans.

'Come on,' she says, 'we're going clubbing.'

'I'm starving. I haven't eaten.'

'Get a kebab on the way.'

'I want a meal.'

'Compromise. Pub.'

In the wake of the burglary, Anna is the first person to notice something suspicious. At breakfast, she corners Miles by the fridge.

'Miles,' she says, 'have you noticed that they left one thing behind?'

'What?'

'The telly.'

'Oh, yeah.'

'Miles?'

'*What?*'

'Who owns the telly?'

'Fuck off, Anna.'

'Delilah, Miles. Delilah owns the telly.'

'That's not funny.'

'I know it's not funny.'

'She was with me. Listen.' Miles takes a step forward, forcing Anna to blink, and retreat a fraction. 'I don't know exactly what Delilah is – but I know what she isn't. And she isn't a thief.'

'Get real, Miles. She did this.'

'Are you jealous?'

'Miles – this is not about you and me. This is about the fact that Delilah has *burgled* our house.'

'I think you're jealous,' he insists.

'You know – they say that when a baby is new-born it doesn't really understand that other people exist. And it – quite naturally – assumes that the whole universe revolves around it. *You* are that baby, Miles. You never got past the first stage – you never found out that not everything on this earth has got to do with you!'

'You're jealous.'

'Miles? Fuck off.'

Chapter 4

Scrambled Egg

Egg's problem is that he doesn't want to be a lawyer. He's never wanted to be a lawyer. He's spent his life following the crowd: going to school, going to university, going to law school – and now he's suddenly arrived, and has found himself to be an adult, supposedly in charge of his own destiny, and he's doing a job he isn't aware of ever having consciously chosen.

Ever since Delilah mentioned that she was writing a book, he's been plagued by his oldest ambition: to be a writer. Even though she was almost certainly bullshitting – there's no way Delilah could conceivably finish a book – it is possible that she had started one. Which is more than Egg has ever done.

To be strictly accurate, Egg's dislike of his job isn't the main issue. The real problem is that it shows. Particularly with him sitting directly opposite Warren at the office. The contrast is obvious to anyone who so much as glances at their shared desk. The pair of them could be an eighteenth-century painting: *Diligence and Dissolution*. Or a modern one: *Arse-Licker and Piss Artist*.

Egg has recently discovered, however, that Warren is a decent guy. Sure, he works like a beast, but other than that, he's O K. He has a big heart. And he can be counted on to cover for Egg when he cocks up.

More than once, Egg has been sent across town to deliver files and documents, or to conduct an interview with an unimportant client, and he has somehow gone astray. First, he finds himself taking a scenic route in order to maximize his intake of fresh air. Then he notices that he is strolling across a park. And suddenly he finds himself in a record shop. Three hours later, he's back in the office, and Warren is all red and sweaty, in a panic over where he's been. Warren then always leans across the desk and whispers the explanation he's given for Egg's absence.

'Thanks, Warren – you're an angel,' Egg always says, trying his hardest to feel grateful. The sad fact is, though, Egg doesn't particularly care whether or not he's found out. While he has a job, it requires a major effort of will to resign. Not to mention all the explanations that would be required by Milly and his parents. If he gets the sack, though – that will be it. He'll have time. He'll be on his own. He'll be able to choose what he *really* wants to do. He'll be able to write.

*   *   *

Delilah may look like a waif, but she comes like an opera singer. No one in the house – in fact, no one in the street – is likely to get any sleep until Delilah has finished her nightly array of orgasms.

Miles is visibly losing weight.

On the morning after the loudest, longest, shrillest series of orgasms yet – performed in the style of Jessye Norman at the Olympic Opening Ceremony – Anna starts canvassing support for an eviction campaign.

Delilah steals, she keeps everyone awake, she leaves streaks of puke in the toilet bowl and she's bad company. Anna has a strong hand. Everyone in the house is convinced. Apart, that is, from a few inches of Miles's anatomy.

Anna calls a house meeting to make a decision on what to do about That Crazy Bitch, as Delilah has been affectionately dubbed.

* * *

For Egg, the worst thing about sleeping (or trying to sleep) with the Royal Opera's *Orgasms 'R' Us* taking place directly above his bed is the effect it has on Milly. It's not that Milly doesn't make a noise when she comes (she doesn't, incidentally, but that's not the problem), it's that the noises keep turning her on. Every night, she cuddles up to Egg, trying to squeeze a hard-on out of him, and for some reason he can't manage it. He's lost interest. Not just in Milly, but in sex. All the pressure of worry about what he wants to do with his life seems to be weighing down on his dick. For the duration of his career crisis, Egg has the libido of a desk tidy. Meanwhile, Milly is randier than she's been for years, and has to be put off with ever more unconvincing lies, ranging from that old favourite, tiredness, to more elaborate concoctions involving pulled muscles and repetitive-strain injury.

Egg's no intuitive genius, but even he knows that pretty soon he's going to have to face A Conversation.

*   *   *

Due to the sexist, lecherous tendencies of the men who run City law firms, most offices have perky, skinny receptionists – all eyes, lips and tits – who are paid to flirt with the partners as much as to answer the phones. Moore Spencer Wright, however, has a more politically correct recruitment policy. As a result, their receptionist is Kelly, who is fat, lazy and thick. She's also a hypochondriac.

This week, her chief malady is indigestion, which she chooses to medicate with six doses a day of pastrami on rye. This proves singularly ineffective, however, and when Kelly finally decides to 'take half a sickie', Kira seizes the opportunity to leap into place behind the telephone console. She's already been watching Kelly work, and has figured out how to operate the system. This is her big chance for promotion.

Meanwhile, on the other side of the office, Egg is having a trauma. He has cocked up. And with the prospect of a sacking looming towards him, suddenly it doesn't look so inviting.

'Shit, shit, shit. Where the fuck is it?'

'What?' says Milly. Walking past, she has seen the look on his face and stopped at his desk, worried.

'It's Spencer. Snidey git.'

'What does he want?'

'He's given me an hour.'

'To do what?'

'Find the statement. I took a witness statement from Mrs Witchell and I've lost it. If I haven't found it by the time Spencer gets back from lunch, I'm dead.'

'That's usually around four o'clock, isn't it?' chips in Warren.

Milly takes Egg by the shoulders, straightens him up, and looks him in the eye. Egg blinks fast. His face is red, twitching with stress. 'Egg,' she says. 'Stop a second. Take a couple of breaths.'

He inhales deeply through his nose, and Milly feels a small amount of the tension seep out from his shoulders.

'Look,' she says, 'you've got an hour. We'll put this stuff in two piles. I'll do half. You do half. It hasn't walked away. We'll find it.'

'You're right. Thanks. You're right.'

With Milly setting the pace, and Egg trying to ignore his pumping heart and surging adrenaline, they methodically look through the two enormous piles of paper. It dawns on Egg as he searches that he's been lying to himself. He needs this job. With the prospect of redundancy staring him in the face, he had lost his cool. He's a lawyer. He has to face the fact. It's not glamorous, it's not exciting, but it's his job. And without it he has no money, and no life.

With five minutes to spare, Milly finds the statement.

'Thank fuck! Thank you. Thank fuck!'

He kisses her.

She smiles and shakes her head. 'You need a Valium,' she says.

'I need a joint.'

*   *   *

It is the end of the week before Anna's meeting to discuss That Crazy Bitch finally convenes. In the intervening period, Delilah hasn't done a lot to shore up allegiances: she's argued with Warren after stealing his yoghurt and spilling a full bottle of his whisky, with Milly after using up all the hot water, and has had an enormous bust-up with Anna over a biscuit. No CD in the house seems to be safe, either, and Delilah also shows all the symptoms of an allergy to Fairy Liquid.

In short, That Crazy Bitch has only one ally.

Anna finally has everyone assembled in the living room (bar Miles, who no one really expected to turn up anyway), and she has barely started briefing her troops, when the enemy arrives.

'House conference, yeah?' says Delilah. 'It's my first one.'

The frosty silence which greets her doesn't seem to put Delilah off her stride.

'We can't decide anything till Miles gets here, can we?' she says.

'What's all this "we" crap?' says Anna.

'Well, I've got a say in this.'

'No. No – *you* are not a part of this bloody house.'

'I am.'

'You are a guest – and one who's totally outstayed her sodding welcome.'

'Says who? It's only you that doesn't like me.'

Anna laughs, and waves an arm at the rest of the group, expecting that she'll be ushering in waves of hatred from Milly, Warren and Egg. Instead, there is a long silence. 'What are you? Silent partners?' says Anna. 'Come on. Tell her.'

'Well,' says Warren, 'we all think that ... in view of ... I mean ... there's a general opinion that ... that ...'

'There's a ground rule,' says Milly. 'No moving-in of girlfriends or boyfriends.'

'What about Egg?'

'He pays rent, you stupid tart!' shrieks Anna. 'And buys food. What do you contribute?'

'The TV.'

'Which no one wanted. What else?'

Delilah is suddenly crying. She makes no attempt to wipe away her tears, and allows them to streak her face with dramatic trails of mascara. 'You can't just kick me out. I've got nowhere else to stay.'

'Well, that's Community Care for you.'

Milly, Egg and Warren look at Anna sharply. She's gone too far. Anna smiles back at them, sarcastically.

'Look,' says Warren, 'we can give her a few weeks, until she's found somewhere else.'

Anna splutters derisively. 'And in the meantime let her rip off the rest of our stuff?'

'I didn't take anything.'

'No. You just let one of your scummy friends do it for you.'

'That's not true. It isn't.'

'Not the tears, please.'

Delilah, by now, is bellowing – a noise strangely similar to one of her orgasms. Her cheeks are black with mascara. Milly's mascara. 'Stop it, all right! Stop it!' she shrieks. 'I didn't steal anything. You want to check my room? Yeah, well go ahead and search it. And me. Search everything. You think I'm dirt, don't you? Yeah, well I'm not. I'm as good as any of you, despite what you think.'

Delilah, now on her feet, stares down at three bowed heads on the sofa. She senses waves of guilt wafting in her direction, and knows instinctively that this is the moment to press home what little advantage she has gained, and to make an exit. Anna, also standing, shakes her head.

'You want me to go away?' says Delilah. 'Fine. I'll go. I'll walk the bloody streets for all you care.'

With that, she flounces out, shortly followed by Warren, who is making vaguely sympathetic clucking noises.

Anna takes a cool drag of her cigarette. 'Well,' she says, 'I think that's what you call a result.'

Miles arrives home from work late to find Delilah in tears, still zebra-faced, at the top of the stairs. A suitcase is perched dramatically on her lap.

'Your friends are bastards. I'm leaving!' she yells.

Miles's first thought is, *That's my suitcase.* He swallows it, and climbs the stairs to comfort her. This proves to be an involved process. Miles is regaled with a long and almost entirely incomprehensible version of the evening's events, from which he is able to draw only one solid fact. It's Anna's fault.

Miles charges into the living room, where all four of his house-mates are chatting in hushed tones. 'It's a bloody conspiracy!' he shouts. 'The four of you have been trying to drive her out from the start. All of you. You're supposed to be my bloody friends!'

'We are,' says Warren.

'Oh, fuck off, Warren, you ponced-up neurotic little queer.'

The atmosphere in the room suddenly stiffens at this unexpected personal attack. Warren blinks.

'Mincing around like some Vaseline-arsed fairy. *I* took your bloody yoghurt,' says Miles. 'Me. Not her.'

Warren stares at Miles, red-faced with anger. 'I see.'

'Course you could've asked around,' continues Miles, 'but no. So much easier to jump to conclusions, isn't it?'

'This is interesting,' says Anna. 'Are you confessing to the CDs as well, then?'

'Delilah's not a thief,' Miles insists.

Anna laughs, derisively.

'Well?' says Miles. 'Where's the proof?'

'I don't need proof –'

'There's a novel concept. No wonder you're not getting much work, Anna –'

Warren jumps in, talking quietly but piercingly to Miles. 'Did you have safe sex?' he says.

Miles, stunned by the question, reels back.

'What?'

Anna points to a used syringe lying on the dining table. 'I found this in your room,' she says.

'What, so she's a drug addict now, is she?'

'You tell me,' says Anna.

'I have licked every part of her body. You'd think I might have noticed the odd track mark.'

'You licked Truelove as well, then, have you? While you've been working late, she's been playing hostess.'

Miles's eyes flick around the room. He can't tell whether Anna and Warren are lying. He suspects they are. Then he sees Egg. When Egg lies, a giant neon sign appears above his head, saying I'M LYING. It isn't there.

Miles turns and leaves, slamming the door behind him. Delilah has vanished from the staircase, along with the suitcase. He pulls on his coat and strides out of the house. Once on the pavement outside, he doesn't know where to go. Switching off his sense of direction, he puts his head down and walks aimlessly, out into the London night.

At the kettle, late in the night, Miles comes face to face with Warren. Miles tries to smile at him, but Warren refuses to catch his eye.

'The answer's no,' says Miles. Warren looks up. 'Did I have safe sex with Delilah? No.'

Warren's expression softens a fraction. 'Then you ought to have an HIV test. Delilah too.'

'Yeah,' says Miles. 'Suppose so.'

Warren drains his herbal tea and leaves the room. Miles stares at the steam billowing out of the kettle, motionless.

Chapter 5

Miles Smiles

Even without the orgasmatron rattling their light fittings, the barrenness of Milly and Egg's bedroom is a problem. They both lie awake at night, pretending to sleep, not touching. Egg stares at the ceiling, worrying that he's impotent. Milly stares at the wall, worrying that she's ugly.

Deciding that Milly's asleep, Egg decides to perform a scientific experiment. Is he, or is he not, impotent?

Ever so slightly, the bed rocks.

Still facing away from Egg, Milly speaks. 'What are you doing?'

'Nothing. Err . . . Crumbs. Crumb-brushing. Crumbs in the bed – itchy bastards.'

'Oh. I thought you were having a wank.'

*   *   *

Miles is smiling. A historic event.

Over breakfast he apologizes to Anna about Delilah, then gives an equally sincere apology to Milly. All over the world, historians are flabbergasted. CNN goes into overdrive. Miles Stewart In Humility Shocker.

So sincere does Miles's change of heart seem to be, that it doesn't even occur to Anna to take the piss. She has an eye for dramatic moments, however, and decides to wait for Warren to arrive. Only then will she genuinely know if Miles is for real.

Warren stumbles in. 'All right?' he says, not catching anyone's eye.

Silence. Rustling of cereal, clanking of cutlery, slurping of tea.

Eventually, Miles speaks. 'Warren. I'd like to take you for lunch. As an apology.'

'That's really not necessary –'

'And for a chat. Really. I want to.'

'OK.'

Anna leaves. All that niceness is too much for her.

The Miles/Warren Yalta Conference takes place in a City wine bar. Although Warren isn't hungry, and hates drinking at lunch-time, Miles insists on buying him a three-course meal, and sharing a bottle of expensive wine.

They stick with platitudes until the food has been ordered, then, as soon as the menus have been whisked away, Miles gets to the point.

'I didn't mean anything by what I said. I was just angry. If you'd had a big nose I'd have said, "Shut up, you trunky git." No hair and it'd have been, "You ponced-up little slap head." But that wouldn't mean that I secretly hate people with big noses. I'm not some closet gay-hater. It's just, when you're angry, you pick up on a person's . . . characteristic and . . .'

'Abuse it.'

'Yeah. Crap, isn't it?'

'What if I'd been black? Would you have called me "nigger"? "Shut up you ponced-up little nigger"?'

Miles finishes his mouthful and swallows, with some difficulty. 'I don't know. What are you? A fucking lawyer or something?'

Warren tips his head back and laughs, enjoying the implicit compliment.

It's funny how an apology can mean nothing – an acceptance of an apology can also mean nothing – but once you've got someone to laugh, you know you're OK. While Warren dabs at his smile with a napkin, Miles sighs to himself. He's in the clear. He's been forgiven.

Now he can get to the point.

He garnishes the friendship treaty with a few extra apologies and, with the arrival of their main course, Miles gets serious. He tops up Warren's glass, leans forward a fraction, and speaks in a lower, more intense, voice.

'This AIDS thing,' he says. 'How do I . . . like . . . am I? . . . What's the situation?'

Warren registers the ulterior motive behind Miles's show of humility and starts on his food. *Hetty men*, he thinks, *what a perpetual disappointment. Just when you think they've shown a bit of depth, they pull something two-dimensional and crap out of the bag. Thank God I don't have to sleep with them.*

After a few leisurely mouthfuls, Warren takes pity on Miles and launches into an explanation: incubation period, risk, tests, precautions, the lot. In short, there's nothing

Miles can do for three months – the length of time it takes for antibodies to show. All he can do in the intervening period is to assess whether or not Truelove is an intravenous drug-user and, if he is, to persuade Delilah to take an HIV test.

When Warren finishes the explanation, Miles doesn't stop nodding. There is a long silence.

'Do you know where she's living now?' says Warren.

Miles doesn't answer. He's still nodding. His eyes have lost their focus, and he looks as if he might be about to faint.

'MILES! Where does she live?'

'Oh! Right. Yeah. Don't know. I've got her mobile number, though.'

'I presume the relationship's over, then?'

'Sort of. Yeah. Drifted apart, really.'

'There is such a thing as safe sex, you know.'

'It's over. We weren't getting on.'

'Listen,' says Warren. 'We *all* let her down. Not just you. All of us.'

Miles doesn't answer.

'If you can find her, I'll help you talk to her. It isn't just you that's under threat.'

'Thanks,' says Miles. 'Thanks.'

*   *   *

Whatever Egg does at work, he gets it wrong. Veering from extremes of diligence to apathy and back again, he always seems to be spotted at his worst moments. O'Donnell keeps on calling him in for 'little chats' and asking in concerned tones about how he's settling in. And when he's spotted swearing vehemently at a broken photocopier, apparently unaware that his abusive conversation is being held with an inanimate object, O'Donnell goes so far as to call in Milly to ask about Egg's mental stability.

Milly does her best to cover for him, but another inevitable 'little chat' follows, during which O'Donnell slips Egg the name and phone number of a therapist.

'I don't believe this!' says Egg, when he gets back to his desk. 'Just because I called the photocopier a cunt, the man thinks I'm a loony. Look what he's given me.'

Egg passes the business card across the desk. Warren glances at it and immediately hands it back. 'She's my therapist, too. Very competent. And only two minutes down the road.'

'You're taking the piss.'

This isn't a conversation that Warren wants to have. He smiles thinly and walks away.

That evening, Milly corners Egg and forces him into The Conversation. She tells him that they don't talk any more, that they don't have sex any more, and that she won't let him leave the room until he explains why he's avoiding her.

Egg finds that he doesn't have an answer. He can tell her that he's fed up, he's miserable, he's pissed off, he's scared – there are plenty of words to describe *what* he feels – but when it comes to *why*, he's stuck.

*

Without telling anyone, a few days later, he visits the therapist.

The appointment, however, isn't a success. The minute Egg sees her room, he's instantly interested in what it's like to be a therapist, and whether she enjoys it. Is it a good lifestyle? Did she always want to be a therapist? Does she get bored of the same old problems cropping up again and again?

He asks her all these questions, but she seems strangely reluctant to answer. She keeps on trying to swing the conversation round to get Egg to talk about himself. But he isn't interested in that. He spends more than enough time worrying about himself. He wants to know what it's like to be a therapist.

On the way out, she gives him a long speech which seems to revolve around the word 'denial'.

*   *   *

Following a brief and rather abusive phone conversation, Miles discovers that Delilah is living with Truelove in a squat: an abandoned tram shed in Manor House. Warren and Miles make the long trek up to north London together. Abandoned tram sheds are never that hard to find, and before long the pair of them are face to face with Delilah.

'I haven't got AIDS!' she screams.

'We're not saying that,' says Warren.

'And neither has he.' Delilah points at Truelove, who is comatose, propped up by a wall.

'How the hell do you know?' shouts Miles. 'He's a heroin addict.'

'No, he isn't.'

'Then why did we find a needle in my room?'

'He's a diabetic. He has to take insulin. Don't you?' She kicks Truelove, who looks up, smiles, and closes his eyes.

'Well, he'd love to answer you, Delilah, but he's off his face on smack at the moment.'

'Take it easy, Miles,' says Warren.

Delilah pushes Miles in the chest and shrieks, 'Are you calling me a liar?'

'Just take the fucking test, all right!' he shouts.

Warren separates them, and drags Miles to the doorway. 'Leave it, Miles. Look – why don't you go home.'

'Sorry?'

'I'll deal with this. Just . . . leave us alone. Please?'

Miles looks at Warren, then down at his feet. Again, he's ashamed of himself. He's never been good at this kind of thing. They don't teach compassion at boarding school. Without another word, he leaves.

When the sound of Miles's footsteps has subsided, Delilah speaks.

'I haven't got sodding AIDS.'

'No, of course –'

'What's the matter? Didn't you kick me enough beforehand? Or you thought you'd come over and make sure I was really fucking down?'

'Delilah –'

'This *is* down, Warren. Believe me.'

'I'm sorry.'

'I never took that yoghurt. I spilt your bloody scotch, but I never took that yoghurt. All right?'

'OK.'

'Say it.'

'You never did. I'm sorry. And even if you had –'

'I didn't.'

'– I'd still apologize. I want to help, Delilah. If you'll let me.'

'I haven't got AIDS.'

'Neither have I. But I still take a test now and again. Just to be sure. It's not as bad as you think. You'll see a counsellor before and after.'

'I don't want a counsellor.'

'I'll come with you.'

'I haven't said I'll do it yet.'

'No. Sorry.'

'And if I go it's 'cause I want to – not 'cause some stingy shithead pushed me into it.'

Warren smiles at her. 'Remind me – what charm school did you go to, again?'

Delilah laughs, and the moment of released tension shatters her defences. A few tears start to flow, then in seconds, sobs are shuddering through her body. Warren puts an arm around her shoulders, squeezes, and waits.

*   *   *

Walking through the park, on the way home from his therapy session, a moment of clarity hits Egg like a Stuart Pearce free kick in the testicles. He sees a crowd of kids playing football and runs towards them, throwing off his jacket and tie, and tossing them on to the grass behind him. He untucks his shirt, rolls up his trouser legs, and charges on to the pitch.

It's simple. A therapist is a happy therapist if she loves therapy. A lawyer is an unhappy lawyer if he hates the law. Egg hates law. Egg hates therapy. There are two things Egg loves. Football – and writing.

He's decided. His mind is clear. Fuck law. Fuck his job. Fuck misery. Fuck money. He's going to do what he wants. He's going to be a football writer. The next Nick Hornby. Only funnier. And less bald.

The kids have stopped playing to stare at the mad businessman streaking across their pitch, doing a strip-tease.

The ball is lying in space, just outside the box. Egg gets to it, head down, and shoots.

The ball sails over the bar, missing by a double-decker bus or two. Egg falls on his back, delighted. Yessss! He's going to be a writer.

Chapter 6

Family Outings

Delilah tests negative for HIV. Miles is three quarters of the way through a bottle of champagne before Warren warns him that they both have to test again, in three months, to be fully in the clear.

Still – panic over.

If Miles could only get out of the Sheringham/Magnitech case, then he'd have his life back. It's not just the workload that Miles objects to – there's something else about this particular case that he hates. There's something sordid about it. One fat cat getting stitched up by another set of fat cats. It's precisely the kind of thing that Miles hates most.

When you tell people you're a lawyer, a lot of people assume you're a git. And when you're working on something like the Sheringham case, you tend to feel that they have a point. There's no right and wrong involved – there's no real justice to be done. Just a lot of sordid greedy wankers with their hands in the till, and you're working for them. You've sunk to their level.

Even if Sheringham is innocent, even if he has been

stitched up by the Magnitech board, Miles hates having to defend him. It's a question of principle.

Or at least he thought it was a question of principle – until Jo pops into his office with one extremely nasty sheet of A4 paper. A list of the Magnitech directors over the last ten years. And roughly half-way down, the name 'Montgomery Stewart'. Miles's dad.

For some reason, this doesn't come as a shock. In the back of his mind, this is exactly what Miles had been expecting. Maybe the name Magnitech had been lodged in his subconscious – an irretrievable trace memory from a conversation overheard at home.

The minute he sees his father's name on the list of directors, Miles realizes why he hates the case so much. By meddling in this kind of City wheeler-dealing, Miles is getting sucked into his father's domain. The hate figure of Miles's entire adolescence – the man who Miles vowed never to emulate – is pulling him in.

With the list of directors crumpling in his hand, Miles walks straight into Hooperman's office, forgetting to knock. He simply *has* to find a way off this case.

'Problem?' says Hooperman, smirking.

'This list. Montgomery Stewart. He's my father.'

'You weren't aware he used to be on the board, then?'

'No. We . . . haven't spoken for a while. Not properly.'

'Well – I think now would be a fruitful moment to rekindle your acquaintance, don't you?'

'I'm sorry?'

'I won a three-quarter-of-a-million-pound settlement once on the strength of a grapevine tip-off. A chap I used to know at college had a wife in the defendant's company. On a case like this, months of trawling through paperwork will never get you as far as a boozy lunch with someone on the inside. And if they're in your family . . . This is priceless, Miles.'

They may have missed out compassion from Miles's school curriculum, but he does have a strong sense of morality. And he can feel himself sinking lower and lower. Still, he grits his teeth, makes that phone call, and goes for dinner with his dad.

It isn't long before Montgomery goes for the jugular.

'The Sheringham case, eh? You sold out after all.'

'Don't.'

'I knew that youthful idealism would disappear eventually.'

'It's called integrity.'

'Well, you can afford a better brand of that nowadays, can't you? Cheers.'

Montgomery raises his glass, and holds it poised above the centre of the table. Miles doesn't move. Montgomery sips, a contented smile playing across his lips.

'Don't be too upset, Miles. A little realism works wonders. Look at the initiative you're showing here.'

'I'm sorry.'

'Well, you're not here to inquire after my health, are you? Have a father-and-son chin-wag about old times?'

'What old times? I never saw you.'

'You want to know what I've heard, don't you? About Magnitech.'

Miles shifts awkwardly in his seat, embarrassed.

Montgomery stares at him archly – relishing the tension. Then he breaks into a smile. 'I knew I'd be proud of you one day.'

Montgomery forces Miles to talk about golf, share prices and Hampshire for the majority of the meal – deliberately prolonging his son's agony. He steers the conversation away from Miles's work, diverting it to his own topics until after dessert, when he casually tosses Miles the information he is after. Sam Bridges, another former director, had tipped him off a year or two back that it would be prudent to throw a few quid into Magnitech shares.

'So he knew the price was about to be inflated?' says Miles, suddenly excited. 'The whole board did. Sheringham was set up. Is that what you're saying?'

Montgomery smiles. 'Would you like some cream? Or do you prefer it black?'

* * *

Kelly, the hypochondriac receptionist, impresses everyone in the office when it turns out that her indigestion is in fact appendicitis. Kira is particularly impressed since this means that for the duration of Kelly's hospital stay, she has a promotion.

Finally happy with her job, Kira focuses on her other main problem. Home. She hates home. Or, more precisely, her stepfather. Even though he has no blood ties with her whatsoever, he has taken it on himself to act as bodyguard of her virtue. His attentions have become so oppressive that with each passing day Kira goes home later and later – doing all she can to spend the minimum amount of time possible in his house.

Kira's favoured hang-out soon becomes Warren's room in Benjamin Street. Although they have been getting on better and better at work, having her in his home almost every evening soon becomes too much for Warren. He can't be expected to act heterosexual *all* the time. And with a spy from his family in the house, he can't relax for a moment.

He starts privately researching speeches along the lines of, 'I love you, Kira, but fuck off.' He knows, however, that nothing he can do will get rid of her. She has slid her claws deeply and irretrievably into his life. There is only one sensible course of action. He has to come out to her.

* * *

Miles reports his father's nugget of information to Hooperman, who is delighted. 'All we need now,' he says, 'is proof that the other directors were privately purchasing shares on the q.t. Ha! We'll get our man cleared, all right. This is excellent.'

Miles frowns, staring at Hooperman suspiciously. 'Is that the reason you chose me? Because of my father?'

Hooperman stands. Ditching the jovial act, he stares Miles in the eye. 'You're here because you're good. Because you've proved you can rise to a challenge. Is that clear?'

'Yeah.'

'Any whispers we hear, Miles, are a bonus. That's all. They act as pointers – short cuts – to a destination already assured. This is a rich vein, though, Miles. Tap into it. OK?'

* * *

Within days of handing in his notice, Egg discovers that he is well suited to life on the dole. Finally, after all the confusion, disruption and fear, his entire existence fits perfectly into one simple equation.

Man + Video Recorder = Happiness

OK, so he's still not having sex with Milly. And she keeps on nagging him to fill in an impossibly complicated application form for some job at the Sports Council. And she frequently asks how long she's expected to chip in for his rent. And they tend to avoid each other most of the time. But one profound, incontrovertible fact reigns supreme. Man + Video Recorder = Happiness.

* * *

Miles would rather lick a cheese-grater than go for another meal with his father. Unfortunately, Hooperman doesn't want him to lick a cheese-grater. He wants him to go for another meal with his father. He wants Montgomery Stewart as a witness.

'Well, this is becoming a bit of a habit,' says Montgomery, drawing deeply on a long, thin cigarette.

'Yeah, thanks for seeing me at such short notice.'

'Always a pleasure, Miles. So – how's the case going?'

'It's progressing.'

'Good.'

As if you gave a shit, thinks Miles.

'Look – last time we met, you gave me some useful information.'

'Did I?'

Someone should take a rolling-pin to that smirk.

'Yes. It's really moved things along. Thanks.'

'My pleasure.'

'Look – I think we can be honest with each other, Dad. We all know that Sheringham's been made a scapegoat, but no one's brave enough to stand up and say so. It's a conspiracy of silence. If you were prepared to tell a court what you told me . . .'

'And what was that?'

'Well, about Sam Bridges and the other directors . . .'

'I must have been pissed. I don't remember saying anything about that.'

'We were sitting right over there.'

'I really don't know what you're talking about. Shall we order? The veal's very good.'

'What exactly is it that you're denying? That we had the conversation or that we had lunch at all?'

'Please don't try to cross-examine me, Miles. Perhaps you'd prefer the chicken?'

'You're unbelievable. I always thought you were a complacent sod. But I wasn't doing you justice. You're actually a corrupt, self-serving bastard!'

'Chicken? Or veal?'

Knocking his chair over as he stands, Miles storms out.

*　　*　　*

Having delayed it as long as he can, Warren finally screws up the courage to tell Kira that he's gay. She doesn't react quite how he expects, though. Instead of all the long pauses and agonized soul-searching that usually follows, Kira just says, 'God – you must think I'm thick.'

Apparently, Warren's straight act isn't quite as good as he thought.

Chapter 7

Brief Encounters

If you're trying to start a career, from the outside it all looks simple. All you have to do is get on the inside.

When Anna got her place squatting in chambers, she thought that was it. She was in. Since then, however, things have proved a lot harder than she expected. She hasn't crossed a neat line from the world of unemployment to the world of business. Instead, she's simply hovering. Half in, half out. With some work, but not enough; some money, but not enough.

The cases she does get, she has no trouble with. Everyone seems happy with her work. But she simply doesn't have enough contacts to keep herself busy. She's a perfectly good barrister, but that's not enough. She needs to learn a far more important skill – how to schmooze.

Her schmoozing starts with Jo – but that doesn't really count. After all, she does want to get work out of him, but she'd also rather like to get him into the sack. For leisure purposes. Still – he's too young. He'd get scared.

Every day begins in Jo's office, seeing what briefs come in, fluttering her eyelashes, crossing and uncrossing her legs, begging for any spares to be thrown her way. Lately, however, there's been nothing. Anna's even had to borrow money from Milly to pay the rent.

Jo gives her some advice. 'You got to go out there to get work.'

'Where?'

'There.' He arcs his arm at the window – a sweeping gesture encompassing the entire City of London.

'Thanks for the tip, Jo.'

'Listen, Graham's having a party. A wine-bar social. Talk to him. Get an invite.'

'And?'

'Schmooze. Who do you think his mates are?'

'Um . . . a broad spectrum of British society?'

'One more guess.'

'A bunch of pushy careerist lawyers on the make?'

'Bingo.'

Ever since her job interview, Anna has never been able to relax with Graham. In fact, she doesn't like him. She's frequently overcome by the urge to put her arm round him, and say, 'Graham – relax. We all know it's hard being a black barrister. But acting like a pompous git really isn't going to help.'

It's never going to happen, though. No one will say it. No one will even get as far as putting an arm round him. Graham is about as touchy-feely as an electricity substation.

And it's not just that he's pompous, patronizing, stiff and humourless. There's something else about him that Anna particularly hates. She's never said it to anyone, because she wouldn't know how to make it sound right, but she can't help feeling that because Graham is black, it's somehow easier for him to be sexist.

The speed with which he took against her is something she recognizes. It often happens to her. Tall, confident and female: you walk into a room, and half the men instantly hate you. It happens all the time. And Graham is one of them. Desire, transmuted into fear, transmuted into aggression.

She knows it's sexism, because she's seen how he operates with the men at her level in the office. Graham doesn't patronize them. In fact, he loves playing big brother. Anna sometimes feels that she can't walk round a corner in the office without bumping into Miles and Graham sharing a secret chat, or a boyish laugh. The Repression Twins, cuddling up to each other – freezing and stepping apart when she comes into sight. Whenever she bumps into the pair of them, they give the impression that she's spoiling their fun by being there – by existing – by daring to possess a vagina.

Still, she swallows her pride, and knocks on Graham's door. This is one situation where Graham's personality will be a help. Normally, the question 'Can I come and do some networking at your party?' would be an embarrassing one. Not with Graham. She only needs to say, 'I'm rather short of work at the moment,' and Graham instantly invites her.

'Come,' he says. 'It will be stuffed with lawyers. Some very bright people.'

'Thanks, Graham. That's kind.'

He smiles. (Sort of.)

'Bring Miles,' he says.

Miles is busy. Working late, as usual. And the party is a disaster. Anna wears her shortest skirt and her biggest smile, but no one wants to talk to her. She's ten years too young to look interesting (i.e., important). Everyone seems to know everyone else. And *no one* seems to have a healthy libido.

Anna hates this. *Only at a party of solicitors*, she thinks. *Here I am: young, sexy, available, and standing alone in the corner buying myself vodka number ten.*

'Chin up,' says a voice. A female voice.

Fuck! Someone's talking to me!

'I'm Sarah Newly. An old colleague of Graham's.'

'Anna. Anna Forbes.'

'Nice to meet you. You'll never get anywhere like this, you know.'

'Like what?'

'Standing in the corner on your own.'

'I'm out of it. I've tried talking to people, but in the last two hours I've just had a series of monologues inflicted on me. No one's asked me a single question. I mean, no disrespect – but talk about self-important pricks. Jesus.'

'Another drink?'

'Yeah. Why not?'

'Great dress.'

'Thanks. Fat lot of good it did me, though.'

'I'm sorry?'

'The plan was, I'd get dressed to kill, so some horny solicitor would give me work in the hope of getting into my pants. No chance.'

'I wouldn't say that.'

Sarah gives Anna a big smile, then turns round and walks to the bar.

Anna twigs. *Oh my God! She was chatting me up.*

* * *

Man + Video Recorder = Happiness

Man + Job Application Form = Misery

Job Application Form + Dustbin = FRRREEDOMMMM!

* * *

As usual, Anna starts the day in Jo's office. For once, there's good news.

'I've got something for you,' he says, brandishing a brief wrapped in the inevitable red ribbon.

'A case?'

Anna wants to cheer.

'Yep. Camberwell, eleven-thirty. Pretty routine, I'm afraid.'

'Who cares?'

'First appearance, criminal damage. Prostitute stickers in phone boxes.'

'What a waste of public money.'

'Yeah? Well you're going to get some of that public money, so don't knock it.'

'Thanks, Jo. I want to have your babies.'

'Yeah, a blow-job'll be fine.'

'My office. Half-past two,' she winks, flouncing out of his office.

Blushing, Jo returns to work.

As it turns out, the case (and the blow-job) don't happen. The defendant is let off with a caution, and Anna is let off with a consolatory drink after work – courtesy of Jo.

The strangest thing about office flirtation is that the second you step outside the office with your flirtation partner, it all either vanishes, or explodes.

With Anna and Jo alone in the pub, for the first half hour or so, the atmosphere is tense. But gradually, as they both get more pissed, and more confident, it begins to look increasingly likely that an explosion is on the cards.

By closing time, it's inevitable.

Neither Jo nor Anna fancy the prospect of facing Miles and the others at Benjamin Street. Given that Jo still lives with his parents, there is only one option.

Back in the office, it seems appropriate to choose Miles's desk.

Jo's love-making technique is what you might call 'enthusiastic'. Papers scatter everywhere. Normally Anna's not a squealer, but this time, simply because she can, simply because it feels sacrilegious, she indulges in a Delilah-style orgasm.

*   *   *

It's the middle of the day. The house is silent.

Egg sneaks into Anna's bedroom, unplugs her laptop, and carries it down to the living room.

He settles himself at the dining table, prises open the computer, and boots up the word processor.

First, he hits the return key eight times. Then sets a tab in the middle of the screen, centre justified. A couple of clicks on the mouse, and he's on Times New Roman, 18 point.

He types.

More Important Than That

A novel about football

No.

A novel of football

No. Pretentious.

A football novel

Cool.

by

Edgar Cook

He'll have to choose a pen-name. Something macho. Like, Dick Beast. *No. Too soft porn.*

Stafford Clench. *Too stupid*.
Armando Clothrop. *Too foreign*.
Stoke Chambers. *That's not bad*.

*　　*　　*

Anna should have known better. If she needed a shag, she should have got one from someone who could handle it. Not from some kid who was guaranteed to turn into a limpet after one quick squirt. And, above all, not from a limpet on whom she was entirely dependent for her livelihood.

The whole thing was a bad idea. A good shag, but a bad idea.

Chapter 8

Bad Dad, Sad Dad

There is a disadvantage to acting pissed off all the time. No one notices when you really are pissed off.

Milly's pissed off. No one notices.

She's fed up with playing mother to a house full of squealing, self-obsessed, perpetually traumatized infants. And as Egg's difficulties go on and on, with no end in sight, she is losing patience with him. She's done everything she can to try and help him – listening to his woes, paying his bills, talking through his ludicrous and ill-thought-out ambitions – but, ultimately, she's *not* his mother. She's his girlfriend. And for months their relationship has been utterly unequal. He takes everything – emotional, physical and financial – but gives nothing. The more Milly thinks about it, the more she realizes that it's like having a child.

There is only one person who, throughout Egg's traumas, asks her how *she* feels. O'Donnell. Her boss.

Egg The Novelist, his latest incarnation, is simply too much for Milly. The whole escapade is such an obvious waste of time that she finds it harder than ever to take her usual patient interest.

She knows what she *ought* to do. She knows what Warren would tell her to do. Talk about it. Tell Egg how she feels. Ask for support. Share her worries with him. But she can't. That's not Milly. She doesn't work like that, and she finds an alternative option – avoiding Egg by staying later and later at work.

Anna's feelers – as you would expect – are twitching. She's sniffed discontent in the air, and keeps on taking Milly out for lunch (proposing lunch, that is – Milly always ends up paying) and asking pointed questions about how things are going between her and Egg.

'Fine,' is the answer Milly always gives. End of subject.

She doesn't even know why she says it. It just comes out. She trusts Anna; she values her opinion; and sometimes she even wants to talk. But the same answer always comes out. 'Fine.'

Occasionally, Milly will be in the middle of an everyday task – standing at the photocopier, for example – and she'll suddenly get the urge to tear all her clothes off and sprint across the office shouting, 'FUUUUUUCK! WHY AM I SO REPRESSED?'

The moment always passes, though. All things considered, it's never really a serious temptation.

*   *   *

Miles's father has an attack of conscience. This may sound a bit like Douglas Bader having an attack of bunions but – well – it happens. Montgomery Stewart decides to take the stand in defence of Sheringham.

73

OK, so maybe there's a tiny weeny ulterior motive. He may have been a terrible father for the last twenty-six years, but that was never his intention. Despite everything, he never wanted to alienate Miles. And after his son's outburst in the restaurant, Montgomery realizes that this is perhaps his last chance to salvage their relationship.

His effort, however, backfires.

With Montgomery as a key witness, Hooperman withdraws Miles from the case to avoid 'professional embarrassment'. Miles, who has been itching for this to happen from the moment the case was assigned to him, is surprised to find himself angry. Very angry. With – naturally – his father.

He goes straight to Montgomery's club, and confronts him.

'You just can't stop interfering, can you? You've got to get involved. Stick your nose in.'

'You're making a scene, Miles. Please sit down. You asked me to get involved.'

'Yeah, but you refused. You had to do it your way.'

'My conscience.'

'Don't make me laugh.'

'After what you told me, I thought it was my duty to come forward and approach Sheringham's solicitors.'

'Bollocks.'

'Look. OK – it wasn't just Sheringham I had on my conscience. I thought that if I came forward as a witness it would mean a successful outcome for your case. I thought it would help you. I know this is your big opportunity.'

'Not any more. Thanks to you, I've been pulled off. Professional embarrassment.'

'What?'

'You have never, ever consulted me about what I want. How do you know what's best for me? You don't even know me.'

'I am trying, Miles.'

'Isn't it a bit late for that?'

'I had no idea my coming forward would take you off the case. But you must have done. Why did you ask me in the first place?'

Miles pauses, caught out. He had initially gone to his father for precisely that reason. Montgomery has done exactly what Miles wanted.

I'm being utterly unreasonable, he thinks. *What's wrong with me? Why am I always like this with my father? Fuck it – what's on telly tonight?*

He storms out.

On Miles's league table of life pleasures, introspection ranks far, far below television.

*   *   *

Milly and O'Donnell are stuck on a tricky divorce case, with a tight schedule before the first court appearance. The workload is a perfect excuse for late nights in the office. He often apologizes for keeping her late, and tells her that she can leave if she wants, but Milly insists on staying. She wants to be there.

Occasionally, after everyone else has left the office, they work with a bottle of wine.

There is an atmosphere. And when O'Donnell – Michael – offers to take her for a meal, she says no, on instinct. Then yes, because she wants to. She feels like it. She would rather go for a meal with Michael O'Donnell than go home to her noisy, stressful, juvenile house.

*   *   *

Hooperman has a birthday party – yet another sterile affair with far too many lawyers around to be fun, so Anna gets pissed to help pass the time. She goads Hooperman into a dance, which everyone finds extremely funny. Except Hooperman. Another cunning career move by Anna.

As soon as she leaves the dance floor, the limpet latches on to her.

'I think I underestimated you,' he says. 'I didn't realize you were ambitious enough to really try and fuck the boss.'

'What?'

'I see the logic. You fucked me 'cause you thought you might get some decent cases thrown your way, but then you thought, "Hang on, Anna, don't undervalue yourself, girl. Why screw the clerk when you can go straight for the big guy?" You don't want to waste your time with East End trash, after all, do you?'

'Are you going to go on like this all night? Because if you are, I'd like to sit down.'

'No. That's about it.'

'I'm going to tell you why I had sex with you, Jo. Can you handle it?'

'Yeah.'

'I did it because I fancied you and I thought it might be fun. And it was fun. I didn't want to go out with you. I didn't want to get married and have your babies. I wanted to have sex with you. I might want to have sex with you again some day and you may turn me down and that's OK, too. But, Jo – don't make me feel like I'm walking out on you and the kids, and for God's sake don't get working-class hero on me 'cause that's a dead cert to put me off for life.'

Jo blinks, taken aback by her fluency. His righteous indignation suddenly seems to have lost its momentum.

'All that . . .' he flounders, '. . . with Hooperman . . .'

'I was having a laugh. Trying to liven things up. I need a laugh right now, 'cause life's a bit crap, and you're not making it any easier.'

'Jesus, Anna.'

'Please. Leave it. I don't want us to be snapping at each other all the time. Please?'

Jo pouts, and frowns. 'You haven't made it easy, you know.'

'Sorry about that. Please?'

Slowly, he smiles. She's forgiven. 'Wanna nip out the back for a quick one?' he says. 'If we don't hang about, we can be back before the brie goes.'

*　　*　　*

For Milly, the pleasure of spending the evening with an . . . with an *adult* – talking about real things in a mature way – is enormous. He even gives her a lift home – stopping, for some reason, at the end of the road rather than directly

77

outside the house. Throughout the meal, it never occurred to Milly that she was doing something wrong. When he pulls up his car at the corner of her street, however, that tiny hint of subterfuge brings home to her the real meaning of their evening together.

She gets out of the car hurriedly, flustered, and after the briefest of waves walks off with her back to him. All her enjoyment of the evening is suddenly spoilt by waves of guilt.

Stepping through the front door, the tense atmosphere instantly hits her. Egg is in the living room with his father, Jerry. She hasn't seen Jerry for months, but before she has a chance to greet him, Egg leaps up from the sofa and starts haranguing her.

'Where have you been? Where the fuck have you been? It's ten-thirty! You weren't at the office.'

'Working dinner. I'm sorry. I should have called.'

'Bloody right you should've. I've been worried. I didn't know what had happened.'

'Jesus! I was busy! OK!'

'Thanks for putting work before me. Again!'

Jerry, looking sickened and upset by the argument, stands up and forces himself between them. His horrified expression stops them in their tracks.

'Dad?' says Egg. 'Are you OK?'

Suddenly, Jerry is crying.

Milly puts her arm round him and guides him down on to the sofa. Egg puts the kettle on, and Jerry explains why he has come. Egg's mother has left him for another man. For two years, she's been having an affair behind his back.

Last night she told him about it, and explained that she wanted to move in with her lover.

Egg, stunned into silence, doesn't react. He has spent the afternoon telling Jerry all about himself. He never even asked his dad how he was.

Milly, her own emotions swamped yet again by other people's traumas, gets up and makes the tea.

Chapter 9

Knight in Shining Leather

Warren likes it rough. Rough and anonymous. He may be a slightly queenie Welshman with a desk job, but when it comes to sex, he likes the whiff of leather, body odour and engine oil.

Although he's a diligent worker, there is one area in which Warren's concentration is slightly less than impeccable. His desk faces the door, and at the entrance of each motor-cycle courier, he simply can't resist a glance up.

When Ferdy walks in: sullen, pouting, with a big black helmet tucked under his arm, Warren's usual glance turns into a double take. *Mmm. Juicy.*

He grabs a piece of paper – any piece of paper – and trots to the fax machine in the foyer.

Ferdy is hovering awkwardly, calling for attention. 'Hello? Hello?'

Kira's not there. The foyer's empty.

'Can I help?' says Warren, his voice ever so slightly a-quiver.

'It's something back from Whitechapel. I need a signature.'

'I suppose I can sign for it.'

Warren has six senses: touch, smell, hearing, sight, taste and sexual orientation. The organ which takes charge of his sixth sense is trembling. It's picking something up. It's bleeping. Morse-code pulses of blood are surging to and from his antenna, spreading the good news. *He's one of us! He's one of us!*

Ferdy passes Warren the clipboard, a fraction slower than necessary.

'We don't normally use you, do we?' says Warren, scribbling his signature.

'Nah.'

'But we do now, I suppose?'

'Yeah.'

'You a . . . local outfit?'

There's a vibe. There's definitely a vibe.

'Callimont Court – just over the road.'

'Oh. Right.'

Stay silent, Warren. Don't say anything else. If he continues the conversation, you're in, boy.

'There's quite a few courier firms round this block,' says Ferdy.

Yeeeaaaahhhhhh! Yessssss!

'Must be . . . uhh . . . competitive.'

'We all get along.'

In for the kill, son. In for the kill.

'So . . . you all . . . meet up after work and stuff?'

'Usually in the pub on the corner.'

'Oh. Right,' says Warren.

Ferdy's radio starts barking, in the strange language comprehensible only to motor-cycle couriers and policemen.

'That's me,' says Ferdy. 'Gotta go.'

Warren nods. *Come on, mate. Say something. Give us a wink. Blow us a kiss. Give me your phone number.*

At the door, Ferdy turns, a hint of a smile on his lips. 'We're usually drinking in there from about six-thirty.'

Bingo.

Kira, who also has six senses, has been hovering a few metres away, listening in on the conversation.

'What was that all about?' she says, knowing exactly what it was all about.

'I don't know . . . yet,' says Warren.

Warren goes to the pub, spots Ferdy, catches his eye, then leaves.

If he's worth getting, he's worth waiting for. You can never harm your chances by playing just that little bit hard to get.

Warren is busy typing up a witness statement, when Kira skips over to his desk. Slightly out of breath, she tells him to come and help her move some boxes.

'Now?'

'*Yes.*'

Move some boxes? What's she on about?

He saunters to the foyer, and finds Kira behind her desk, grinning like a maniac. He's about to ask her what she's up to, when Ferdy appears.

'You come for the letter?' says Kira, with a rather poor attempt at an innocent smile.

'Yeah,' says Ferdy, answering Kira, but staring at Warren.

'There you are, then,' says Kira.

Ferdy takes the letter and puts it in his bag without even glancing at it. His gaze is still trained on Warren. 'Did I see you at the pub the other night?'

'I might have popped in.'

'Suppose we missed each other,' says Ferdy. 'Never mind. We're in there most nights.'

He turns and leaves. *Mmm. Nice arse.*

'Boxes?' says Warren.

'Oh! My mistake! They've gone,' says Kira.

One of Warren's main reasons for coming out to Kira was so that she'd stop trying to set him up with women. Oh, well. Clearly, she'll never get off his back. But at least now her efforts are useful.

Ferdy's pub is a noisy, grungy, stinking, hostile shithole full of pissed leather-clad drop-out bikers spoiling for a fight. Warren loves it. He can barely contain his lust.

Ferdy and Warren find the nearest thing the pub can offer to a cosy corner (two sticky stools just outside the bogs), and shout a conversation at each other over the deafening music. Warren nods and smiles and agrees with everything Ferdy says, even though he can barely hear a word of it. Not that this makes for an unsuccessful evening. Warren is in bliss. As long as he can stare at Ferdy's long, dark hair, rugged jaw and kissable lips, he's happy.

Ferdy, it emerges, is hardly the world's greatest conversationalist. But for Warren, this is good news. Less talk means more action.

Knowing that the shag of a lifetime is in the bag, Warren plays it coy when they emerge from the pub – just for the pure theatre of it.

'Well, then,' says Ferdy.

'Right.'

'Fine.'

'Great. So – what are you going to do with your bike? You can't drive.'

'I left it in the pound at work.'

'Right.'

'What about you?'

'Me?' says Warren. 'Oh . . . cab, I think. I might try and find a busier street.'

'Why don't we share a cab? Back to your place. Have a few cans.'

'OK. If you like.'

That night, the house shakes. Jerry, kipping on the living-room sofa, concludes that a tug-of-war is taking place in one of the bedrooms.

Chapter 10

Father Figure

It's not unusual to get jostled in London. When Milly, walking along the street with O'Donnell, is almost knocked off her feet by a rollerblader, she feels the usual mix of rage and impotence. It doesn't occur to her to do anything about it. O'Donnell, however, immediately shouts at the rollerblader to stop, chases after him, rips off his Walkman, and demands that he apologize.

The rollerblader, reluctant to engage in a debate about public rights of way, punches O'Donnell in the face.

O'Donnell immediately punches him back: hard, fast, knocking him flat on his back.

All Milly's anger instantly floats away, and she is left with one thought. *Phwooaarr! What a man!* She knows that the standard reaction in these circumstances is to mince up in your high heels and prise the men apart, begging them to stop. But no. She wants O'Donnell to hit him again. Punch the fucker. Make him bleed.

This moment of – let's face it – pure, unadulterated masculinity opens the floodgates of Milly's lust. Egg has lost interest in her, and O'Donnell has been flirting like a teenager. For weeks, she has been burying herself in legal papers, pretending that nothing's going on, but now she realizes what she wants. O'Donnell. She wants to shag him. A long, slow, dark, naughty screw with her boss is *exactly* what Milly wants.

She has to talk to someone about it. She needs advice. There is only one place to go.

'Anna?'

'What?'

'Do you like older men?'

'*Yeah!* It's the way forward. I've had enough of boys.'

'Have you ever been out with an older man?'

'I've shagged a few. I haven't been out with one. But I'm not like you – the longest relationship I ever had lasted three months.'

Anna's about to go on and describe her three-month affair, but she stops. She senses an admission in the air. One of Milly's rare moments of openness is creeping over the horizon.

Anna takes a sip of wine, leaving a long silence – luring Milly towards an admission of what's on her mind.

'This thing with O'Donnell punching that man . . .'

'Yeah. What?'

Milly stares at the wall, smiling slightly.

'For God's sake,' says Anna, 'the suspense is killing me.'

'OK. I fancy him.'

'Oh my God. Oh-my-God-oh-my-God-oh-my-God.'

'What? Don't.'

'You're so sweet. I love you so much. Don't ever go out of my life.'

'What?'

'I thought you were going to say something serious.'

'It *is* serious. I fancy him.'

'Well, of course you fancy him. He's got self-assurance, dignity . . . and an American Express card. Tell me everything. Is he flirting with you?'

'Well – sort of.'

'He's not bad-looking. I've seen him. Is he married?'

'Yes.'

'*Fab!*'

'I'm having fantasies about him.'

'It's fine to have fantasies. Life would be so boring without fantasies. Let your mind roam free, that's what I say. I mean – I can see it. O'Donnell is an old-style man. Egg is a bit of a lad and a bit of a SNAG. Lovely, but a SNAG.'

'What's a SNAG?'

'Sensitive New Age Guy.'

'Right.'

'There is one thing about older men, though. Major drawback.'

'What?'

'They wear Y-fronts.'

*　　*　　*

Warren is in love. He's never felt like this before. This is it! The real thing. Life suddenly looks like a Coke advert.

As a result, he isn't really thinking clearly when he leaves a message on Ferdy's answerphone.

'Hi . . . it's me. Hope you're feeling OK because my body's still aching. Not that I'm complaining. I haven't had sex like that since I was at college. Listen, why don't you get a bottle of wine and come over? If you're very good I'll let you shake my maracas.'

Ferdy does come round. But he doesn't bring a bottle of wine. And as soon as his motor-cycle helmet comes off, it's clear that he is not happy.

'What the fuck do you think you're doing?' he says, his voice reverberating with suppressed anger.

'What?'

'Leaving that fucking message on my parents' answer machine.'

'Your parents? You live with your parents?'

'Yeah.'

'Oh, shit. I'm sorry. I didn't realize.'

Warren, despite himself, and despite the fact that he's in serious danger of getting beaten up by Ferdy, can't avoid letting out a little laugh.

'It's not funny, you arsehole. I've just spent the last two hours trying to convince my dad the message was a wind-up.'

'Sorry. Doesn't your dad suspect?'

'There's nothing to suspect. I'm getting married. In two weeks.'

'You're joking, aren't you?'

'No. I love her, and I'm marrying her.'

'So what happened last night? You were taken over by aliens from the planet Poof?'

'Last night didn't mean anything.'

'It did. You *know* it did.'

'Look – last night wasn't . . . how I felt. Isn't how I feel. I was drunk. Things were . . . confused. I'm not –'

'So confused that you flirted with me, invited me to the pub, got me pissed, and rogered me into another dimension for six hours?'

'Just keep away from me. Stay out of my life.'

'So confused you had a tube of KY and a packet of mint condoms in your jacket?'

'You call again and I'll kill you.'

'What are you going to do – shag me to death?'

Ferdy snarls, turns from the door, and climbs on to his bike. Revving hard, he roars off.

'Have a nice wedding!' calls Warren, his voice drowned out by the retreating motor bike.

*   *   *

The arrival of his dad has changed everything for Egg. It dawns on him that there is a simple explanation for his recent actions. He's been in a depression. A selfish, self-indulgent, blinkered depression. Compared to the genuine horror that his father has just been through – with a twenty-six-year marriage falling apart into acrimony and betrayal – his life is peachy. OK, so he started as a lawyer and realized that he didn't like it. So what? Big deal. He has to get on and do something else with his life. And if he really does want to be a writer, he can't expect just to

89

live off Milly until he sells his book. It can take years to write a book. He must get a job, pay his way, and generally get himself started again.

The first step on his new life has to be with Milly. He has been undervaluing her and exploiting her. He must explain to her what he's been through, apologize for acting like a child, and get their sex life started again.

On reflection, he decides to take those three in reverse order. Sex first, apologies later.

As a novelist, Egg knows a thing or two about feminine psychology, and decides that the best way to rekindle Milly's interest in sex is with a touch of pornography.

'Look what I bought today,' he says, just as Milly gets into bed. He has to act fast, or she'll be asleep.

'What?'

'A book.'

'What book?'

'This.'

From his bedside table, he picks up a copy of *The Taking of Princess Selina* and passes it to her. She glances at the cover, cackles, wrinkles her nose, and turns away.

'I bought it for you,' he says. 'It's written specially for women. So it's – you know – tasteful.'

'If I want one of those books, I'll buy one myself.'

'Yeah, but you wouldn't.'

'I did. I bought a sex book.'

'What – a namby-pamby therapy book? What we need is honest-to-god no-nonsense porn. I'll read a bit out to you –'

'Egg. I'm not in the mood.'

'I'm just getting to the bit when they insert the wooden penises.'

'Wooden penises?'

'Yeah – to prepare her for her master.'

'Sick.'

'It's fantasy.'

'It's sick.'

Milly turns her back, and a vision floats into her head of O'Donnell – naked, with a huge wooden penis. Mahogany.

With a smirk, Milly closes her eyes and tries to drift off – already looking forward to her night's dreams.

*　　*　　*

All week, Milly and O'Donnell work late on the divorce case. The details, however, aren't *that* complicated. It occurs to Milly that this will be one of the most thoroughly prepared divorce cases in the firm's history.

Then the inevitable happens. O'Donnell asks Milly out for supper again. Her heart racing, with as casual a voice as she can manage, she agrees to go.

Over the meal, O'Donnell continues to flirt, and makes all the right noises – flattering her looks, praising her work, and telling her how long it has been since he last had a meal with a beautiful young woman. Milly, however, senses that something is wrong. The atmosphere isn't quite right. Perhaps it's the slightly apologetic overtone in his voice. Whatever it is, Milly somehow gets the feeling that rather than representing the culmination of something, the meal represents a termination. O'Donnell, she can tell, is trying to back off.

Outside the restaurant, they hover for some time – neither of them making a move to hail a cab. The real issue of the evening still hasn't been discussed.

'Milly,' he says, eventually. 'I have to make an apology. This whole thing . . . I've been . . . It just isn't going to happen.'

Milly blinks and swallows. Only a surge of anger – at herself, for her weakness – stops her tears.

'I think you're lovely,' he says, 'but we're not going to have an affair.'

'It's OK –'

'Believe me, I –'

'It's OK. Really.'

'There's nothing I'd like better than to have sex with you. But we work well together. It would be wrong to jeopardize that.'

'I'm going.' She has to leave fast – without crying – with her dignity intact.

'See you tomorrow,' he says, smiling. Forcing eye contact out of her.

'Bye,' she says, looking up at him.

He leans down and gives her a dry, quick peck on the lips.

'Bye,' he says.

There is a moment's pause, with neither of them moving, before he leans forward again, and gives her another dry kiss on the lips – this one lingering a fraction before he withdraws.

'If you kiss me like that again, I'll have to kiss you back,' she says.

Time stops, London vanishes, while Milly and O'Donnell lose themselves in a deep, long, passionate kiss.

The roar of a motor bike, speeding past inches away from them – a thick pony-tail of dark hair flying behind the rider – unfreezes the world. Pulling apart, they stare at each other, speechless.

Without a word, Milly turns and walks. She has betrayed her ideals, she has betrayed Egg, and she has humiliated herself in front of her boss. Everything about their kiss felt wrong.

She travels home, disgusted with herself, and with the situation she has created. She simply isn't cut out for deceit.

Chapter 11

Let's Get It On

Egg's dad, Jerry, knows no one in London. Unable to go back to Manchester, where he would have to face the reality of his collapsed marriage, Jerry spends most of his time at Benjamin Street. For Egg, in his unemployed state, this is rather like having your guilty conscience wandering around the house making you cups of tea.

Egg tries to be sympathetic about Jerry's problems, but is so shocked by what has happened that he can't manage anything very helpful. Jerry tries to be sympathetic about Egg's unemployment, but is almost overwhelmed by the desire to give him a slap and tell him to get on with his life. The two of them, in fact, spend most of their time prowling around the house, avoiding each other, and waiting for the others to come home. Not that Egg has much to look forward to on Milly's return, these days. He's mainly waiting for Miles to get back, so that they can watch telly together or go to the pub.

Jerry, although he hasn't quite admitted it to himself, is particularly waiting for Anna. He admires her. She's everything he isn't: forthright, confident, in control. She is also extremely kind, and seems genuinely concerned about what went wrong with his marriage. They have spent several long evenings talking, by candlelight, about his life and how things turned out so badly. Only the nagging worry that she finds him boring spoils his enjoyment of their time together.

'I shouldn't be talking about myself,' he says, as this fear rises. 'Tell me about you. How was your day?'

'God,' says Anna. 'Say that again. That was incredible.'

'What? How was your day?'

'No – start from, "I shouldn't . . ."'

'I . . . shouldn't be talking about myself. Er . . . how was your day – tell me about yourself.'

'Thanks, Jerry. My day was . . . pretty dull. In fact – I had no work today. Tomorrow I'm going to court – to apply on a publican's behalf for the renewal of his licence to serve liquor. Another day at the cutting edge of litigation.'

'But – generally speaking, you'd say you're in the right job? I can tell that you are.'

'Maybe.' Anna smiles. *My God*, she's thinking, *this is what you're supposed to do with your time. I'm an adult. I should be doing this. Having mature conversations with . . . with exchange of opinions, reflections on what really matters, genuine concern. This is what life's about. This is real communication.*

At that moment, just as Anna is reshuffling her life priorities, the light switch flicks on, and Miles walks in. With Jerry and Anna blinking in the glare, the atmosphere is shattered.

95

'What are you doing in the dark?' says Miles.

'Could you switch the light off, please,' says Jerry – a hint of ice in his voice.

Miles flicks the switch, returning the room to candle-light, but not before he has spotted a bottle on the coffee table.

'Oh – whisky,' he says, charging for the sofa. 'D'you mind?'

Jerry shrugs, and Miles plucks a used glass from the coffee table, peers into it, gives it a couple of shakes, and pours himself a generous slug. Plonking himself heavily on to the sofa next to Anna, he sighs contentedly.

A distinctly chilly fuck-off-Miles silence hangs in the air. Miles can feel the hostility being beamed at him, and decides to settle in for a chat. There's something about Jerry he doesn't like. The way he always hangs around Anna is creepy.

'So,' he says, smiling at Jerry, 'what happened in the football?'

'I'm sorry – I don't follow it.'

'It was an international. Well – we lost. I was just wondering how much we lost by. I know we lost 'cause we can't win in Europe. I mean – they pass the ball. We don't pass the ball any more. It's a great shame.'

'We all know how knowledgeable you are about foot-ball,' says Anna, with blunt scorn.

'I can't understand how it happened that we stopped passing the ball. You would have thought you couldn't play football without passing the ball. But you can. We do.'

'Fascinating, Miles. We were having an interesting conversation – me and Jerry. You'll probably want to go to
bed.'

'No, no, no. I love conversation. Don't mind me.'

There is another silence, which Miles fills with a noisy
slurp of whisky.

'Cantona,' he says. 'Now he can pass the ball. But he's
foreign, isn't he?'

Anna knows exactly what Miles is up to. He's warning her
off Jerry. He feels threatened by the presence of an older
man – in particular an older man who appeals to a younger
woman. Miles can't handle it, and he's trying to come
between them.

In the circumstances, there is only one possible course
of action.

*　　*　　*

Warren is stumbling around the world in a death-of-love
depression. Everything is difficult. Everything hurts.
Inanimate objects conspire against him. Life feels like a
Sensodyne toothpaste advert – innocent things zapping
you with a lightning bolt to the jaw just when you least
expect it.

Ferdy, once a leather-queen biker boy, now a Catholic
bridegroom, is gone for good.

*　　*　　*

'You're good at that,' says Anna, rolling over and reaching
for the packet of cigarettes on her bedside table.

'I've had some practice,' says Jerry.

'You're *really* good at it.'

'Twice a week for twenty-five years.'

'Twice a week? That's not bad.'

'Every day for the first year.'

'Let's see – fifty-two weeks in the year – call it a hundred times. Twenty-five years. Plus, say, an extra five hundred. That's three thousand fucks. Blimey.'

* * *

Milly has no talent for keeping secrets. From the moment she tells Egg that she spent the evening having dinner with O'Donnell, she knows that he suspects something. She has done nothing worse than a kiss, but she knows, just from the guilty way she told Egg about their meal, that she gave him the suspicion she has had sex with O'Donnell.

She hates herself for hurting Egg, she hates herself for lying, and she hates herself for what she has done. Above all, she feels bitter. Other people – Anna – do what they want. They fearlessly have sex with whoever takes their fancy. But Milly – having spent her whole life obeying the rules – steps out of line once – just a silly, adolescent snog – and she feels the whole edifice of her life collapsing. Her relationship and her work – two things in which she has invested years of her life – are suddenly under threat.

It's not fair. *Why* is goody-two-shoes Milly never allowed to break the rules? Why is her world so much more vulnerable than everyone else's?

*

It's a ridiculous situation, and she has to get it under control. Arriving at work, she marches straight into O'Donnell's office, and speaks without even greeting him. 'I'm really glad it turned out the way it did,' she says, assertively.

'I've been thinking about you,' he says.

'I mean it. I'm really glad.'

'Are we still friends?'

'Yes. I just want you to know – it's got nothing to do with you – but you do know Egg, and I want you to know it had nothing to do with him. Me and Egg are not splitting up or anything like that.'

'Good.'

Milly turns and leaves, an aggressive look on her face, and walks to her office. She slams the door.

That evening, Milly takes Egg out for a meal.

'What's wrong?' she says. He is behaving more sulkily than ever.

'What do you think is wrong?' he says. He looks slightly red around the eyes.

'I don't know. I can guess – but I don't know.'

'I don't want to talk about it.'

'You want me to read your mind?'

'Yeah – please.'

'I can't read your mind, Egg.'

'OK. Did you fuck him?'

'Egg!'

'Sorry. Start again. Did you have sex with Mr O'Donnell?'

99

'No!'

'But you thought about it, didn't you?'

'I didn't do it.'

'So you did want to?'

'Well – maybe for a moment. So what?'

'What do you mean, "So what?"'

'It was a phase.'

'You can't have "phases".'

'Don't tell me what to do.'

'OK – I can't tell you what to do. But this is what I'm going to do. If you have sex with another bloke while you're going out with me – I will leave you. Understood?'

Something in the way he says this breaks the atmosphere. This is the closest Egg has come in months to showing Milly that he cares for her. Milly, touched – genuinely moved – by his sincerity, reaches out an arm.

'Understood,' she says, taking his hand.

At last – contact. The pair of them have made contact.

'So you never fancy anyone else, then?' says Milly, with a sceptical smile.

'Well – I wouldn't say that,' Egg admits, reluctantly.

'Who? Go on.'

'That Spanish girl in the deli,' he says. 'I wouldn't mind going around the houses a few times with her.'

'Anyone else?'

'Anthea Turner.'

'Oh, please.'

'What?'

'I think I'd prefer not to know that.'

'There you go then,' he says, relieved that he can keep the remaining few hundred names to himself.

'Egg,' she says. 'I'm sorry if I've been . . .'

'What?'

'Just – sorry for not being supportive. I just – don't know how I feel about you leaving the firm . . . not working.'

'I am – I'm writing. Trying to get a part-time job.'

'I know. I know. It's not you. I just – haven't worked out how I feel.'

'That's OK. You can be clear in being confused,' he says. 'That's fine.'

'I know I moan about it, but I don't mind paying the rent. Honestly. But . . . I do wish you'd make more of an effort. You know – change the sheets just once a year or something.'

'OK. Once a year.'

'Every other week?'

'Every other week,' he says. 'But – before I change them . . .'

'What?'

'I think we should get them dirty.'

'OK.'

'Like – now. This evening.'

'Good idea.

Milly and Egg arrive home, hand in hand, to find the house full of people, with the lights off and music thumping. Anna is in the hall, dancing with Jerry.

'What's going on?' says Egg.

'Impromptu party,' says Anna, shouting over the music. 'As of half an hour ago.'

'What for?'

'Birthday.'

'Whose?'

With a sideways nod, Anna indicates Jerry.

'Oh, shit. Sorry, Dad. I didn't realize. I would have got you something, but –'

'Shut up, Egg. That's the best present you've given me in years,' says Jerry – pointing at Egg and Milly's hands, still clasped. Instinctively, they both let go, blushing.

Anna leans forward and kisses Milly on the cheek. 'I love you both,' she says, kissing Egg as well.

Despite Milly's first instinct – to resent any intrusion into her personal life – she realizes that she's been caught out. Everyone in the house must have known that things with Egg were going badly. And now, it must be equally obvious that (for the evening, at least) they are a happy couple. She puts her arm round Egg and smiles.

Egg, in shock at this unprecedented public display of affection, beams.

'Piss off in there and get a drink before I vomit,' says Anna, shoving them into the living room.

The first thing Milly sees is Miles, standing by the drinks, staring at Anna and Jerry. You can almost see the cogs in his head whirring.

'I hate that,' he says, as Milly approaches.

'What?'

'The way Jerry clings on to Anna all the time. It's disgusting.'

'Miles – they're having a . . . thing. Didn't you know?'

Miles tries to take this information in coolly, but fails. His face reddens, and he leaves the room.

'Egg,' says Milly. 'Wait here.'

Milly, glass in hand, trots into the hall, squeezing between Jo and Kira, who are wedged in the doorway, discussing the relative merits of *Captain Pugwash* and *The Magic Roundabout*. She grabs Anna's arm, tugs her into a private corner, and whispers in her ear, 'I think Miles is upset.'

'Miles?' says Anna. '*Upset?*'

'I always thought you and Miles – I mean, I know you play games. But really . . . Jerry is –'

'Upset about Jerry and me?' Anna can barely contain her joy at this idea.

'Yes. Are you deaf?'

'Just checking.'

'Don't you like Miles any more? Why don't you go upstairs and seduce him right now.'

'Jesus, Milly. Your blood's up this evening.'

Milly blushes and smirks, trying to cover her embarrassment by taking a generous swig of wine. The wine (or is it paint stripper?) takes the smile off her face.

'If I have sex with Miles, you'll have to hospitalize me afterwards,' says Anna.

'He's upstairs,' says Milly, retreating.

Alone for a moment, Anna swivels her head. No sign of Jerry.

Swiftly, she climbs the stairs, stepping over a semi-comatose Warren, who is burbling something about sexual deprivation, and how it's all the Pope's fault.

Jerry, emerging from the toilet, spots Anna's feet just as they disappear from the first-floor landing.

Outside Milly and Egg's bedroom, Anna – slightly out of breath – spots Miles.

'There you are,' she says.

They look at each other. Miles doesn't speak. Anna seems lost for words.

Then they hear a voice – Jerry's voice – wafting up the stairs. 'Anna? Anna?'

It's getting louder.

'Quick,' says Miles. He takes Anna's hand, and drags her into the nearest room.

Jerry's voice is now immediately outside. In the darkness, Miles makes out a wardrobe and fumbles it open. The pair of them bustle in, just in time to hear the bedroom door open.

'Anna? Anna?'

There is a brief silence, then the click of a closing door.

Miles and Anna stay in the wardrobe, listening to each other's breathing.

'Do you think he's gone?' asks Miles.

'Oh dear,' says Anna, shuddering with repressed laughter. 'It's tragic.'

'Did you not find him a bit, sort of, wrinkly?' asks Miles.

'Well, he wasn't all sort of firm, and . . .' With one

finger, she pokes Miles in the stomach. '. . . firm. Let's get out of here.'

Miles opens the wardrobe door, and sees Milly and Egg inching towards the bed, tearing one another's clothes off. The pair of them are too wrapped up in one another to notice the shaking, talkative wardrobe.

'Shit.'

He clicks the door shut again.

Even through half an inch of wood, the noises are unmistakable. Full-on sex. Full-on sex after a long gap.

'Oh, my God,' says Anna. 'This isn't happening.'

'Let's go,' says Miles.

The wardrobe pops open, and they make a dash for the door, eyes averted. Milly, on her back, sees the two figures sneaking out of her room and recognizes them by silhouette. She smiles. 'Yes! Yes!' she says.

Inside Anna's bedroom, on the top floor, Miles jams the door shut with a tilted chair. Neither of them speaks, as they step outside on to Anna's balcony.

Part Two

Chapter 12

Last Tango in Southwark

Anna wakes up with Miles in her bed. Braving a faintly rancid whiff, she kisses him on the lips. *This could be it*, she thinks. *This could be the one.*

Miles grunts and rolls away, lost in sleep.

Anna hops out of bed and down to breakfast. The house is scattered with party debris, with a beery smell in the air. The kitchen floor is sticky. Only one other person is at the table – not her ideal breakfast partner, given the circumstances. Jerry.

'Hi,' she says, trying not to sound too happy.

'Hi.'

Jerry, curiously, looks less miserable than he ought to. 'I think I'm going to move on,' he says. 'Get a place of my own.'

'Jerry . . .'

'What? Look – I've no problem with last night, Anna. Really.'

'Right.' *As if.*

'I mean it. I've no regrets. I just hope Miles appreciates what he's got. I know I did.'

Jesus. What a gent. She wants to snog him right there over breakfast, by way of thanks.

'I've got to get ready. I'll see you, Jerry.'

She kisses him on the forehead and skips up the stairs – tea in one hand, toast in the other. Life is good. Men are great. Sex is fantastic.

She bumps into Miles outside the bathroom. He looks rough. His hair seems to have five partings, all at different angles, and his face is a delicate shade of grey-green. He is also dressed in a suit, and seems to be heading for the front door.

'Hi,' he says.

'Hi,' says Anna. 'You off, then?'

Tension. There is definitely tension.

'Yeah. Got to be in court by ten.'

'Right.'

'Must've been wasted last night,' he grunts.

'Yeah?' *What's he getting at. What's he saying?* 'Yeah – I was pretty out of it myself.'

'Pretty stupid, really.'

'What was?' *What was? What was?*

'You know. Getting pissed like that. Court case this morning. Not very professional.'

'No. Suppose not.'

'Right. I'll see you later, then,' he says, shuffling towards the stairs.

'See you.'

'Bye.'

'Bye.'

Christ. That was fucking tense. Although the sex was great – it was even a laugh – Anna and Miles seem to have woken up in a Harold Pinter play.

Miles gets through his court case in the same way a corpse gets through a funeral. Afterwards, he downs a pint or so of water in the Gents, and heads for chambers. First port of call, as ever, is Jo's office.

'Good party, was it?' says Jo. His tone of voice somehow adds to these four words, 'You look like shit and I know what you did.'

'Yeah, not bad,' says Miles, toppling into the nearest chair.

'What about Anna? She enjoy herself?'

There is no point in resisting. To avoid the topic is simply to prolong Jo's pleasure.

'OK, so you know. What's she said about it?'

'Nothing. Why?'

'No reason. I just wondered if she'd mentioned it, that's all.'

'Nah, mate – she's keeping shtum. Probably embarrassed it ever happened, eh?'

'Yeah, well, if she'd slept with you, maybe –'

'So what's the problem, then?'

'Who said there was one? We're fine,' says Miles, defensively.

'So – you two an item, then?'

'I don't know. We haven't really talked about it.'

'Well – you would have done if she was interested.'

'Not necessarily. We've been busy.'

'What about this morning? You must have woken up together.'

Miles hesitates for a second, caught out, and Jo pounces. 'Oh. Like that, is it? Well – she's blown you out, ain't she?'

'I don't think so.'

'Face it, mate – she's a one-night-stand merchant. Always was, always will be.'

'Yeah – well maybe that's all I was after.'

'Right.'

Anna, about to enter Jo's office, pauses unheard outside the door. Miles's voice brings her up short, and she listens, intent – and increasingly outraged.

'Look, Anna's a good shag – I admit – but that doesn't mean to say I want a long-term relationship with her. Might be more work than it's worth. Who knows?'

'Believe it.'

'Anyway – living together – might get a bit awkward, mightn't it?'

'Bound to.'

'I'm going to take her out for lunch – have a word with her about it.'

But Miles isn't going to take Anna for lunch. She has already stormed out of the building, and is standing on the pavement taking urgent steps to rectify the lack of nicotine in her bloodstream.

Bastard. Bastard.

She stamps down the street, heading for Milly's office.

*

Over lunch in Lincoln's Inn Fields, Milly tries to calm Anna down. After a full description of the eavesdropped conversation, Milly manages half a syllable of comfort, 'An –' before Anna sets off again.

'I promised myself that if I ever went for it with Miles, I'd take it slowly. Not like last time – jump into bed and not see him again for four years. No. This time, I'd do it properly. Make the bastard beg.' Anna, staring at the grass, doesn't see Milly smirk.

'Sorry.'

'About what?' says Anna, distractedly.

'Well – I was the one that suggested you go and seduce him.'

'Don't be daft.'

'I think he really does like you, though.'

'Yeah – well, I'm a "good shag", aren't I?'

'Oh, come on. Blokes talk like that to each other all the time. We do the same.'

'Excuse me, but I would never, ever, refer to Miles as a "good shag".'

'Bad then, eh?'

Suddenly, sex isn't such a touchy subject for Milly. Anna thinks for a second, chewing over her memories of the previous night. 'No,' she says, smiling slightly. 'Makes it even worse, doesn't it?'

'Look – you haven't even talked to him. How can you know what he's thinking? He's probably just as worried about you.' Anna instantly laughs at this idea, but Milly presses on – not caving in to Anna's pessimism. 'Why don't you tell him how you feel?'

'And be humiliated even more? I don't think so.'

'That's just stupid.'

'Well I am, aren't I? You know what I think? I think he did it 'cause of me and Jerry.'

'How d'you mean?'

'Well – bit of a blow to his ego, wasn't it? Older guy moving in. I think he just wanted to prove something to himself. And I let him.'

Just when Anna thinks her life can't get any worse, it doesn't. It gets better. She arrives back from lunch to find a big, fat brief waiting for her in Jo's office. A proper case too – criminal damage – something you can get your teeth into. After her prolonged self-pitying lunch with Milly, she only has a couple of hours to read the entire brief and prepare for court.

At least work has been going well lately, she reflects, just as she bumps into Miles in the doorway.

'Anna – can I have a word?'

'Not now. I've got to read this.' *Yes! Perfect timing.*

'What, you've got more work?' Since being bumped off the Sheringham case, Miles has been having a thin time.

'Asked for her specially,' chips in Jo – ever the professional stirrer.

'How come? What – have you done something for them before?'

'No. I give blow-jobs to their senior partner.'

Anna turns and leaves the room. Her sarcasm is back in place, and she's even made an exit. What more could she hope for? She walks to her desk – the confident bounce back in her step for the first time that day.

Even better, Miles is trotting after her. She can hear him.

'Anna! Wait!'

'Look, Miles. I've got about half an hour to read this –'

'We did fuck last night, didn't we? I mean, tell me if it was some peculiar nightmare but I was under the impression that you quite enjoyed it.'

Anna doesn't reply. She has the upper hand for the moment, but can feel her control of the situation slipping away.

'I just wanted to say,' Miles adds, 'that we might at least have the guts to talk about it.'

'OK. When?

'Yeah, well – since you're so in demand it'll have to be later. I'll be in the pub around the corner from about six. Join me there if you like. It's up to you.'

Jo – who has an impeccable sense of drama – chats affably to Anna on her return from court at ten to six. He can tell she's in a hurry, and only when Anna has a coat on and is half out of the door does he chip in with, 'Oh! Hold up a minute. Hoopie wants a word.'

'What about?' says Anna, exasperated.

'Oh, yeah. He confides in me about everything.'

Anna sighs, tosses her coat over a chair, and heads down the corridor.

*

Although it's only five past six, Miles has a forlorn look on his face as he checks his watch. Either she's deliberately late – on a power trip – or she's not going to show up at all – also on a power trip.

Oh, Jesus. Hooperman's in one of his expansive moods.

'Sit.'

He's also opening a bottle of wine.

'I'm hearing good things, Anna. Very good indeed,' he says, pouring a generous glass and thrusting it into her hand.

'Thank you.'

'Good?' he says, expectantly, eyeing her glass. Hooperman, for some reason, is drinking mineral water.

Anna assumes his question refers to the wine, but isn't quite sure. 'Yes, fine thanks,' she replies, carefully choosing a catch-all phrase to suit whatever he's referring to.

'Excellent. So, tell me – what have you been working on lately?'

Oh, no. The bastard's decided he wants a sodding chat.

Fucking pissing slagging power-tripping bitch. Fucking typical. I'll give it one more pint, and I'm off. Just one more.

Miles spots a girl – blonde, a touch bland but relatively fit, seemingly on her own – and decides to salvage something from his disastrous evening.

'What are you drinking?' he says.

Chat-up lines have never been Miles's strong point. But then, he doesn't seem to need them.

*

Hooperman leans forward to top up Anna's glass. Just in time, she slides her hand over the rim.

'Err, no. I'm fine, thanks. I'm . . . meant to be meeting someone later.'

'Oh, I see.'

'Well, it's just Miles actually.'

'Nothing important, then?'

'No, well . . .'

Despairingly, Anna watches Hooperman refill her glass.

'You see – I've called you in to talk about a tenancy. You've been here a few months now and I thought perhaps we might discuss the situation.'

'Oh, right. Yes. I'd like that very much. Thank you.'

Pretending to scratch her wrist and rub her chin, Anna checks her watch. *Shit! Quarter to seven.*

Miles, well into his fourth pint, is blissfully unaware of the dent that alcohol has made in his charm. His chat-up victim, almost asleep, hasn't spoken for half an hour.

'It's pathetic, really,' he continues. 'I mean, I slept with her years ago. It was just a one-night stand, you know? She's obviously just been storing it up – waiting for a chance to do the same thing to me. Yeah – like I care. I mean, it'd only work if I really liked her. And I don't. So where's the victory in that, eh?'

Anna – having eventually escaped Hooperman – appears in the pub, and spots Miles deep in conversation with the blonde girl. She feels her tension about being late and her worry over letting him down instantly transform themselves into one emotion. Anger. Pure rage.

She plucks a partly drunk pint from a vacant table, charges up to Miles, and tosses the beer in his face. Feeling a depressing lack of triumph at this gesture, she runs out of the pub. Miles chases after her, shouting.

'Anna! Anna – wait!'

Although she knows she should just run away – indignant and aloof – Anna can't stop herself turning round and confronting him.

'Was that how you wanted to tell me? Let me show up and see you with someone else?'

'No.'

'You spineless shit!'

'I was talking to her about you! Where the hell were you? We said six o'clock.'

'I got delayed. Hooperman wanted to see me.'

'And how was I supposed to know?'

'You're right. It was my fault. Now fuck off!'

'Will you just listen?'

'No. You listen, Miles. It's over. OK? I've given up taking pity on you. You were the worst shag of my life the first time around –'

'I knew it was about that.'

'– and the second time lived right down to expectations.'

'Yeah, well you weren't so bloody hot yourself.'

'I was a fucking result and you know it!'

'No. You were a result for Jerry, Anna. You'll find that people under the age of thirty have slightly higher standards.'

Anna draws breath – amazed that Miles has somehow found a way of sinking even lower.

'What did I see in you?' she says. 'What did I see that made me think we could ever have a relationship?'

'You don't want a relationship, Anna. You just want to cut my balls off.'

'Well, I'd have to find them first.'

Anna is about to knock on Milly's door, but stops herself, hearing the sound of energetic (if relatively discreet) sex. She presses on, up the extra flight of stairs, to bed. Life is shit. Men are bastards. Sex is a con.

Chapter 13

Underhand Tactics

Kira arrives at work to find a display of six fluffy pink cuddly gonks on the front of her desk. Sitting in her chair is Kelly, tutting and shuffling papers from drawer to drawer.

Kira is speechless with horror.

'Hiya,' says Kelly.

'What are you doing here?'

'I don't know who's been covering for me but this place is a mess. Nothing's where it should be.'

'I thought you said you weren't coming back? Your mum said you'd got another job.'

'Dozy cow. I applied for one but they didn't want me. So I'm back here, worse luck.'

'Does O'Donnell know?'

'Well, he should do. Mum said she'd phone him and tell him I was OK.'

Kira, with a mildly psychotic look in her eyes, heads for O'Donnell's office.

Kelly calls after her, 'Get us a coffee, will you?'

*   *   *

Word spreads fast that Hooperman is putting Anna up for a tenancy. If she can keep a steady flow of successful work going for a couple more months, she'll be in.

The source of this gossip is, unsurprisingly, Anna. She's telling as many people as she can about her triumph – particularly when Miles is within earshot. On the surface, she may be telling Jo that she's up for tenancy, but really her comments are aimed out into the corridor. *See, Miles. I'm on the up. One bad fuck can't drag me down.*

Jo, sizing up the situation, wanders into Miles's office to give him a brief (and to indulge in a good old stir). 'A B H and affray in a pub on the Mile End. 'S all in there,' says Jo, tossing the papers on to Miles's desk.

'Cheers.'

'Anna seemed pretty up this morning. Is that 'cause of the tenancy, then? Or –'

'Did you know about that?' says Miles, peeved.

'No.'

'There's little enough work as it is. What's Hooperman playing at?'

'She's a good barrister.'

'Series of flukes.'

'Well, don't get too paranoid about it, eh? I mean, it's not definite or nothing.'

Miles lights up a fag, suddenly tense. 'Yet. Just wait till she's worked her way through the rest of chambers. Me down. Sixteen other poor bastards to go.'

'No joy, then? Last night?'

Jo is in heaven. Miles is possibly the easiest person to wind up in the history of the legal profession.

'Well, I blew her out if that's what you mean.'

'Right.'

'Ask her if you don't believe me. She found me chatting up this blonde girl and went psycho. It's ridiculous. We can't seriously take her on – I mean, what if she flips out like that on a client?'

'She won't. Look – just 'cause you two had a bust-up –'

'That's got nothing to do with it. She needs help. That's why I blew her out. I just didn't want to be the one carrying her until she got it.'

'Well – don't feel too bad about it, eh?' says Jo, as insincerely as he can manage.

'I don't intend to.'

Back in his office, Jo fingers the other new brief of the morning. In fact, it's more or less the same brief. Two co-defendants with different solicitors – requiring a pair of barristers able to work as a team.

He smiles warmly, with a slightly evil glint in his eye, as Anna sweeps into his office. 'I've got something for you,' he says.

*   *   *

O'Donnell, having invited Kira and Kelly into his office to settle their dispute amicably, immediately regrets this decision.

'I didn't know my mum hadn't phoned,' whines Kelly.

'Well, you should've done it yourself, then, shouldn't you? See? She's useless,' whines Kira.

'I've been ill.'

'The only reason she's here now,' says Kira, 'is 'cause the job she applied for fell through.'

'That's rubbish.'

'You liar!'

'I never applied for another job! I like it here.'

O'Donnell, waves of tiredness sweeping over him, somehow can't bring himself to wade in.

'You said you hated it.'

'No I never. It's not my fault I had appendicitis.'

'If it *was* that.'

'What's that supposed to mean?'

'All right,' says O'Donnell. 'Let's –'

'Probably just a stomach-ache from stuffing yourself stupid.'

'I had peritonitis! I could've died! Look.'

Kelly lifts her jumper, revealing an angry-looking scar on her abdomen. O'Donnell suddenly feels woozy.

'That could be anything,' says Kira. 'Someone probably harpooned you by mistake.'

'Are you calling me fat?'

'I'm surprised you can waddle through the door.'

'Be quiet!' cuts in O'Donnell, finally. 'One more word and I'll sack the pair of you.'

Silence descends, and the pair of them look at their feet, chastened. O'Donnell sighs, trying to brush aside his weariness, and settles into headmaster mode. They can both keep their jobs; they can learn to behave like adults; and, above all, they can leave him alone.

* * *

'You're *what*?' Miles shrieks.

Anna grins, through gritted teeth. 'I'm representing the second defendant – Philip Becks.'

'This is a joke, right?'

'No.'

'Shit! Jo's done this on purpose.'

'Miles. Sit down.'

'Excuse me?'

'Look – I'm not overjoyed about the situation either, but since they are co-defendants it might help to know what line you're planning to take.'

Miles slumps into his chair and stares at Anna, his features puckered into a scowl. 'Yeah, well just don't fuck it up for me, all right?'

'And vice bloody versa – I've got more riding on this than you.'

'Let's just try and be professional, shall we?'

'You try. I already am.'

Why does Miles feel he's losing this argument? Why does he want to thump her?

'Well, we'll see about that, won't we?'

Weak, Miles. Weak.

'Look,' he says, 'your instructions should be the same as mine. We're taking a self-defence line.'

'I'm not admitting to any part in the violence.'

124

'That's a bad word to use for a start. If you start labelling my client's actions as violent – '

'There are three witnesses who'll do that.'

'I'm not worried about them. They're shaky. Look – just follow my line of questioning.'

'Don't patronize me, Miles. I'll take the line I see fit.'

'Which is?'

'My client was attempting to restrain the assailant – that's all.'

'Mine too. So it's exactly what I said in the first place, isn't it? Self-defence.'

How is Anna going to put up with Miles's smugness? How is she going to avoid thumping him?

Miles's pride has been tickled. He doesn't trust Anna. At stake is not just a legal but also a phallic victory. She wants to put one over on him. He can tell. And the only way to deal with it is to put one over on her first.

He arranges an informal meeting in the pub with his client, Terry Cole. No charge. Strictly informal. Just to sniff out the territory.

In the pub on Chancery Lane, Terry isn't difficult to spot. A hundred men and women in dark pin-stripe, and one bloke in a purple shell suit with a shaved head and several kilos of gold on his fingers.

'Terry Cole?' inquires Miles, out of politeness.

'Yeah. How could you tell?'

Because you might as well have the word THUG tattooed on your forehead, mate. 'Intuition.'

Miles settles Terry down with a couple of pints, and tries to gauge the case's weak points. There seems to be no shortage. Fortunately, the biggest one is Terry's co-defendant, Becks. Apparently, he's 'a shitter'.

It's going to be a hard case to win. Terry is the kind of person who clearly has a rather generous, and enthusiastically enforced, interpretation of 'self-defence'. Proving him to be an innocent man set upon without provocation by a gang of motiveless bottle-wielding maniacs is going to be a tough one.

*   *   *

Although Kelly is rarely afflicted by much curiosity about legal matters, something stops her from hanging up when she puts Egg's call through to Milly. Hearing the words 'I've had a hard-on all day just thinking about you', Kelly presses the phone harder against her ear.

'I'm feeling it now,' says Egg.

'Egg!'

'You do it too.'

'What?'

'Go on. Slide your hand up your skirt. Are you wet?'

'Egg!'

'Go on. Do it. I love you.'

All five lights on the switchboard are flashing angrily. *Shit*. Kelly abandons Milly's call and returns to work.

Five minutes later, Milly's line is still busy. The blind on her office door is down.

*   *   *

Anna only needs to clap eyes on Becks to know that he's flaky. Even asking him in a friendly way to go over his statement, he contradicts himself and falls apart. He also smokes neurotically, and has the guilty body language of a three-year-old with a full nappy.

Miles clips into the court-house with Terry, looking confident and smug. Terry approaches Becks and plucks the cigarette from Beck's lips, threateningly.

'All right?' says Terry, steely-voiced.

Becks shudders and looks away.

Miles drags Anna aside. 'How is he?' he whispers.

'Fine.'

'Doesn't look it. Don't fuck this up, Anna.'

'I've said he'll be fine. Just spend a lot of time on the prosecution witnesses. That way I'll have lunch-time to pump him up.'

'Fancy a beer?' says Terry, loudly.

Anna whips round. 'Not you,' she says, taking Becks by the hand and dragging him away. 'You're coming with me.'

Terry watches her go – more than a hint of lechery in his gaze. 'I'm glad she's on our side,' he mumbles.

In the court-house café, Anna sits Becks down and eyeballs him. 'Your statement's bollocks, isn't it?'

'Eh?'

'Just tell me the truth. You went down there looking for that man.'

'No.'

'I need to know. That way if you veer off your statement

127

I can put you back on course. Now you went down there to find him, didn't you?'

'Terry did, yeah. He'd smacked one of his mates earlier.'

'Why did he take you?'

'Drive him. He's been banned.'

'So he picked a fight, then waited for the guy outside. What about the bottle injury on his head?'

'Did it himself. He's a nutter.'

'Did you know why you were taking him there?'

'No. He don't have nothing to do with me, usually.'

'Well that's the statement you should make.'

'Eh?'

'We blame the whole thing on Terry Cole.'

'No way, man.'

'Fine. Then you'll almost certainly be convicted.'

'I'll be convicted anyway.'

'If you stick to what really happened then there's a chance you'll get off. It's your choice.'

Slowly, Becks nods – staring at the floor. Then he looks up, catches Anna's eye, and nods more firmly.

'Let's be clear about this. You're instructing me to run a cutthroat defence? Yes?'

'Yeah.'

'Then I'll have to do what my client says, won't I?' says Anna, trying not to smile.

*　　*　　*

'Bye,' says Milly, on her way out of the office – leaving early for the third time that week.

'Bye,' says Kelly, grinning broadly.

Milly pauses. 'Are you OK?'

'Fine.'

'Why are you grinning like that?'

'No reason.'

'You sure you don't need more time off?'

'I'm fine. Just happy to be back.'

Shaking her head, Milly steps outside and rushes home to Egg.

* * *

Miles storms out of the courtroom, fury pumping through his body. That was too much. This means war.

'Miles! Miles!' Anna is trotting after him. 'Hang on a minute. I'm sorry. He changed his mind at the last minute. What else could I do?'

'How about telling me, for a start? I didn't have a chance in there.'

'There wasn't time.'

'"Miles. We're changing our line." Not too complicated, is it?'

'I couldn't say it when Terry was there.'

'You could have whispered it to me any time. Shown a bit of professional bloody courtesy.'

'Look – I was following my client's instructions.'

'What? He thought that up for himself, did he? Cutthroat defence?'

'That's right.'

'I doubt he could even spell it.'

Miles turns and marches back to chambers, dreaming of revenge.

Chapter 14

The Bi Who Came in from the Cold

A ring at the doorbell and Warren, finally reconciled to being young, depressed and single, is face to face with Ferdy.

'All right?' says Ferdy. 'Remember me?'

Warren is too shocked to answer. Judging by the look on Ferdy's face, this isn't a love call.

'We can do this here,' continues Ferdy, 'or we can go upstairs. Might be better in private, don't you think?'

Warren, his mouth opening and closing like a goldfish with jaw-ache, is rooted to the spot. Wordlessly, Ferdy marches past him and up the stairs. After a few deep breaths, Warren follows and finds Ferdy in his room, standing by the window. *Not so pissed you can't remember which is my room, then*, he thinks.

'It was my wedding at the weekend,' says Ferdy. Something in his intonation makes this sound curiously like a threat.

'Oh. How did it go?'

'Well – after my fiancée got your call about me, not so fucking good as it happens.'

'What?'

'Don't fuck me about, man. You told her, didn't you? Just like you told my old man.'

'What are you talking about?'

'She found out I fuck men. She called off the wedding. Is that plain enough for you?'

'And you think I told her?'

'Sweet little revenge, was it?'

'I wouldn't have wasted my phone bill,' says Warren, with an emphatic contempt that brings Ferdy up short.

Ferdy shuffles from foot to foot, then speaks in a more conciliatory tone. 'Well, who was it?'

'I don't know. How many other men have you shagged?'

Hmm. Pausing to reflect for a moment, Ferdy realizes that there are an awful lot of people who could have phoned his fiancée. His anger at Warren has been a defence against any real reaction to her desertion of him. In a surge, he suddenly realizes that his life is a mess. One phone call, and years of stability have been yanked away from under him. He's floating, with nowhere to land.

'My parents kicked me out,' he says, quietly.

'Yeah?'

'Can I stay the night?'

Warren shoots him a confused look, and Ferdy immediately jumps to clarify the situation. 'Just . . . crash, you know? Nothing gay. I'm not like that.'

Warren shakes his head. Recognizing an advanced case

of denial, he raises an eyebrow and leaves the room. 'I'll get some bedding,' he says, closing the door behind him.

* * *

Since sorting things out with Milly, a few things have fallen more clearly into perspective. With Jerry gone, Egg has been alone in the house all day, and has had plenty of time to think. More accurately, he's had plenty of time to write, which he hasn't been doing. Instead, his solitary hours have been dedicated to thinking about why he's not writing.

And he has finally reached a conclusion. Several conclusions:

- He's not writing, because he's shit at it.
- And he hates it.
- He's never going to be a writer.
- So he has to decide what to do with his life.

OK, so they're not what most people would call conclusions. But for Egg, it's progress.

He has found a new way to focus his days, however. Shopping. Warren, tasting one of Egg's stews, suggested that they start a house kitty – twenty pounds a week each – with Egg's labour as his contribution. Egg, despite thinking that this was a great idea, told Warren to piss off – more on instinct than anything else. After all, it's always wise to keep some minuscule semblance of masculinity intact. You never know when you'll need it.

Everyone pleaded and flattered Egg until he agreed. Now, he is a professional housewife – and loving it. The shopping is boring, but Egg has discovered that cooking for an appreciative audience is an amazing sensation. Finally, he has found an outlet for his creativity.

Egg spends several days pondering how great it would be to make your living by cooking, before he realizes that he might have found a solution to his problems. *Oh my God*, he thinks:

- I can get a job as a chef.

Shit! He's found an answer. Something he wants to do with his life. He'll have to start at the bottom, but it's what he wants to do. It's a career. He can spend his life feeding people – satisfying hunger. What a great way to make a living!

Egg instantly feels sure that after all the prevarication and indecision and false starts, he has finally made a genuine decision. This is something he's going to stick at. And in this sudden moment of clarity, he sees that his entire life up to this point has been a blur.

That's how I'll explain it to Milly, he thinks. *The world slipped out of focus so long ago that I've forgotten when it happened, and I've forgotten what clear vision feels like. But now – I've been given a pair of glasses. And that pair of glasses is cookery.*

So maybe the analogy falls at the last hurdle, but it's a cool way of putting it. Milly will understand. She does wear contact lenses, after all.

*　　*　　*

Before leaving for work, Warren wakes Ferdy and tells him that he can stay as long as he likes.

'I'll get a place of my own,' says Ferdy. 'Don't worry, I won't –'

'Take – your – time. Honestly.'

'What will the others say?'

'I'll talk to them.'

'Don't think they're going to like it.'

'What's there to not like?' says Warren, smiling. And he means it. Ferdy may be a wreck, in denial about his sexuality, and perpetually surly – but the bastard still manages to be utterly loveable.

Warren floats off to work – in love again – still with Ferdy, but this time he's a heterosexual.

Chapter 15

How to Get in Bed by Advertising

Egg wanders down Borough High Street, asking in all the cafés if they need any kitchen help. All except one give him the brush-off. His single ray of hope is an average greasy spoon, but the girl in the kitchen seems cool. She's called Nicki. Leyton Orient supporter, but these things can't be helped. She tells him that someone just left, and she'll ask the boss about work, on condition that he promises never to mention Manchester United in her kitchen. He promises. With his fingers crossed.

* * *

Miles doesn't quite remember how it happened. He remembers beer. More beer. A joint or two. And calling up the Lonely Hearts answerphone service at *Time Out*.

Egg, who evidently has a clearer memory of events, proudly shows Miles the new issue. A few pages in from the back is a Lonely Hearts advertisement circled in blue Biro.

Athletic six-foot barrister, twenty-six, with classic good looks, seeks attractive, adventurous woman for fun, friendship and mutual pleasure. Do you like dining by candlelight and taking every minute as it comes? Then call me. I really want to meet you.

Egg pisses himself laughing, expecting Miles to cringe with embarrassment, but he doesn't rise to it. He just raises an eyebrow, smiles wryly, and rereads his ad.

The next day, Egg doesn't laugh quite so much when Miles gives him a figure.

'Twelve? In twenty-four hours?' says Egg.

'Yup.'

'That's unbelievable!'

'I didn't know there was so much of it out there,' Miles crows.

'So what's next?'

'I don't have to answer them. That's the beauty of it. I mean some of these are definitely Vauxhall Conference, aren't they? "I love anything by Andrew Lloyd Webber."'

'This one's OK,' says Egg, flipping over the page in Miles's notebook. 'Judy.'

'Yeah . . . she sounds up for it. I called her.'

'What did she say?'

'Seeing her in an hour.'

'What?'

Miles nods, smirking.

'Shit! Aren't you nervous?'

'No,' Miles lies, confidently. Not because he wants to

deceive Egg. It's just practice – preparation for an evening of bullshitting followed by sex. What can possibly go wrong?

*　　*　　*

Warren feels he can't chuck Ferdy out. The guy needs help, and everyone close to him seems to have turned their backs, but having him around is driving Warren mad. Ferdy veers between macho in-the-closet belligerence, and not very macho attempts to suck Warren's cock. Although there are few things Warren would enjoy more than a good old-fashioned Mexican blow-job, he has vowed not to succumb. He refuses to open himself up, only to be spurned again next time Ferdy changes his mind.

So, life in Benjamin Street is an exercise in temptation resisted. Meanwhile, Warren's work is no escape. He's been roped in by O'Donnell to help Milly with a heavy workload. Given that Milly is well known in the office as a champion stress queen even when she's underworked, this is hardly a joyous assignment.

With his friend and house-mate suddenly transformed into his boss, and his live-in ex-lover veering between John Inman and Burt Reynolds, it is increasingly difficult for Warren to have any clear fix on life.

*　　*　　*

Judy turns out to be all right. *A bit plain, but worth a once-over*, is Miles's instant estimate. He turns on the charm (i.e., bullshit), labours all evening to appear likeable, then, at the last minute, just when all the drudgery is about to pay off, she tells him that she's going home. Home! On her own!

'Give me a call when you're free,' she says, on her way out. 'We could go to a film.'

Yeah, right. Likely.

*   *   *

Milly doesn't like chatty, and she doesn't like ingratiating.

She arrives at work to find a new trainee sitting opposite Warren. Rachel. Chatty, ingratiating Rachel.

*   *   *

Only slightly daunted by his waste of effort with Judy, Miles arranges a date with his second choice: Cora. One glance is enough to reassure him that this is a more likely prospect. Cropped blonde hair, black clothes, blood-red lipstick – clearly, this one puts out.

And she does. Without much encouragement. Unfortunately, however, Miles is sprawled on her sofa with his shirt off and his trousers down when Cora's husband turns up in a dressing-gown and tries to join in.

Miles runs. He sprints. He discovers leg muscles he has never used before to get him out of that house.

*   *   *

Working for Milly is as bad as Warren expected. Milly's definition of 'thorough' falls into most other people's interpretation of 'pathologically anal'. And if you're work-ing for Milly, you have to tighten up your sphincter to match hers.

When Warren is called in by Spencer – a senior partner – and asked to assist on a major case, this is not just a priceless opportunity to further his career, it's a chance to get away from Milly. Trying to conjure an apologetic expression for his face, Warren rushes straight for her office.

'I've just been in with Spencer,' he says. 'He wants me to assist him on a child-abuse case.'

'Oh. I see,' says Milly, tightly.

'It's dealing with social services, that sort of thing.'

'Does O'Donnell know?'

'Spencer's talking to him.'

'Right.'

'Aren't you pleased for me? It's a great opportunity.'

'I am, it's just . . . I've got so much on at the moment. I need you.'

'It's only for one case. And there's Rachel . . .'

'She doesn't know the ropes like you do. Warren – I know you're excited. It's just a really bad time right now. We'll talk about it later, all right?'

Next thing Warren knows, he's been summoned to O'Donnell's office and told that it would be 'unwise' to leave Milly at such a busy time.

Warren returns to his desk utterly downcast. Bastards. The pair of them have pissed on his fire for their own ends. He doesn't have a choice. He's stuck with Milly until she tells O'Donnell that he's free. Cow. And she's supposed to be his friend.

*   *   *

Although Miles has made Egg promise not to tell anyone about the Lonely Hearts advert, there comes a point when he simply can't hold it in any longer. He lasts a few hours, then he just *has* to tell Milly. And Anna.

He feels guilty – he knows he shouldn't have betrayed Miles – but when Milly and Anna start drafting a fake reply, it's more than Egg can manage not to join in. It's an awful thing to do to your friend, but – really – you'd be mad not to. It's Milly who does the voice: throaty, languorous, and with more than a hint of soft-porn ultravixen.

'Miles – I think we should meet. My name is Maria. I hope you are a man who knows what he wants, because I know what I want. And I warn you – my standards are high. If you are stylish and sexy, then I'll be in Bar Excel at nine tomorrow night. If you have any doubts about yourself, don't bother. I'll be waiting.'

*   *   *

With his avenue of escape blocked off, Warren's tedious workload depresses him more than ever. After another day of boredom and tension with Milly, he decides to do something to cheer himself up. The universal panacea. Random sex.

He downs a bottle of wine in his bedroom, psyching himself up for action, then puts on a lumberjack shirt, and heads for Highbury Fields.

He spots a few guys prowling around in the bushes near the Gents, and picks out a well-built (though hardly gorgeous) man in a baseball cap and tight jeans. They eye each other up, and play a brief game of cat and mouse together. Neither of them, however, is in a teasing mood, and within minutes they have found their way into the Gents, where they snog greedily.

Warren isn't thinking clearly. He's pissed. And when a man clatters into the Gents, shouting something, Warren has hardly even noticed him by the time the man in the baseball cap has punched out the intruder and fled.

Warren looks down at the unconscious man, worried that he's hurt. He puts a finger under his nose to see if he's breathing, and is far too confused and scared to understand the significance of the police radio barking for attention in the man's top pocket.

'Are you all right?' says Warren. 'Can you hear me?'

A fist then hits Warren in the back, pushing him over on to the stinking, wet floor. His hands are tugged behind him, while he tries to keep his nose clear of the puddles on the floor. He hears shouts, and feels cold metal clamping around his wrists.

*   *   *

'You two take a seat,' says Anna, pushing Egg and Milly towards the corner of the bar.

'He might not even show,' says Egg.

'I know him. He'll show.'

'Who knows what's going on in his head?'

'I saw him tonight. He had his Paul Smith on.'

'So?'

'He always wears that when he's seriously going for it. Can't wait to see the look on his face.'

'Hope he sees the funny side,' says Milly.

Anna smiles. 'If he won't, I will,' she says, departing for a bar stool. She opens her mouth to order a beer, but before she can speak, the barman places a bottle of champagne in front of her. There is a card resting against the bottle. MARIA, it says.

Anna lifts the card, unsure of what this means, then turns it over. On the other side, it says, GOTCHA.

She turns round, and sees Miles reclining at an alcove table, with a glass of beer raised as a toast. A smug grin glows from his face.

The four of them arrive back at Benjamin Street several pissed hours later, with Miles protesting vehemently to Anna that Maria wasn't his type, and that he wasn't remotely convinced for more than a second. The phone is ringing as they walk in. Milly answers.

It's Warren. He's been arrested. Milly tells him to calm down and sit tight. She's on her way.

By the time all the statements have been taken and forms filled in, it is the middle of the night. Milly, holding Warren's arm, walks him out into the street, where they wait for a taxi.

'I thought I'd be there all night. That bloke . . . I thought he was dead.'

'Concussion,' says Milly.

'He's in hospital.'

'He's stable.'

'It wasn't me,' says Warren. 'There was . . . I didn't touch him.'

'I know. They've got your statement. They'll find the other guy.'

'But if they don't –'

'They will. They'll drop the GBH. Gross indecency. You're looking at a fine, no more.'

'They wouldn't talk to me for ages. Just kept me waiting in that room. And this officer was just staring at me for . . . what . . . an hour?'

'I know.'

'Then he said – really quietly in my ear – "Do you want a nice cup of tea, you fucking AIDS carrier?"'

Milly doesn't know what to say. She wants Warren to stop talking – to calm down – but he's still in shock.

'It wasn't my fault,' he continues. 'I didn't have a chance to think. I didn't know if it was a mugger or . . . or a queer-basher or what. But GBH!'

'You didn't do it. We'll sort it out.'

'Sorry . . . to call you out . . .' says Warren, fighting off tears.

'I thought about passing it on to Rachel. She wants the experience.'

Warren barks a half-laugh half-sob.

'I'm glad you called me, Warren. And I'm sorry we fell out.'

'Yeah . . . so am I.'

With Warren looking almost feverish, Milly reaches a

hand up to his shoulder. He bows his head, and they fall into an awkward hug – Warren fighting to hold in his tears.

Chapter 16

Going Under

Warren knows how fast bad news travels, so the first thing he does at work is to go and see O'Donnell.

O'Donnell chews over Warren's description of the night's events, and attempts to look sympathetic. In fact, he looks as if he's just swallowed a turd.

'And you've done this before?' he says.

'Yeah.'

'What, regularly?'

'Fairly.'

'You've never considered this sort of problem might arise?'

'Well, no . . . not really.'

'You . . . must be a bit shell-shocked.'

'I'm OK.'

'Are you?'

'I think I'd just like to get on with my work.'

'Of course.'

'It's not like I'm ill, or anything.'

'But if you did want to take some leave, that would be perfectly understandable under the circumstances.'

'Thanks for the offer, but I don't think that'll be necessary.'

O'Donnell takes another swallow at the turd – which doesn't seem to be going down too smoothly – and smiles, thinly.

'Warren – I will have to mention this to the other partners. And, of course, to the Law Society.'

'Right.'

'But I do appreciate your candid account.'

'Well, I'd rather you heard it from me.'

O'Donnell goes to the door and opens it – boss-speak for 'Piss off out of my office.' 'I'll keep you posted,' he says. 'And . . . I'm sure you'll appreciate the need for discretion.'

Warren steps out into the open-plan office, and walks to his desk, feeling as if everyone in the room is staring at him. He spots Kira and Milly in the corner by the photocopier, deep in conversation.

Rachel looks at him, concerned. 'All right?'

'Fine and dandy,' says Warren with a sigh, not catching her eye.

'Hi, Warren,' says a voice, coming from directly behind his chair. Warren turns to see a man in a suit, with a mac draped over one arm, who he doesn't recognize.

'Hello?' says Warren.

'How's it going?' he says.

'All right, thanks. Do we . . . have an appointment?'

'Brian Beecham.' The man offers a hand, which Warren shakes. 'I wonder if I could just ask you a few questions . . .'

'What about?'

'It's just for the local press.'

'I'd rather not, thanks.'

'It's going to come out sooner or later, you know.'

'Yeah, well –'

'I'm just offering you the opportunity to set the record straight.'

'How did you find me?'

Brian smiles and takes a small notepad from the top pocket of his suit. 'Don't worry about that. Tell me what happened last night.'

'No way.'

'This won't take long.'

'I've got nothing to say to you.'

Kira, sensing what is happening, charges over. 'Are you getting hassled, Warren?'

'Let me deal with this,' says Milly, also suddenly appearing by his desk. 'Kira – would you call security, please.'

'You don't need security. I can sort this,' she replies.

'Kira – security.'

The reporter, realizing that his moment has passed, tucks the notebook back in his top pocket and sighs, mock-affably. 'Warren?' he says.

Warren leans forward, almost spitting in the man's face. 'Read my lips. No comment.'

Warren storms off, which the reporter takes as his cue to leave.

'Will someone tell me what's going on?' says Rachel.

Milly ignores her, and follows the reporter to the door.

*   *   *

Ferdy walks into a chemist shop and lurks behind a stack of deodorants. He just wants to see her. He picks up a couple of cans of Impulse, and pretends to browse.

Then he hears her voice. Mia – his ex-fiancée – serving a customer. Ferdy panics. Dropping the deodorant, he steps to the door, takes one square look at her, and runs away.

*   *   *

Warren stumbles through his day's work, and goes for a drink with Kira and Rachel afterwards. They try and say the right things to him – but at the moment, Warren feels that he needs a different kind of support. After one pint, he offers a few excuses, then heads home to talk to Ferdy.

He finds Ferdy sitting on the sofa, a fully-packed bag at his feet. 'What's this?' says Warren.

'I've found a bedsit.'

'Right.'

'I'm moving out.'

'Tonight? You've decided to go tonight?'

'Yeah. I didn't know where you were.'

'And you have to?'

'It's a good time, isn't it?'

'Excellent. Absolutely brilliant. Great timing, Ferdy.'

'I thought it's what you wanted.'

'OK . . . of course it is. Go. Piss off. Nice knowing you, and all that.'

Ferdy isn't expecting Warren to take it like this. He doesn't know what to say.

'Warren – I'm really sorry about –'

'So you know then?'

'Yeah. Miles and Anna told me just after you left. Could you go down?'

'Yes. I could end up staying for ... what ... two or three years. But don't let that bother you. You just ride off into the sunset and have a nice life.'

'Fine,' Ferdy says, stung by the sarcasm. He picks up his bag and takes one step towards the door, before he is halted by Warren.

'Ferdy. Don't leave now. Please stay.'

'What for?'

'I want you to stay around while this is going on. I need you here. D'you understand?'

Warren, suddenly feeling all the energy drain out of his body, sinks on to the sofa. Despair sweeps over him, and he buries his face in his hands.

Ferdy hesitates, then leaves his bag by the door and walks over to the sofa. Sitting down, Ferdy reaches out an arm and pulls Warren towards him. For the first time, Warren allows himself to cave in to tears. He buries his face in Ferdy's chest and sobs.

Arriving at work, Warren is immediately summoned by O'Donnell, who tosses a local paper on to the desk in front of him. Warren reads the headline. GAY SOLICITOR COPS GBH CHARGE. The blood drains from his face as he scans the text of the article, picking out both his name and the name of the firm.

'You've not seen it yet?' says O'Donnell.

Warren shakes his head, unable to think of any reaction to this bizarre form of public humiliation.

'Warren – I'm really sorry,' says O'Donnell, with only the lightest hint of sincerity.

'So am I.'

O'Donnell leaves a long pause before pointing out that, 'Moore Spencer Wright take their image very seriously.'

'I know,' Warren replies.

'We really can't have the firm brought into any kind of disrepute.'

Warren nods, while O'Donnell leaves another awful silence. 'Can I be as honest with you as you were with me?' he says, eventually.

Warren nods.

'Frankly, this isn't something which is going to be over and done with overnight. It's going to drag on.'

'I know.'

'I think you'll find it very difficult to get on with your work. You're going to be under a great deal of strain and pressure.'

'What's this actually leading up to?' says Warren, foreboding hitting him in the stomach.

'Well,' says O'Donnell, 'I want you to consider something.'

'I'm not into hara-kiri,' says Warren, attempting – with a staggering lack of success – to inject a more jovial note into the conversation.

O'Donnell allows Warren's comment to sink into the carpet before continuing. 'What I'm suggesting is that you consider tendering your resignation.'

'You want me to *resign*?'

'Think about it. You could leave here with a good, strong reference.'

'And go where?'

O'Donnell coughs, lacking an answer.

'Is that really what you want me to do?' says Warren, outraged.

'I want you to do what you consider best under the circumstances.'

Warren walks out of O'Donnell's office, and staggers blindly to his desk. He sits down, then immediately stands up again, grabs his coat, and leaves the building.

* * *

Miles answers the door to find an angry-looking pug-faced woman on the doorstep.

'Is Ferdy staying here?' she demands.

'Possibly,' Miles replies.

'Look, don't be a prat. Just answer the question.'

'Pardon?'

'O K – are you the one he left me for?' she says, stepping into the house.

'Excuse me? Are you ill?' says Miles.

'Where is he? I want to see him.'

'This is a wind-up, yeah? You're one of Anna's mates.'

'I'm Ferdy's fiancée, and I was going to marry him until you moved in fluttering your big eyelashes and wiggling your skinny backside about.'

Miles finds this a little hard to take in, and tries to shut the door.

'Get this,' she continues. 'You're not the first. Whatever he told you. And tell him not to come round to where I work, either.'

A gentle shove in the chest is required before she is outside, and Miles can close the door. Not funny, he thinks. That kind of thing is not funny.

Ferdy has to go. Soon. After all, Miles's reputation is at stake. Word gets round about this kind of thing.

*　　*　　*

Warren wakes up the next day with a clear head. He has decided what to do. There is no way that he is going to allow a slimy git with hairy knuckles to intimidate him out of a job. It has taken years of work for Warren to leave his dreary, small-minded valleys past behind, and if he loses his job now, he's right back where he started. No – Warren is going to tough it out.

He puts on his suit, and heads purposefully for the office.

Once there, he heads straight into O'Donnell's room – uninvited – and takes a seat. O'Donnell, by the look on his face, wasn't expecting Warren back quite so soon.

'I've never hidden what I am,' Warren says. 'It's my choice and I'm proud of it, however difficult it is for other people to come to terms with.'

'This is not about your being gay.'

'Isn't it?'

'No, it isn't.'

'I never laid a finger on that officer. His testimony will bear that out.'

'I'm sure it will.'

'So why should I resign?' Warren eyeballs O'Donnell. 'It would be like me denying who I am.'

'You've made your mind up, then?'

'Yes.'

'You're absolutely sure?'

'Yes. Absolutely.'

'Then, Warren, I regret to say that you offer me no alternative but to ask you to leave.'

'You're sacking me?'

'We're terminating your contract and putting the whole matter in the hands of the Law Society.'

'I'm fired?'

'I'm sorry . . .'

'I don't believe this.'

'I'll see to it that you receive four weeks' wages and a good reference.'

'This can't happen. You can't do this to me.'

'I think you'll find we can. Please believe me, Warren, when I say this is nothing personal.'

Warren walks out of O'Donnell's office, his mind blank. Suddenly, his future is a void. He feels nothing, other than shock at his incapacity to know how to react. There is no scale against which to measure what has just happened. He pulls on his coat and leaves the office, thinking that these are exactly the same motions as leaving the office for a lunch-hour. Only this time, he is leaving the office for ever.

Walking down the steps into Chancery Lane tube, Warren notices the strangeness of travelling against the flow. Other people are still trudging out of the station on the way to work. But Warren is going home. It's still morning, and Warren is pushing against the crowds, heading home.

Chapter 17

Unusual Suspect

Egg loves his new job in the kitchens of the local café. Although what he's actually doing is pretty basic – wiping tables, washing up, bits of chopping – he knows at once that the atmosphere of a restaurant kitchen is somewhere where he's happy. You're on your feet *doing* things, instead of sitting on your arse barking into a phone all day. Also, there's music on, and no matter how hard you're working, you can always chat.

Work-chat is an entirely different activity to mates-chat. It's a unique skill. And it's one at which both Egg and his kitchen partner, Nicki, excel. The art is to talk with no end in sight. The conversation has to last all day, since it's the only way of keeping yourself entertained. The art revolves around your ability to throw away your conversational filter. If you try and say only interesting things, you'll run out after half an hour. You have to say anything that comes into your head – no matter how stupid or bland – and then hope that your partner remoulds it and tosses it back to you in a slightly different shape. Done correctly, you can start at nine o'clock discussing Leyton

Orient's defensive weaknesses, move on to mid-eighties one-hit wonders, then take a journey via Limahl's haircut to the worst job you ever had, your favourite type of cheese, the role of the United Nations in a post-Cold War world, the reason for the hole in the side of Biros, then back to Leyton Orient's defensive weaknesses, and suddenly it's six o'clock and you're going home without realizing that you've done a day's work.

In short, Nicki and Egg get on – perfectly.

*　　*　　*

Milly arrives at work on the day of Warren's ID parade feeling stressed. She has promised that she'll be at the police station to help him through it, but it's going to be hard to get out of the office in time.

The first thing Milly sees as she walks in is Rachel, working at Warren's desk. Milly stares at her, stunned.

'I like to see what's going on in the rest of the office,' Rachel explains, indicating the better view she now has.

'Really?' Milly says, through thin lips.

'It's OK, isn't it?' smiles Rachel, ingratiatingly.

'Course. Why not?' says Milly, stamping off. It suddenly occurs to Milly who Rachel reminds her of. She's like Miles – with the same pushy, aggressive, ambitious ruthlessness – only worse, because while at least Miles is honest, Rachel hides it under a simpering, sweet-faced, butter-wouldn't-melt exterior. Yes – Milly hates her. She's hated her from the second she walked into the office, and with every minute they work together, Milly hates her more.

*

Milly puts her head down and works without a lunch-break, managing to get to the police station to meet Warren just before the parade.

Through the glass, Milly can't help feeling that Warren acts exactly like a guilty man, and when the police officer indicates that number seven – yes, Warren – should stand up, Milly's heart skips a beat.

With Warren standing and the other eight men sitting, the policeman – a livid bruise around the corner of his mouth – stares for a long time. Milly tries to give Warren an encouraging look, but he can't see her through the mirrored glass. Warren is sweating in his suit, and his mouth has run dry.

Eventually, the policeman speaks. 'He was there at the scene, but he didn't attack me.'

Outside the police station, Milly and Warren hug. The GBH charge has been dropped. With a hearing the next day, they can only convict him of gross indecency. He's in the clear. The worst that can happen is a fine.

Milly has to race back to work, but as she leaves, she sees Ferdy pull up on his bike. It is obvious from Milly and Warren's body language that the parade has been a success, and Ferdy lets out a little cheer.

'Pub,' he says, climbing off his bike and putting an arm round Warren.

Milly arrives back at the office, half an hour late for her three-o'clock appointment. However, no one is waiting for her at reception.

'Any sign of Mr Slater?' she says to Kelly.

'He's in with Rachel.'

'Rachel?'

'Yeah. They're using your office.'

Milly marches to her office, and stares through the glass at Rachel sitting in her chair. Rachel's eyes flick up, and they see each other. Milly opens the door and walks to the desk, eyeballing Rachel. For a few seconds, they stare at each other in silence.

'Thanks for covering for me,' says Milly, eventually.

'No problem.'

Rachel stands, and takes up her usual hovering position, a few inches behind Milly's chair.

*　　*　　*

Ever since being mistaken for Ferdy's lover, Miles has barely concealed his resentment of Benjamin Street's permanent guest.

Watching the usual crap on telly one night, Miles finds himself on the sofa with Egg and Ferdy.

'Pub?' says Egg.

'No,' Miles replies. 'I brought some work home.'

'More fool you. Ferdy – fancy a game of pool?'

'Yeah, great. I'll get my wallet.'

'Oh, sod it,' says Miles, unable to face the thought of being left out. 'Twist my arm. I'll come for a quick half.'

With Ferdy heading up the stairs, Miles turns to Egg. 'If he orders a pink gin, you're a dead man,' he spits.

*

Over their game of pool, Egg turns to Miles. 'Do you think a man and a woman can ever be just good friends?'

'If you're shagging the arse off each other, then yes,' replies Miles.

'No, I mean – boy meets girl – no sex.'

'No way.'

'He's right,' says Ferdy.

'What – and you'd know?' scoffs Miles, before turning back to Egg. 'So who is she?'

'Nobody,' says Egg.

'Nobody you work with?'

Egg shuffles and fiddles with his cue. Miles can always see through him. In fact, everyone can always see through him. Egg gives up, and drops his guard. 'OK – so it's Nicki – at the caff. It might be my imagination, but I think there's something going on. I can't quite put my finger on it.'

Miles and Ferdy both laugh. Egg immediately realizes that he has lost control of the conversation. The whole confession thing was a bad idea. Unless you count 'Is she a dog, or what?' as useful and sympathetic advice, the two guys proceed to give Egg only minimal help with his dilemma.

*   *   *

With Anna acting for him in court, Warren gets only a fifty-pound fine.

A free man at last, Warren takes Anna for a celebration drink in a pub near the courtroom.

'How long before the Law Society makes its mind up about you?' she says, sipping a glass of wine.

'Anything up to a year. I don't really know.'

'What are you going to do?'

'Sort my life out. Settle down. Get married. Have triplets.'

'That should cover it. Same again?'

'For sure.'

*   *   *

When Nicki asks Egg to go for a drink after work, he doesn't know how to react. He doesn't know what kind of drink she has in mind. Does she mean a drink, as in a drink – or a drink as in . . . a *drink*.

He tries to react coolly, and fails. 'Tonight?'

'Tonight.'

'Well, err . . . I've got to make a phone call. Make sure nothing else is on.'

'Fine – go on then.'

Egg walks to the phone, and hovers. If he says no, she'll be offended. He might even get the sack. There's nothing he can do about it. He has to go.

Egg sits at a wobbly pub table with Nicki, noisily munching on his crisps. All their ease of conversation has vanished.

'So what's Milly up to tonight?' says Nicki.

'Milly?' he replies. *Shit! This is it! It's her chat-up line. She's moving in on me.* 'Errr . . . why d'you ask?'

'Just wondered.'

'She's working late.'

'How long have you two been together?'

'Five years.' *You hear that? Five years.*

'Two more to go, then?'

'Sorry?'

'Before you get the itch.'

Jesus. She really is going for it.

'No. Not me and Milly,' he says, emphatically. 'We're sound.'

'I was joking.'

'Right. I know.'

Egg takes a big gulp of beer, hiding behind his glass for a few moments while he regains his composure. 'What's your other half doing tonight?' he asks, hopefully.

'Looking for me, with any luck. Single girl, Egg. Footloose and fancy free.'

Right. OK. Can't delay any longer. It has to be said.

'Nicki?'

'Yeah.'

'I'm no good at this. I mean – some blokes can, but I can't. I know it's daft, but I . . . it wouldn't be right. Am I making sense?'

'Totally.' She stares at him, a slight scowl on her face. 'What are you on about?'

'Don't get me wrong – I think you're really attractive . . . and funny . . . and sparky . . .'

'Sparky? I think I know what's coming next.'

'Yeah?'

'Yeah. You're bored and you want a bit of sparkle in your life.'

161

'Nicki – you're a great girl . . . woman . . .'

'You were doing all right with girl. Calm down, Egg – before you self-combust. Do you really think I fancy you?'

'Well . . . no . . . not really.'

'Not really? Or not at all?'

'Not at all. Really.'

'What are you like?'

Nicki is shaking her head. Suddenly, the situation is both more embarrassing and less embarrassing than before. Egg, however, can't help feeling relieved.

'You're a nice guy, Egg, and I really enjoy working with you – but there's no question of us having a thing together. You're in a relationship. And, to be honest, you're not my type.'

'Let's have another drink, eh?' he says.

'I'll go.'

She stands and walks to the bar, still shaking her head. Egg sighs, and sinks into his chair. *Thank Christ. It's over. That was worse than a job interview.*

*   *   *

Warren arrives home at around midnight, and finds the whole house waiting up for him with a bottle of champagne. To Milly's barely disguised horror, Rachel has also come round to join in the celebration.

Something in Warren's bearing as he enters punctures the atmosphere. He no longer looks relieved – but has a purposeful manner, as if the week's events are now entirely forgotten and he has moved on to something new. Under his arm is a huge bundle of brochures, which he dumps on the table.

'What's that?' says Anna.

'I'm leaving. For Australia,' he says.

'How long for?' she says.

'As long as it takes.'

'When?' says Ferdy.

'Soon.'

'Are you serious?'

'Why not? We all spend our lives dreaming of the big trip and when the moment comes we're either skint or we get cold feet. I'm unemployed – with a nice lump sum – what should I do? Invest in a PEP? Or have a ball?'

The room is stunned into silence.

'Don't worry. I'll send you a postcard,' he says, reaching for the champagne.

Chapter 18

He's Leaving Home

Rachel lives with her parents. But she doesn't want to live with her parents. It's no fun. She wants to move out and live in a house-share – somewhere where there are more people to chat to – preferably people with the same interests as her – ideally, with the same type of career.

Although Warren hasn't even left yet, Rachel is angling for his room.

Miles, who first caught sight of her at Warren's post-trial celebration, likes her. He likes her breasts; he likes her hair; he likes her face – for him, she's the perfect house-mate. For the others, she also seems ideal. Pleasant, smiley, chatty – she's the kind of person who is easy to live with. Only Milly is against her. Because only Milly realizes that Rachel is Satan.

Rachel's technique for getting into the house starts with a charm offensive aimed at Milly. She smiles a lot, buys Milly lunch, then drops leaden hints into Milly's food. 'I want to move out of my parents', but I don't want to live in a studio flat . . . I don't want to live in a house full of strangers, either . . . How did you manage to get your place together? . . . Sounds like an ideal set-up . . . You're really lucky . . . Warren says he'll really miss you . . . Was it Egg who invited him in?'

Milly finds herself incapable of digesting her food at the mere thought of Rachel living in her house. She smiles sweetly, and answers all of Rachel's questions, pretending not to understand the hints.

The human warmth bouncing between the pair of them spreads through the café, and within ten minutes the place is empty, and the waitress has clinical depression.

When Milly arrives home from work to find Rachel sitting at the dining table, asking Egg how he managed to get the house-share together, telling him that it sounds like an ideal set-up and that he's really lucky, then asking who invited Warren in, Milly walks up to Egg, and kisses him deeply on the lips, right in front of Rachel. She then whispers a sexy greeting and drags him upstairs, without a word to Rachel.

Miles, however, immediately comes to the rescue, and offers Rachel a glass of wine. He even drinks the wine himself – a sure sign that he's out to impress. They sit together on the sofa, sipping their drinks, and Rachel proceeds to ask him how he got the house-share together, who invited Warren in, and whether they've found a replacement for him.

*

The following morning, over breakfast, they have the conversation that Milly has been dreading.

'Right – what are we going to do about the room?' says Miles. 'We need a decision.'

Milly flinches. 'Do we have to talk about it now?'

'He's right,' says Anna. 'I don't particularly want to lose a month's rent.'

'Yeah. Which we do if we advertise,' says Miles. 'So – has anyone got any candidates?' There is a tense silence. After scanning the table for a response, Miles continues. 'What about Rachel?'

'I like her,' says Anna.

'She's nice,' says Egg.

'I don't see how anyone could not like her,' says Milly, through gritted teeth. And she means it. It is hard to dislike Rachel. She's an utterly friendly, likeable person. Unless you can see through her – in which case, SHE'S SATAN.

Milly stares hard at Egg. She has primed him for this discussion, knowing that if she attacks Rachel, everyone will accuse her of being uptight, or bossy, or jealous. Egg, however, refuses to catch her eye.

'I know she's looking,' says Miles. 'She's got some kind of running feud with her parents at the moment, and she's ready to move in pretty much straight away.'

Egg, finally, can't ignore the burning sensation on the back of his neck – a laser imprint of Milly's stare. He coughs. 'Is it such a good idea to have another lawyer?' he offers. 'I mean – it's better to have more of a mix. Isn't it?'

'I'm sorry,' says Anna. 'Are we boring you?'

'No, it's just . . . sometimes it's nice to have a change of scenery.'

'What are you *getting* at?' says Miles, impatiently.

Milly sees her chance to jump in. 'I agree with Egg. Rachel is lovely but we're in danger of becoming a bit cliquey if we only hang out with lawyers.'

'Thanks,' says Egg, trying not to smile.

'That's stupid!' Miles is exasperated. 'Rachel's perfect. She's a good laugh, she's got a heart of gold –'

'Breasts . . .' says Anna, ignored by Miles.

'– even Anna gets on with her. Why should we risk someone we don't know?'

'You're forgetting Ferdy,' says Milly.

'Yes, I am. So why don't we have a vote?'

'I think Warren should have a say in this,' says Milly.

'Bollocks,' says Miles. 'He won't have to live with it. What's wrong with Rachel?'

'What's wrong with Ferdy?' replies Milly. 'What's wrong with *you?*'

'Jesus! I just don't see why there has to be such a drama about everything!' shouts Miles, melodramatically.

*   *   *

Warren's leaving party is a blast. Although Miles finds it impossible to relax – deeply unsettled by the gay contingent – everyone else has a laugh. Ferdy has such a great evening he even manages to smile a couple of times. He also gives a touching, not-entirely-platonic farewell to Warren on Anna's balcony. Ferdy's night is only spoilt when, at two in the morning, he takes a peek at Warren's room – which he assumes he is about to take over – and finds Rachel asleep on the bed.

Although he's flying on Monday, Warren has taken a big decision. He decides to leave on Saturday morning for Wales. He's going to visit his parents, and tell them the truth about what has happened to him. After twenty-six years, he is finally going to come out to his family.

A group gathers round the front door to see him off. Kira, almost crying, is the first to give him a hug. Warren hugs her back, and tells her to keep an eye on Ferdy.

Warren loads his stuff into a taxi, then turns to see his house-mates lined up on the pavement. 'Right,' he says, 'who's first for the snog of the millennium? No fighting, please. Form an orderly queue.'

Milly dashes towards him and leaps through the air into his arms. Struggling under the weight, and taken aback by the strength of emotion in her grip, he staggers a little, then puts her down. Anna steps forward and gives Warren a long, sloppy kiss on the lips.

Egg gives him a warm hug, then Warren turns to Miles. There is a moment's hesitation before Miles reaches out one arm for a handshake. He then stoops, and kisses Warren's hand. This makes the other three whoop and clap, so Miles relents, and gives Warren a hug.

Kira then dashes out of the house, and dumps a huge parcel in Warren's hands. 'This is for chasing blokes,' she says.

Warren gets in the taxi and drives off, waving through the back window at his friends as they recede into the distance. Once round the corner, he rips open the parcel on his lap and pulls out two giant red shoes, *à la Wizard of Oz*. Turning them over, he sees that they are a set of rollerblades.

If he can't pull in Sydney, in a pair of bright red designer rollerblades, then he'll never pull again in his life. Maybe he can give them a try-out that weekend, on his parents' street. Then again, maybe not.

Chapter 19

The Spare Room

Miles steps out of the shower, just as Ferdy walks in. His body surging with panic, boosted by homophobia and a touch of phallic insecurity, Miles leaps for a towel and covers himself.

'Sorry. It wasn't locked,' says Ferdy, smirking.

'There is no lock. Shit!' Miles is trembling slightly, as the adrenaline rush hits his bloodstream.

'You're usually in here much earlier,' says Ferdy.

'What?'

'I thought you usually –'

'I – I – don't want to discuss it at this particular moment.'

'Right,' says Ferdy, taking a couple of steps towards Miles and plucking his toothbrush from a shaving mug.

'Get the fuck out!'

'OK.'

Ferdy turns for the door, takes a couple of steps, then spins round. The towel is still firmly up.

'Sorry. Toothpaste,' he says, nipping back to the sink for a tube of Colgate.

'Out!'

'He's got to go,' says Miles, marching into the kitchen for breakfast. 'Every time I turn around, there he is – gawping at me.' He looks around the room for support, but everyone just stares at him, smirks plastered across their faces. Anna seems particularly amused. 'House meeting. This evening,' he says. 'We're going to decide who gets that room.'

Everyone nods, still smirking.

Minutes before the house meeting is due to start, Rachel arrives to pick up some tapes she left behind at Warren's leaving party. 'How are things going at work?' she says to Anna.

'Fantastic,' Anna replies, with heavy sarcasm. 'If I ever get a case, I'll be unstoppable.'

'You shouldn't worry. It'll pick up,' says Rachel, her head cocked on one side.

Anna curls her lip and heads upstairs to fetch Egg and Milly for the meeting.

Milly enters the living room to find Rachel succumbing to a major onslaught of flirtation from Miles. When Miles starts flirting, you don't need a degree in psychology to detect what's going on. While Rachel is hardly falling on to the carpet and spreading her legs, from all the eyelash-fluttering and hair-flicking she's doing, Miles is certainly getting a response.

Milly grits her teeth. 'Hello, Rachel,' she says.

'Hi.'

Rachel looks at Milly and stands up. The temperature in the room seems to have dropped by a couple of degrees. 'Well, I hope you'll be considering me,' she says. 'Outgoing, single female who's out a lot and loves to clean.'

'Sounds good to me,' says Egg.

'Doesn't it?' says Miles, his mouth awash with saliva.

'We'll certainly keep you in mind,' says Milly, ushering Rachel to the door.

'Thanks. Bye everyone.'

'Don't forget your tapes,' Anna smiles.

'Oh, yeah. Right.'

This time round, the discussion over who gets the room is more honest. Milly refuses to live with Rachel. Miles refuses to live with Ferdy.

Eventually, they settle on a compromise – an ad in the *Standard*. Someone with no baggage. Emotional baggage, that is. Suitcases are allowed.

Then they argue about what to put in the ad. Miles wants to specifically rule out Christians, nutters and kids. Anna wants to rule out facial hair.

* * *

Ever since the first house party – for Jerry's birthday – Kira has been reeling Jo in. After a complex military operation of phone calls, missed phone calls, exposed cleavages, and a ruthless lack of sex, she finally has him on the rack.

The final manoeuvre to clinch her victory comes on

their third date. He is driving her to the cinema in his Volkswagen Beetle, when he pulls up in a lay-by and looks at her with a cheeky glint in his eye.

God, he's gorgeous. How am I going to hold back?

'Why have you stopped?' she says, acting confused.

'We've got some time.'

'We have to get tickets.'

'We'll be all right.'

He leans over and kisses her – a long, wet snog.

Phwoar! You're good at that.

She pulls back, and manages to look flustered. 'I don't think this is a good idea.'

'Relax,' he says, kissing her again.

This time, Kira can't hold it in, and she kisses him back – drawing herself excitedly towards him as she feels her brain doing a loop the loop. Moving closer, her arse gets a sharp poke from the gear stick, which brings her to her senses.

'Ow!' she says, flopping back into her seat and forcing her facial muscles into a frown.

'Look. Why don't we move into the back? We can stretch out.'

'You must be joking.'

'OK – we'll stay put.'

He leans towards her again, but this time Kira pushes him away.

'That's not what I'm after, OK? If you can't handle it then maybe you should take me home.'

Kira crosses her arms and pouts, staring ahead as if in an offended sulk. Jo's face falls. 'Kira – I'm sorry. We'll go to the pictures, all right? I didn't mean anything by it . . .' he stammers.

'Well . . .'

Jo starts the engine and they drive off. Kira has to look out of the side window to stop him from seeing her grin. *Gotcha!*

She knows her plan has worked perfectly when, after the film, they go for a chaste walk, holding hands, and he even puts his coat around her when she gets cold. He drops her off at home with a peck on the cheek.

At last, she can relax. He's under her thumb. Finally, she can shag him.

* * *

If there are three letters Miles despises most in the alphabet, they are D, I and Y. He grits his teeth, however, and stops off on the way home from work at a hardware store.

After two humiliating hours on his knees, wrestling with a screwdriver and more pieces of fiddly aluminium than you would ever have thought necessary for such a simple piece of equipment, Miles stands, satisfied.

He closes the door, and slides the bolt to and fro a couple of times.

Yes. At last, the bathroom is safe from prying bisexual eyes.

* * *

The response to the *Standard* advertisement isn't promising. After an entire evening of interviews, the house still can't decide. There's Muriel who works in a women's refuge, but Anna rejects her for wearing socks with sandals; there's Salim who Milly rejects for insisting on talking to her in Urdu; and a multiplicity of others who Miles simply thinks are wankers. Egg isn't bothered.

The argument rages for so long that Miles eventually leaves the room in despair to make a phone call.

He returns with a shifty look in his eye.

Half an hour later, the doorbell rings, and Miles leaps up to answer it. Rachel steps into the hall, laden with two heavy bags, and gives Miles a big hug.

'I'm so pleased,' she says.

Egg watches, agog, from the door to the living room.

Rachel grins, broadly. 'Hi, Egg. I hope you don't mind. I thought I'd move a few things in. Just to get started.'

'Er, yeah. Fine,' Egg replies, retreating to the living room, while Miles helps Rachel carry her bags upstairs.

He shows her to her room, watches her hang an ornamental brass R on the wall, and is just sitting down on the bed for a good long chat, when Ferdy enters.

'Er – Miles. You're wanted downstairs,' he says.

'Yeah. I bet I am.'

Miles skips through the door and down to the living room. An awkward silence is left behind him.

'Sorry to burst in like this,' says Rachel. 'Miles thought it would be all right to move a few things in.' Ferdy nods, stony-faced. 'And I'm really sorry about the room. I know you wanted it as well.'

'It's all right,' he mutters.

Rachel smiles at him, kindly. 'This is going to sound really pushy, but do you have any idea when you might be moving out?'

In the living room, Milly is screaming at Miles. 'What the hell do you think you're doing?'

'I don't believe you,' Anna adds. 'You're a walking hard-on.'

Miles has to shout to make himself heard. 'Hang on! We were getting nowhere and –'

'So you thought you'd make a unilateral decision?' says Anna.

Miles turns on her. 'Milly asked you to move in without asking me –'

'That was different!' shouts Milly. 'What you've done is completely out of order. Isn't it, Egg?'

'It's not on, Miles,' he says. 'But . . . you know . . . seeing as Rachel's moved her stuff in . . .'

Milly's face is now red with fury. 'Over my dead body! OVER MY DEAD BODY!'

The front door slams, and the room suddenly falls into a tense silence, with no one sure who has walked out. Whoever it was would certainly have heard Milly's shouts.

Ferdy enters the living room. 'Just seeing Rachel out,' he says. 'She's going to move in properly at the weekend.' He looks around the room, stirring their embarrassment a little longer, then goes back upstairs.

Milly, suddenly feeling guilty at what Rachel must have overheard, is the first to speak. 'Look – I like Rachel,' she says.

'Yeah, right,' says Miles.

Egg sighs. 'Look – why don't we go back to the interviews, then?'

'This is ridiculous. We'll never decide on one of them,' says Anna. 'It's between Rachel and Ferdy. Let's vote and get it over with. Majority rules.'

Anna interprets the room's silence as acquiescence. 'Right. Who votes for Rachel?'

Miles's hand shoots into the air, like an excited schoolboy. Egg's hand also twitches towards the ceiling, but one of Milly's laser beams smarts him in the eye, and he scratches his ear, then puts his hand back in his lap.

Miles scowls – a moment richly enjoyed by Anna and Milly. 'Ferdy!' they shout, in unison.

Ferdy clomps down the stairs, and nonchalantly accepts their offer of the room. 'What about Rachel, though?' he says.

'God – that's going to be really awkward,' Miles spits.

Milly, calm at last, speaks to Miles in the most patronizing tone she can muster. 'I think you've done enough, Miles. I'll tell her myself – at work tomorrow.'

Milly steps into the office with one task on her mind. It's going to be painful, it's going to be embarrassing, but she's going to enjoy it.

Rachel greets her warmly, as if they are suddenly better friends than ever.

'Hi,' says Milly. 'Did you get home all right, then?'

'Yeah. Thanks.'

'Good. Umm –'

'But getting into work this morning . . . what a nightmare. Glad that'll be over soon.'

'Yes. Umm –'

'We can come in together. Get some work done on the tube.'

'Look. There's been a misunderstanding about the room. Miles shouldn't have told you it was yours. We were still deciding.'

'Oh.'

'We've agreed on Ferdy, I'm afraid.'

'Oh. Oh – I see.'

'I'm sorry, Rachel.'

'No – I'm sure it's the right decision. It's all right. No hard feelings.'

Although neither of them say anything, the words 'Over my dead body' hang in the air between them. They both know why Rachel wasn't given the room. Milly frowns sympathetically, and walks to her office.

*　　*　　*

For the second time that week, Miles sleeps through his alarm. The first he sees of his bedside clock it says 8:50, and he has ten minutes to get to work.

He curses, shakes his head, leaps out of bed, and dashes for the bathroom. His vision is still a little blurry, but he immediately senses a presence in the room. Blinking himself out of the vestiges of his sleep, he sees Ferdy drying himself.

'Shit! There's a lock on the door,' says Miles, averting his eyes. 'Why don't you use it?'

Ferdy shrugs. 'Sorry,' he says, drying his balls roughly, then tossing the towel over his shoulder. 'I thought you'd all left.'

'Look – I'm late. D'you mind hurrying up a bit. I want to get in.'

'I've had my shower,' Ferdy replies, dabbing at his hair with the towel. 'Go ahead.'

Miles half turns, and catches sight of Ferdy, stark naked. Competitive instinct and natural curiosity fleetingly take over Miles's brain, and he simply can't stop his eyes from flicking downwards. He manages to look away almost instantly, but not before he has caught a glimpse of something dark, wide and weighty.

'I'll wait until you've finished,' says Miles, heading off with his head down.

'Don't worry. I won't look.'

'Forget it,' says Miles, slamming the door.

Alone in the bathroom, Ferdy smiles.

Chapter 20

Smashing

Rachel comes round to collect her stuff. She removes her brass R from the wall and Ferdy, by way of apology, asks her to stay for supper. He's cooking one of his mum's recipes for a house meal. Only Miles is excluded, since he 'doesn't eat Mexican food'.

Miles, however, spotting Rachel at the dining table with the others, plonks himself down and demands a plate.

'You said you didn't want any,' says Ferdy.

'No I didn't.'

'Yes you did,' says Egg.

'The menu's changed a bit since then,' says Anna, nodding at Rachel.

Rachel, embarrassed, asks the group whether they eat together every night.

'No,' says Miles. 'We're almost never in at the same time. It's a shame – I love cooking for people.'

Milly and Anna involuntarily crack up. Miles on the pull – in fact, the mere sight of Miles making an effort to be nice – is a hilarious spectacle.

'Yeah. Pork pies are his speciality,' says Egg.

*

Miles, helping Rachel out of the door, offers to take her for lunch. She tries to squirm out of it, but when Miles offers to take you out, it's rather like the police offering to take you in for questioning. You go. Not because there's any threat involved – just because you know that by resisting you will only make things worse for yourself.

She manages to get out of the door without having arranged anything specific, but within a couple of days he has persuaded her to have a drink with him after work.

On the day in question, Miles wakes up with a spot on his forehead. In the office, Jo happens to be toying with a flyer from a local salon. 'What's that?' says Miles, catching a glimpse of the text.

'Voucher for a salon.'

'A "salon"? What do you mean, "salon"?'

'You know – they do haircuts, shaves, massage –'

'A hairdresser?'

'– manicures, pedicures, facials, hair removal.'

'Hair removal?'

Jo reads aloud from the leaflet, ' "Eyebrow, back and leg waxing –" '

'Backs! It's a salon for queer Neanderthals.'

'Don't knock it. Women love a well-groomed man.'

'What do you know? You're not exactly whisking Kira off her feet.'

Jo suddenly clams up and reddens. 'She's not like that.'

'Like what?'

'Like . . . other women.'

'Yeah, right.'

'Piss off, Miles.'

*　　*　　*

Ferdy rings Mia, his ex, but she hangs up on him. He wants to talk to her. He *needs* to talk to her. He also needs his stuff. Since she dumped him, he's been living out of a holdall.

After days of agonizing, he eventually rides round to her flat. She isn't there, so he decides to wait. He knows it's stupid to waste time hanging around outside her house, but he somehow can't make himself leave.

After an hour or so, a shiny BMW pulls up, and Mia steps out. She clops to the front door without seeing Ferdy, and the car drives off.

Ferdy stands in shock for a while – it simply hadn't occurred to him that she could be seeing another man so quickly. Then, slowly, he climbs on to his bike and rides home.

*　　*　　*

Jo goes straight from work to the men's beauty salon, as an investment in his prospects with Kira.

One of the faces next to him, almost entirely hidden behind a mud pack, seems familiar. The brown face turns, sees Jo, and does an unmistakable double take.

'It's you, isn't it?' says Jo.

'Of course it's me,' Miles sighs.

'You look like you should be playing a banjo.'

Miles scowls. 'No one finds out I've been here. Got it?'
Jo nods, though without much conviction.

*   *   *

Anna's work situation is desperate again. With the tenancy vote coming up, it's more important than ever that she has lots to do, but for a while now she's had almost nothing. Things are so bad, in fact, that she decides to call Sarah Newly – the lesbian solicitor who tried to chat her up at Graham's party.

Sarah, with more than a hint of lasciviousness in her voice, invites her for a meal.

It takes Anna hours to prepare for her supper with Sarah. For the twentieth time, she hops into Milly's room and asks for advice on her outfit.

'What do you think?' she says. 'I want to convey the perfect balance of "I am not a dyke – not that I think there's anything wrong with it," combined with, "Please give me work."'

'That jacket says it all,' Milly enthuses.

'Why do none of my skirts go past mid-thigh? Why?'

'Because you've got great legs and you enjoy showing them off.'

'And look where it's got me.'

'Just wear what makes you comfortable.'

Then Egg walks in and eyes Anna up and down.

'Wow! You look great!' he says.

Milly smiles. Anna beams, and sighs – finally reassured that she looks OK 'Thanks, Egg.'

'Have you got a hot date?' he says.

Anna's face falls. 'Excuse me. I'm just going to change. Again.'

*   *   *

Miles emerges from his facial with his spot glowing brighter and redder than ever before. He feels as if he has a wind-sock growing out of his eyebrow. Still – he can't stand Rachel up, so he heads for the pub determined to switch on the charm and compensate for his bad day.

Sitting by the bar, she looks a peach. Yes – if this goes well, all his problems will be forgotten. He walks up to her and kisses her on the cheek. 'I've had a shit day . . . until now,' he says, looking deep into her eyes.

Rachel's posture stiffens slightly. 'You're very sweet, but –'

'I am sweet. You have no idea how sweet. Why don't you cancel your plans for later and let me show you how sweet I can be.'

'I can't, Miles.'

'We'll go back to my place, have a bottle of wine –'

'I really like you . . .'

Finally, that phrase halts Miles's momentum. 'There's a but coming, isn't there?' He shakes his head. 'This has been such a shit day.'

'I've just had a relationship end badly,' she explains.

'We're not all the same, you know. I'm –'

'It's just – I need some time.'

'I'm not going to pressure you,' he insists.

'No, of course not. But, to be honest, I find the idea

of getting involved with you while Anna is still in the picture –'

'There's nothing,' Miles interrupts. 'We had sex a couple of times. It's over.'

'I don't know –'

'No. It's over. I feel nothing for Anna. Less than nothing.'

'Not you. Her. I think she's still interested.'

'No.' Miles chuckles. 'I don't think so.'

* * *

The minute Anna sits at the table with Sarah Newly, she blurts out the truth – insisting that her phone call wasn't a come-on. She just needs some career advice from a woman solicitor.

Reluctantly, Sarah seems to take this information on board. However, as the evening progresses, and as the second bottle of wine is finished, it slowly dawns on Anna that she is being chatted up.

'Design, comfort, mileage – a loser in every category,' sighs Sarah.

'They can look pretty impressive.'

'D'you think?' says Sarah, shuddering. 'I think they're hideous. Pathetic when they're small – grotesque when they're big. All those purple veins . . .'

'The problem starts when you rev up the engine . . .'

'Power and size. That's all it's about.'

'Everything's humming,' says Anna, 'you're doing ninety – and suddenly . . . that's it. They've run out of fuel.'

'Who needs it?' says Sarah, with a glint in her eye.

'And all those guys at my office! Jesus! If I could just find an island of sanity in an ocean of testosterone . . .'

Sarah reaches forward, and cups her hand over Anna's. 'That could be arranged,' she says.

Anna looks at Sarah's hand and thinks for a moment. *OK. So a woman's holding my hand. It doesn't feel that bad. It's just a hand. Hands don't have a gender, really. No. This is wrong. I'm not into this.*

Anna pulls her hand away, and gives Sarah an apologetic smile. 'You know – in spite of all its shortcomings, I still am rather partial to the penis.'

Sarah smiles back, mischievously. 'Whatever you say.'

*   *   *

Ferdy tries to talk to Mia at the chemist's shop, but it doesn't work. He explains that he wants his stuff back, but she takes this as an insult, and thrusts a set of keys into his hand. Nothing he says to her comes out right, and he walks away with the keys, feeling as if he has made the situation worse. He has missed his opportunity to apologize.

Using her keys, he lets himself into her house that evening. Hearing the door open, she walks to the door, and looks strangely freaked-out to see him.

'I thought you'd come while I was at work.'

'I wanted to talk again.'

'Ferdy,' she says, 'there's something you don't know.'

A male voice rings out from the living room. 'Who is it, Mia?'

'You remember Seb,' she says, suddenly sheepish.

Seb, a guy who until recently worked with Ferdy – rugby-player type – walks into the hall, towering over the two of them. 'Course he remembers me,' says Seb, warmly reaching out a hand.

'I just came to pick up my things. Maybe I should come back.'

'No. It's fine,' says Seb. 'Better do it while I'm here. In case you need a hand or something. Drink?'

'No thanks.'

'Go on. Have one. Get us some lager, will you, babe?'

'I don't think Ferdy wants one,' says Mia, nervously.

'No? All right. So – still doing the courier bit, then?'

'Yeah,' replies Ferdy, still not catching his eye. 'I hear you moved on.'

'Set up my own company.'

'Right.'

'Best move I ever made. Business is fantastic. Just bought a nice new car, didn't I?'

'Yeah . . . well, I'll get my things together.'

'They're in the spare room,' says Mia, ushering him away from Seb. 'I'll just get you some bin bags.'

Ferdy is on his way out of the flat, carrying two full bags containing all his junk, when Seb stops him by the door. 'You know,' he says, 'I always had my doubts about you. You never really fitted in, did you? I should have guessed.'

'Guessed what?' says Ferdy, his hackles rising.

Seb smiles, affably. 'I'm not going to stand here and

pretend. You're a shirt-lifter. I should have known all along that you were queer.'

Ferdy steps out of the flat, lugging his bags.

'Seb!' says Mia, horrified. She steps outside and halts Ferdy before he goes down the stairs. 'Ferdy, I'm sorry. This was a mistake. I should have told you.'

'Did you have to tell him about me?'

'I didn't. He told me.'

Ferdy scowls, and strides down the stairs.

Outside, he dumps his bags on the pavement, and stares at the brand-new BMW in front of him. He steps towards it, and spits on the boot. With the cuff of his leather jacket, he rubs in the saliva, bringing up a shine.

He looks around. A house over the road has a skip outside, and a stack of building materials piled high in the front garden. Ferdy crosses the street to see what he can find. On the edge of the lawn is a discarded piece of scaffolding pole – roughly three-feet long. A perfect length. Easy to wield, but heavy.

He starts with the tail-lights. Using the pole as a mini battering-ram, the plastic shatters with pleasing ease. The headlights, too, cave in with a surprising lack of effort.

One giant swing, propelled with all the joy and violence of satisfied revenge, shatters the windscreen, spreading shards of glass all over the bonnet and upholstery of the car. Ferdy spits again, this time directly into the car, and walks away.

*　　*　　*

Anna arrives home from her date – meal, that is – and finds Miles slumped on the sofa, a bottle of beer in his hand, looking utterly depressed.

'Hello,' she says, cheerily.

'You're in a good mood,' he replies, phrasing it as an insult.

'Yeah. You're not.'

'Mmm . . .'

'So,' she says, 'how did it go with Rachel?'

'Great . . . fine. We're just good friends, really.'

'She turned you down, then?'

'It's your fault, actually. She's got this idea you still fancy me.'

Anna chuckles. 'She said the same thing to me about you.'

'Barking,' says Miles, after a considerable pause.

'Completely twisted,' says Anna, filling another long silence.

The door clatters shut, and Ferdy walks in, carrying two swelling bin bags. He grins at them, broadly. 'Night,' he says, then walks upstairs, still smiling at his private joke.

Chapter 21

When the Dope Comes In

Suddenly, out of the blue, there is a vibe with O'Donnell again. Milly is showing him a document one morning, when he says, with no warning, 'I like your earrings.'

In effect, he might as well have said, 'I still haven't forgotten that we almost shagged.'

He covers Milly's embarrassed response with one of his pep talks about her workload, and how well she's managing, then proceeds with the meeting as if nothing has been said – casually signing papers and discussing legal technicalities.

Milly is on her way out of the office, still feeling confused by O'Donnell's behaviour, when he suddenly says, 'I'd like you to come to Paris.'

Milly's heart stops for a moment. What does he mean? Then she remembers that a European Law Conference is being held there at the weekend. The question remains, though. What *does* he mean?

'To the conference?' she says.

'Yes. I've just got the programme. It's going to be

impossible for one person to cover the whole thing.'

They stare at each other across the office, each struggling to read the other's mind.

'What do you think?' he says.

'Um – I think it's not that simple,' says Milly.

'It could be. It would be,' he replies. She looks out of the window, then down at her feet. 'Milly – you're my most experienced assistant. I need you to be updated on European law.'

'Can I think about it?' she says, eventually.

'Of course you can. Mull it over for a couple of days.'

Milly walks back to her office, conflicting emotions racing through her mind. She can't decide whether to be excited, scared or angry.

She won't go. She can't go. But every time she sees O'Donnell talking to Rachel, she finds herself rethinking. Just watching the way Rachel flirts with him causes Milly to seethe with jealousy. Rachel *always* seems to be in O'Donnell's office – usually on false pretences, Milly suspects. And she always hovers by his door – chatting, laughing and fluttering her eyelashes for minutes on end after she has finished whatever work they have got through. It makes Milly furious that Rachel can be so openly flirtatious in such an unprofessional manner. She's only a trainee, for God's sake. Milly knows exactly what she's up to. She is blatantly using her looks to further her career, and O'Donnell's falling for it. The whole thing is disgusting.

*   *   *

Miles refuses to come in on Ferdy's blow, on the grounds that it comes through Spain, and Spanish stuff is always cut with henna. Egg and Anna both chip in, and the first test run produces extremely promising results. Clearly, this dope isn't cut with anything. It is *very* good. Anna resists temptation, and after a few puffs heads upstairs to work.

Miles wanders in just as Ferdy and Egg are beginning to lose it, and out of pride refuses to smoke. Only when Ferdy leaves on a munchies run (in search of strawberry-and-kiwi Snapple, a dark-chocolate Bounty, a Boost and a packet of Maltesers) does Miles succumb.

Within minutes, Miles is wasted. This stuff is good.

The doorbell rings, and Egg gets up to answer it. 'People who forget their keys can't come in!' he shouts through the door, assuming that it is Ferdy on the other side.

The letter-box flap lifts a fraction. 'Hello. It's the police,' says the letter-box. 'Could you open the door please?'

Egg doesn't recognize the voice. It slowly dawns on him that this isn't a wind-up. He dashes into the living room. 'It's the police!' he says.

Miles leaps to his feet, stubs out the joint and shoves it into a stack of magazines. He picks up the dope and stuffs it into his pocket. Seeing the ashtray, he shoves it under the sofa. He then leaps to the stereo, stops the CD, and switches the music over to Classic FM. Spotting a half-burnt stick of incense in the sideboard, he fumbles for a box of matches and lights it. Egg runs to the window and back, for no apparent reason. He can't decide whether the curtains, or the windows, should be open or shut.

'Let them in,' says Miles, blinking and rubbing his cheeks.

Egg walks into the hall, takes a couple of breaths, and opens the door with a hospitable smile. Two policemen walk in.

'Sorry about that,' he says. 'I was just in the middle of something.'

'It's all right,' says one of the policemen. 'Sorry to call so late, but we've tried a couple of times in the day and there's been no one about.'

'Right.'

'Are you Ferdinand Garcia?'

'No.'

'Is he in?'

'No. I'm afraid he's not.'

'Would it be all right if we left him a note?'

'Yeah – sure. Come through.'

In the living room, Miles is sitting on the sofa, flipping through a magazine at top speed, in the hope that this will disguise his shaking hands.

'This is Miles,' says Egg. 'These two officers are going to leave a note for Ferdy.'

'Right. How do you do?' says Miles, standing to shake them by the hand. As he stands, he is suddenly aware of the huge bulge in his pocket – a Golden Virginia tin stuffed full of dope. 'Err . . . actually, Ferdy *might* be in,' he says. 'He's right at the top of the house so you never know. I'll just go and have a check.'

Miles gives a casual smile to the policemen, saunters into the hall, then sprints upstairs, heading directly for the bathroom. With his co-ordination in ruins, he fumbles the tin from his pocket and tips the contents into the toilet. He flushes, hides the tin behind the bathroom sink, and scrabbles in the closet for some eye drops.

'He's not in his room,' says Miles, back downstairs. Egg, he sees, has made them each a cup of tea. *Smart move, Egg. Why not ask them if they want to stay for* Sportsnight?

'Are you all right?' says Egg. 'You look like you've been crying.'

'They're bigger than you think, these houses,' says one of the policemen.

Miles is just trying to figure out whether this is a veiled comment on the suspicious length of his absence when the front door slams, and Ferdy walks in, carrying a bag full of sweets.

'Are you Ferdinand Garcia?'

'Yes.'

The policeman explains that he is investigating an allegation of criminal damage to a car outside a flat in Colliers Wood. Ferdy reacts smoothly – frowning with concern at the crime, and offering without hesitation to answer all their questions.

The policemen interview Ferdy in the hall, while Miles listens intently at the door. Ferdy offers a slick alibi, giving a precise time when he left Mia's flat, and saying that he came straight back to Benjamin Street for a regular Friday-night house meal.

Miles spits with fury on the other side of the door, but when the police interview him, he backs Ferdy up – saying that he was in all evening, and Ferdy arrived home in time for their regular Friday-night meal.

The second the door closes on the policemen, Miles sprints upstairs to Ferdy's room. Ferdy is sitting on his bed. He listens to the rapidly approaching footsteps, thinking, *I'm a fan, and here comes the shit.*

'That was totally out of order!' Miles shrieks, bursting in. 'Totally out of order! I can't believe what you just did. I don't know anyone else who would do that.'

'Did they question you?' says Ferdy.

'Of course they questioned me. And Egg – who can't say anything without pissing himself.'

'I wasn't that bad,' says Egg, appearing at the door.

'What did you say?' Ferdy asks.

'What do you think I said? What could I say? I backed you up. I had to, because you had totally fucking stitched us up!'

'It sounds like it worked out OK, though.'

'How can you be so stupid? It's only just started. They're going to do house-to-house inquiries, they're going to check your route home, and if any witnesses come out of the woodwork we are all in deep shit. It's perjury! You can get seven years for that. You've compromised my entire career to cover your own arse.'

'I'm sorry.'

'So you fucking should be,' says Miles, storming out of the room. At the door, he turns back to Ferdy and says,

'I flushed your gear down the bog. The tin's behind the sink.'

*   *   *

Over lunch, Milly asks Anna's opinion about her invitation to Paris – expecting to get some direct, clear advice. What she gets is rather more direct than she had in mind.

'The real question is – do you want to sleep with the guy? If you do, go to Paris. If you don't, don't.'

'I don't know what I want.'

'If you want to fuck everything up, break Egg's heart, gatecrash a marriage and jeopardize your job, then it's a great idea.'

'It's exactly the sort of thing *you*'d do.'

'Yeah, but I'm not you. You're a good person. That's your cross.'

Back in the office, Milly goes to see O'Donnell and tells him that she can't go to Paris – her workload is too much at the moment, and it would be unwise to distract herself from her client work.

O'Donnell pauses, sighs, then responds pointedly. 'Well – I can't pretend I'm not disappointed, but I think you're very wise and very professional.' He looks at her and blinks a few times. 'A model of discipline.'

She knows what this means. He wants to sleep with her, but he knows they shouldn't – and he is passing over to her the responsibility to make sure that they don't.

Sexual tension hangs in the air like a fine mist of rain.

'Don't say that,' she replies.

'Well, you are, and I admire it.'

Milly walks out, feeling slightly weak at the knees.

Milly leaves the office late, and walks to the tube with Rachel. 'Got anything nice planned for the weekend?' she says.

'Well, I didn't,' Rachel replies, 'but now I think I might do a bit of clothes shopping tomorrow.'

'That's nice.'

'O'Donnell's asked me to go to the conference in Paris.'

Milly's heart leaps into her throat. This is the worst possible outcome. She tries to control her voice, while she decides what to do. 'Gosh. You must be delighted.'

'If you weren't so indispensable here, I'm sure he would have asked you,' says Rachel.

'What are you going to buy?'

Milly doesn't listen to Rachel jabbering on about clothes. Her mind is racing. Suddenly, without really being fully aware of the decision she is taking, she leaps in, cutting Rachel off in the middle of a sentence. 'Oh, God. I've just remembered I was supposed to fax that report to Mrs Walters. It can't wait till Monday. Sorry.'

'I'll wait for you.'

Milly is already walking back to the office. 'No – don't. I'll see you on Monday.' She turns, and breaks into a run.

'Have a nice weekend,' Rachel calls after her.

Milly bursts into O'Donnell's office, out of breath. 'I panicked about Paris,' she blurts. 'I'm sure I can catch up with work. I was being neurotic. I'd like to change my mind.'

O'Donnell's face falls. 'But Milly – I've . . . I've made other arrangements. I don't think I can change them. I wish I could. I . . .' He stands and tries to touch her arm – his face drooping with regret.

'No,' says Milly. 'Sorry. Sorry. I shouldn't have asked.'

'No. You should. Don't be sorry.'

They stare at each other, and Milly suddenly feels hot, tired, confused and embarrassed. 'I'm sorry.'

'It's all right.'

She turns and runs away – out of his office, out of the building, and down the street.

Chapter 22

She's Gotta Get It

Anna is having a good week until Hooperman tells her that the firm is about to vote on her tenancy. This is exactly what she wants, but the news that her fate is about to be decided hardly makes for a relaxing week. Still, it couldn't have come at a better time. Sarah Newly has been providing a steady supply of work for the last month, and, on the whole, Anna has been winning. Her latest is a prostitution case – extremely interesting, but a tough one to win.

Hooperman has always been a big champion of Anna's, and she knows that he has deliberately timed the vote for a strong moment in her favour.

Miles, meanwhile, is in a slump. His flow of work has almost dried up, and every time he steps into Jo's office there seems to be a fresh brief lying around from S. Newly at Rankin Jamal, destined for Anna.

'So who's S. Newly?' he says to Graham – who knows everyone.

'Sarah Newly? She's a solicitor.'

'And?'

'She's very good. Does a lot of criminal – with Rankin Jamal.'

'Are they good?'

'Yes, they are. Very right on. Quite a few of them are gay.'

'Is she gay?'

'Yes.'

'She's a dyke?'

'Yes. Why?'

'Because she can't stop briefing Anna.'

Graham laughs, a knowing twinkle in his eye. 'Oh, really? That sounds about right.'

'What do you mean?'

'Nothing. She's a friend. She's great. But she'll always give things a try.'

Sarah isn't trying it on with Anna, though. Yes, they've been having a lot of meetings together – and, yes, they've even gone out for the odd drink – but the focus of everything is strictly work. And she's happy to send her briefs to Anna, because she is rapidly developing a genuine respect for her work. The girl is sharp, witty and an excellent barrister. Oh, dammit – she fancies Anna rotten. But the poor girl does seem to be irredeemably heterosexual. For the time being, anyway.

All the gossip in chambers is about Anna's tenancy. Angus, one of the senior partners, watches her on a drink-drive case, and is impressed. When Miles overhears Graham commenting on this, he can't resist chipping in.

'What – he's going to vote for her on the strength of that?'

'I don't know – but he did think she was good.'

'Yeah – good with boozers and tarts. It's the Jane Austen approach – stick to what you know.'

Graham laughs and shakes his head. 'She's bright, Miles.'

'I know she's bright, but she's also a head case.'

'Most chambers members are.'

'Not like that.'

In the week building up to the vote, Anna's reputation in chambers is more important than it has ever been. As a rule, she never cares what people say about her behind her back but, in the circumstances, her growing awareness that Miles is conducting a whispering campaign against her makes Anna extremely anxious.

'He's even got the clerk cracking jokes about briefs from Lesbos,' she tells Sarah, over a drink in a City wine bar.

Sarah seems unsurprised. 'They can't handle you. You're clever and successful, but your skirts are too short and your legs are too long.'

'No – that's Barbie.'

Sarah persists, casually demolishing Anna's flippancy. 'You can't be everything at once, because that's a threat, so they undermine you. I don't mean in an organized way. It's not even conscious. It's a . . . deeply entrenched thing. It's how hegemony works.'

'Well, it's working. I'm never going to get tenancy.'

'Stop it. If you start thinking your fate is sealed, then it will be.'

'What else can I think?'

'You can think, "Right – I'll play a long game. I won't compromise my nature, but I'll keep my corner clean and do my work well, and sooner or later they will have to reward me."'

'Why should it be such a fucking trial?'

'Because men run the world, my love.'

Watched by Graham, Anna pulls a high-risk but utterly successful defence in the prostitution case. Afterwards, she walks back to chambers with Graham. Or rather, he walks; she floats.

Anna is so high, she can barely stop herself gabbling. 'I got completely carried away cross-examining the boy-friend. I just heard this character demolition pouring out of my mouth and I couldn't bear to stop.'

'Well,' says Graham, shaking his head slightly, 'that's what got her off.'

'Only because her previous didn't go in,' she laughs.

Graham tries to burst her bubble. He doesn't trust Anna's strategy. 'I can't believe your attitude. You took a huge risk on your client's part and you seem to think it's funny.'

'Don't worry. I won't try it again. I couldn't afford the toilet paper.'

Graham can't resist a smile. But, although Anna won an impressive victory, what he saw has in fact turned him against her. Or rather – it has confirmed what he always thought of her. She's unreliable. A maverick.

Hooperman summons Miles for a meeting, and challenges Miles to justify himself. 'I think Anna's sparky, capable, stimulating . . . yet I hear that you've been bad-mouthing her in chambers. I'd like to know, what is the precise nature of your feelings against her?'

Miles squirms in his seat. 'I don't have any feelings against her. I have some reservations about her, that's all. I have reservations about almost everyone I know.'

Hooperman squints at Miles, and speaks with a shade of sarcasm. 'When she first arrived, you thought she'd make a good barrister. What happened?'

'Nothing.'

'So you haven't been waging a hate campaign?'

'I think you must have been quoted edited highlights,' says Miles, confidently.

'Maybe so. Still – I think you ought to exercise more restraint in future. Chambers is a delicate organism at the best of times. When personal feelings come into play, the results can be ruinous.'

'It's really nothing like that.'

'Good. I think she'll be an excellent tenant.'

Miles walks back to his office, feeling more resentment towards Anna than ever before. Everything's so much easier for her than it is for him. Just because she's a woman, she's got Hooperman feeling sorry for her, and some dyke throwing more work at her than she can handle. It's discrimination. It's sexual discrimination. If you're a white male with a public-school accent, no one will ever do you any favours. It's not fair. Not that Miles expects favours from anyone. He just wishes there could be a level playing field.

Back at chambers, Jo tells Anna to peel herself off the ceiling and go home. The vote has been shifted to that evening.

On the way back to Benjamin Street, Anna stops off at an off-licence for three packets of maximum-tar cigarettes and two bottles of Soave.

No one has much to contribute to a debate about Anna's merits and flaws, so Hooperman moves directly to a vote.

'For?'

Hooperman counts the hands, and jots down a number.

'Against?'

Two hands go up – one of them, Miles's, rather coyly.

'And abstentions?'

Graham puts his hand up, looking at Miles with a rather thoughtful air.

The phone rings. Milly, Egg and Ferdy, sitting in empathetic silence, stare at Anna. She picks up the receiver.

'Hello?'

She pauses, and listens for a couple of seconds, then breaks into a grin. Three whoops go up, and it is suddenly impossible for her to hear what Hooperman is saying. He understands – and congratulates her briefly, then tells her to go out and get drunk.

* * *

For Jo, too, the waiting is over. Rather like a medieval knight, he has survived the ordeal and his fair maiden is ready to parcel out her reward.

Kira's mum and stepdad are on holiday in Tenerife. After one quick drink in the pub, she utters the six magic words, 'Jawana come back ta my place?'

In a style rather dissimilar to that of a medieval romance, they spend the night fucking noisily in Kira's parents' bed.

* * *

Music is pumping and drink is flowing at Benjamin Street when Miles arrives home.

Anna sees him and leaps across the room – swamping him in a bear-hug.

'I did it! I did it!'

'I know you did,' he says, pulling a bottle of champagne out from under his coat.

'You voted for me?' she says.

He smiles. 'Course.'

Anna kisses him, underneath her elation quietly regretting that she had been so suspicious of him. 'Miles – I love you. You're a darling.'

'Forget about it. Congratulations,' he says, and uses the pretext of opening the champagne to turn away from the group. As he twists the wire from the cork, his face sets into a stern, rather guilty-looking stare.

Chapter 23

The Perfect Partner. Almost

The office is oddly quiet for a few days, and Milly vows that when Rachel and O'Donnell return, she will make a fresh start. She'll try and be professional with O'Donnell, and less bitchy with Rachel.

Just the sight of them wafting in late from the airport together, however, upsets Milly's plans. They suddenly look more comfortable than ever together – so comfortable, in fact, that Milly's mind fills with paranoid thoughts. She can't help feeling that something has happened between them. In some way, O'Donnell has cheated on her.

Milly tries to repress her jealousy, and decides that despite her feelings, she can still try and begin afresh with Rachel. If nothing else, a friendly lunch together is probably the best way to find out what really happened.

Under the pretext of getting Rachel out of the office to talk through the conference notes, Milly invites her to a sandwich bar for lunch. Rachel chats away as usual, and

Milly slowly directs the conversation to the subject of Paris.

'I had to leave my credit card in the hotel in case I went crazy. All those fabulous clothes.'

'I'm beginning to wish I agreed to go, now,' says Milly, pointedly. And accidentally. She seems to have a put-Rachel-in-her-place gland which takes over her metabolism at unexpected moments.

Rachel looks slightly stung. 'O'Donnell asked you to go?'

'Yes, but I was too busy. Didn't he mention it?'

'No, I don't suppose he had any reason to.'

Milly suddenly feels satisfied. It is obvious from Rachel's behaviour that nothing happened in Paris between her and O'Donnell. In fact, it was always obvious. Milly feels cross with herself – with her paranoia. She has always despised irrational behaviour, and is now exhibiting it. She emerges from her self-absorption to find Rachel gabbling on about how supportive O'Donnell was at the conference.

'O'Donnell?' says Milly – suddenly alarmed by the variety of possible meanings for the word 'supportive'.

'Yeah – he's a sweetheart.'

'Why?'

'Less attractive men have to work harder at it, you know. They've got more tricks up their sleeve.'

'He's not that bad-looking,' says Milly, trying not to sound defensive.

'God, Milly – you don't fancy him do you?'

'*No.* Anyway – he's married.'

'He isn't married any more.'

'What do you mean? Of course he is.'

'They've separated. He's got his own flat in town.'

'He told you this?' Milly suddenly feels sweaty all over. She knew that O'Donnell had been flirting with her lately. *Oh, God – this is terrible news. And marvellous news. Oh, God.*

'Yes. It just sort of came up. Are you all right?'

'Yes – I'm fine. Listen – we'd better be getting back.'

They walk to the office in silence, with Milly forcing the pace – a couple of steps ahead of Rachel in order to conceal her face.

*　　*　　*

Sarah Newly expects, and deserves, a thank-you from Anna. Quite which form this thank-you is supposed to take is a matter of some concern to Anna. They have arranged to go for a meal together, and Anna is certain that Sarah will make a move on her.

As soon as they have ordered food, Anna pitches in – reeling off a prepared speech. 'Right. Here goes. I am very grateful for your help, Sarah. The work your firm put my way really swung it for me. So thank you. Thank you very much.'

'Very gracious,' says Sarah, smiling saucily, and tipping her glass to Anna.

The meal proceeds with more sexual tension than an episode of *Baywatch*. Sarah insists on flirting shamelessly – passing forkfuls of food across the table to Anna, and Anna simply can't help responding in kind – telling Sarah that her food melts on the tongue. Just when Sarah seems to be getting excited about her prospects, Anna explains that her problem in life is that she's programmed to flirt with anyone. She can't help herself.

'Anyone?' says Sarah, sceptically.

'Yep. Anyone. Sad, eh?'

'You don't seem sad to me.'

'That's because I enjoy it.'

'Whether you like the person or not?'

'I suppose I enjoy it more if I do.'

'And you like me?' says Sarah, leaning forward on to her elbows.

'Of course I do.'

Sarah smiles. 'The difference with me is – I can only flirt with people I *really* like.'

Anna coughs. Their flirtation started blatantly, and has become less subtle ever since. Anna doesn't want to bottle out – on principle, she doesn't believe in bottling out of anything – but Sarah does seem to have pushed things to a point at which Anna can only retreat. Either that, or advance into *extremely* new territory.

The trouble is, barring the one rather obvious stumbling-block, Anna has found her perfect partner. Intelligent, sexy, great job, ambitious but not arrogant, sensitive, nice car, GSOH, fancies Anna like mad *and* respects her. Sarah's perfect. Almost perfect.

Anna coughs again. 'I'm just going to the toilet,' she says.

*　　*　　*

When O'Donnell asks Milly if she minds working late, Milly shakes her head and shrugs.

Over the next few hours, she gets almost no work done. Her mind races with conflicting thoughts and emotions. She can't possibly know what to think or say until she knows the situation with O'Donnell's marriage. If Rachel was telling the truth, then Milly's suspicions have been proved right. The decision now is all hers.

As soon as the office has emptied of other workers, Milly walks into O'Donnell's room.

'Finished for the night?' he says.

'Are you and your wife separated?' Milly replies.

O'Donnell, surprised by this uncharacteristic directness, freezes. 'I'm sorry?'

'Rachel told me that you and your wife are separated and you've got a flat in town. Is it true?'

O'Donnell scratches his nose and thinks for a second. 'Yes.'

'I didn't know whether to believe her.'

He sighs, and turns to her with a sympathetic smile. 'I should have told you.'

'Rachel seems to know everything,' she spits.

'Is that why you're angry with me?'

'I'm not angry. I just like to be kept informed.'

'About my private life?'

Milly's anger suddenly falters. She feels caught out. She has pitched the whole thing wrongly, and – yet again – has embarrassed herself. She turns for the door. 'You're right. Why should you tell me about your private life. It's none of my business.'

He stalls her – speaking calmly, and looking her directly in the eye. 'The reason I didn't tell you is that I thought it might be too . . . provocative. I thought you might have felt compromised, given our history.'

'You obviously think I'm a very weak person,' she says, her confidence returning a fraction.

'I think you're a remarkable person,' he insists.

'And Rachel? Do you think she's a remarkable person, too?'

O'Donnell clenches his jaw, and Milly realizes that she might have gone too far. 'I'd better go before I talk myself out of a job,' she mumbles, scurrying for the door.

'Milly! Wait. Please listen.' Milly stops with her hand on the doorknob, but doesn't turn. 'Rachel,' he continues, 'is a charming, attractive woman. I like her, yes, but if I was going to risk jeopardizing my position . . .'

He takes a couple of steps towards Milly, touches her gently on each upper arm, and turns her to face him.

'. . . it would be with somebody far more desirable.'

They stare at each other, their faces only the smallest kissing distance apart. Milly blinks and turns. She has lost control of the situation. Without speaking, she leaves, closing the door behind her, and walks slowly out of the office. Through his venetian blinds, O'Donnell watches her go.

Chapter 24

Wish You Were Queer

Ever since Warren left, Ferdy has been neither in nor out. Sitting on the porch, as the saying goes. Under her cousin's instructions, Kira has been doing her best to improve Ferdy's sex life – setting him up with several old mates of Warren's, but it hasn't worked. If there's one place in the world that makes Ferdy feel straight, it's a gay club. One glimpse of a roomful of skinny queens dancing to crap music, and Ferdy becomes convinced that he's a fully-fledged heterosexual.

However, when a Glaswegian plumber with tight muscles, thick red hair and a cheeky grin comes round to mend the boiler, Ferdy has an instant rethink. As the plumber screws the front back on the boiler, and asks if there's any more work that needs doing, Ferdy realizes that he doesn't want to let this man out of his house.

'You just do plumbing?' says Ferdy, fixing him with intense eye contact.

'Oh, no. I'm a general handyman,' he replies, staring back, not blinking.

'It's just – there's a loose socket in my bedroom.'

The plumber answers by raising his eyebrows. Then he smiles. 'Better take a look, then, hadn't I?'

Twenty minutes with this particular handyman, and you *know* your sexuality.

Ferdy sighs and lights two cigarettes. OK, so he's gay. Now he can get on with his life.

*   *   *

Ever since the tenancy vote, Anna has felt slightly warmer towards Miles. Despite his perpetual hostility towards her, and his general sulkiness, and his homophobia towards Ferdy, and his competitiveness, and his vanity, and his selfishness, and . . . this list could go on indefinitely. Basically – despite everything, when it came to it, he voted for her. He did the necessary, and proved himself to be on her side. And when someone is on your side, even if they get on your nerves, they're a friend.

*   *   *

Although Egg and Milly haven't exactly entered the sexual Gobi Desert of earlier in the year, their relationship has gradually turned semi-arid. Milly is preoccupied by her own roving lust, and Egg has become obsessed with cookbooks. In bed at night, given the choice between a good old-fashioned shag and an analysis of modern courgette technique, nine times out of ten, Egg takes the modern option.

After twenty-six years of pissing around, he has finally found his *métier*, and he feels he has to make up for lost time. Nicki's giving him a useful grounding at the café, but Egg now has big plans. He is – officially – the next Marco Pierre White. He's decided. The only problem is money. He's got no cash to get to catering college. He has tried to get a loan from the bank, but the manager laughed in his face and told him to piss off and get a life. Not literally. That was the subtext.

So he has decided to start from the bottom. The first step is to improve the café. And with the boss on holiday in Ireland, he arranges with Nicki to stay open one night for a Tex-Mex evening, with Ferdy as culinary consultant.

*   *   *

Jo won't tell her what it is, but Anna can tell that something big is in the air. She can smell it. Now that she's a tenant, with months of licence applications and driving offences behind her, she's hoping for some work that she can get her teeth into. And with the odour of a big case permeating the office, the moment seems ripe for a quick schmooze with Hooperman.

She taps on his door, which he opens, carrying a glass of thick grey liquid. 'I'm drinking my lunch today,' he explains. 'Mixed vegetable juices.'

They both frown at his drink for a few seconds, before he abandons it on a shelf and heads for his desk. 'So,' he says, 'before I send out for something more appetizing, tell me your troubles.'

'No troubles at all. I just wanted to say how chuffed I am about getting tenancy.'

'It's no more than you deserve. How's practice going?'

'I'm getting plenty in the magistrates, but I'm keen to do more up in Crown.'

'Well, of course you are.'

'It would be nice to be led on something. Get a bit of experience . . .'

'Miles will be fighting you on that one.'

'No change there, then,' she says, with a chuckle.

This comment, however, triggers a pained reaction from Hooperman. He thinks for a moment, grimacing slightly, then speaks in an avuncular tone. 'If things have been a little touchy between you since your tenancy vote, you should let it go.'

Anna frowns, unable to respond, while the implication of this comment sinks in.

'You're a tenant now, anyway,' he continues, 'and what's done is done.'

Anna's jaw slackens as it dawns on her what Hooperman means. Miles voted against her. He's been lying all this time. She fights to contain her anger and shock.

'It's got nothing to do with Miles and the vote,' she says, struggling to keep her voice steady.

'Good. That is big of you. Now – I think I'll order a sushi.'

Anna walks into Miles's office. He's not there, so she sits in his chair and waits. Physical violence is out – she knows that – but she can't actually think of what she can say. She just has to tell him that she knows, and let him know that she despises him.

Miles enters, and gives her a what-the-hell-are-you-doing-in-my-chair look. 'Are you lost?' he says. 'Your desk is down the corridor, isn't it?'

'Yes, it is.' She stares at him, biliously.

Refusing to rise to the bait, Miles plays it cool. 'Right. If we've got that clear – I've got a lot of work to do.'

'So have I,' she says. 'Despite your efforts.'

Anna still isn't moving. Miles, hovering above his chair, stares at her, quizzically. 'What is this, Anna?'

'You didn't vote for me.'

Miles swallows, and tries not to react. Anna stares at him, observing his agonized silence.

'How do you know that?' he says, eventually.

'How I know isn't the point, is it?'

Still trying to appear unruffled, it takes Miles a long time to think of a response. 'Well you got it, anyway.'

'You knew how hard I worked. How much I wanted tenancy. And you lied about it. Just blatantly lied.'

Anna stares at him, but Miles fails to meet her gaze. He blinks and looks away.

Anna stands and walks towards him. 'Yeah,' she says, almost touching his face with her nose. 'I'm not sure I'd know what to say if I were you.'

She slams the door behind her.

* * *

Graham has received a major brief from Rankin Jamal – probably the biggest thing the firm has had since the Sheringham case. The press have already got hold of the story – involving a schoolgirl who is accusing a teacher of rape, while he claims that it was an affair that went sour.

216

Graham is going to need assistance on it, so he immediately thinks of Miles. Although Anna has already had a sniff, and is nagging him for the work, he has chosen Miles. He works hard, he's more trustworthy, and he's far easier to get on with. All Graham needs now for Miles's participation is the approval of the solicitors.

The solicitor concerned, however, is a certain Sarah Newly, who Anna just happens to have asked out for dinner that evening. Anna also just happens to be wearing an *extremely* short skirt.

'Nice wine,' says Anna. 'Just what I needed. I've had a pig of a day.'

'Anything in particular, or just overwork?' asks Sarah.

'I wish.'

'So why don't you say why you're inviting me out for dinner all of a sudden?'

Sarah leans back in her chair, and gives Anna an affectionately suspicious look. Anna hesitates, but realizes that she can only be honest. Clearly – she has already been rumbled.

'The Aylmore case? Sorry to be so obvious.'

Sarah smiles, suggestively. 'Oh, I've been a little obvious myself in my time.'

'So can you ask for me?'

'Why should I?'

'A woman on the defence team makes the defendant much more plausible in a case like this.'

'Especially a woman as intelligent and attractive as you are?' Anna smiles, awkwardly. This flattery is obviously leading somewhere. 'Of course, I did consider asking for you.'

'And?'

'I'm still considering.'

Anna pauses to absorb the tidal waves of lust gushing over her, and tries to redirect the conversation. 'We could be a good team.'

'I think so.'

'I mean professionally.'

'I think we could be more than that,' says Sarah, reaching round the table and touching Anna's thigh.

'I know,' says Anna, slightly coolly.

'I don't think you do. I really fancied you from the start. But now it's more messy than that. I've fallen in love with you.'

Anna stares at her, dumbfounded. 'I'm flattered, but . . .'

'We like each other, don't we?'

'I have thought about it. But I've never . . . I just don't think it's me.'

'How do you know until you've tried?'

In a surge of decisiveness, bolstered by residual anger at Miles, Anna decides that Sarah is right. You can never be sure until you've tried. And the only way to try is to grasp the nettle.

She leans across the table, places her fingers behind Sarah's head, and pulls her into a kiss. A long, slow, deep, wet snog. The volume of chatter in the restaurant falls, as heads turn.

Anna wipes her lips and leans back in her chair. She

smiles at Sarah, who appears to be in shock. 'I'm sorry,' Anna says. 'I've tried now – but it doesn't do it for me.'

'Pity.'

Sarah's cool surface, for once, has been rumpled – and she doesn't like it. She stands. 'I'd better go. I'll get the bill on the way out.'

Without looking back, she leaves the restaurant.

* * *

The Tex-Mex meal with free tequila shots to get people in the mood turns into a tequila-abuse session with random dips that no one particularly notices. Ferdy baits Miles into a drinking contest which proves staggeringly one-sided, and Egg, whose evening has been disastrous from start to finish, is left with the task of peeling Miles off the pavement and getting him home in a taxi.

With the evening raking in a total loss of twenty-five pounds, Egg decides to have another tactical rethink. Serving decent food in a café is a waste of effort, and doesn't make business sense. He has to find some way of getting into the restaurant trade.

* * *

Anna arrives at work to find a bunch of flowers on her desk, with a card, reading 'Welcome on Board – Rankin Jamal.'

Anna calls Sarah, who acts as slick and calm as ever. 'You can't blame me for trying, can you?' says Sarah. 'I didn't mean to embarrass you. I hope I didn't . . .'

Anna realizes that everything is all right as long as Sarah

can appear in control. Anna immediately assures Sarah that she wasn't embarrassed.

'Let's forget all about it,' says Anna.

'Good,' says Sarah. 'So it won't be in the way. You know you got it on merit. Entirely on merit.'

Anna thanks her, not entirely convinced, and hangs up the phone, just as Miles walks past her office and clocks the flowers. He does a double take and pauses in her doorway.

'Nice flowers,' he says – fishing.

'From Rankin Jamal, to welcome me aboard.'

'You got the brief?'

'That's right.'

Miles – a hangover beating on the inside of his skull – is slow to respond. He's confused, since Graham had already offered the work to him.

'Congratulations,' he says, eventually.

'Don't choke on it, will you?'

'Look – I'm pleased.'

'Don't give me that bullshit. You're sick as a pig,' says Anna, every syllable ringing with delight.

'Forget it. My head hurts too much to fight with you.'

Miles hobbles off down the corridor, as Anna plucks at her bouquet.

She invites Jo for a lunch-time drink to celebrate her triumph, but he also has a tequila hangover, and turns her down.

'I'll take no excuses,' she says. 'You've got to get pissed with me this lunch-time, and that's final.'

'Congratulations, Anna,' says Graham, appearing at her shoulder.

'Thanks. I'm really looking forward to it.'

'We'll be starting work after lunch, so it might be best not to be pissed,' he says, swanning out.

Chapter 25

The Plumber Always Rings Twice

Ferdy notices, for the first time, that there's something wrong with the radiator in the bathroom. He's not exactly sure what the problem is – he can't quite put his finger on it – but he figures that the safest thing is to call the plumber anyway.

*   *   *

For weeks now, everyone in the house has known about Miles's new girlfriend. At least, everyone knows he's got one, but he never lets anyone see her, and he never talks about her. In fact, Miles treats his girlfriend in the way that most people treat lice.

It's clear, however, from his newly discovered taste in reading matter – art books, history books, *books*, in fact, at all – that he is trying to impress her. The lice factor, it seems, applies more to his house-mates than his girlfriend. He'd rather take her out every night to concerts at the Barbican and for expensive meals than allow her to see the brash and diffuse people he lives with.

Her name, apparently, is Francesca, though she is more commonly known in Benjamin Street as Miles's imaginary friend.

*   *   *

Since O'Donnell left it up to Milly to decide what is going to happen between them, she has developed a new tactic for dealing with him. She avoids him.

It's from the Graham Taylor handbook of tactics. And it's having predictable results. Milly is becoming increasingly tense, increasingly jealous of Rachel, and increasingly dependent on hot baths for her mental health. O'Donnell, meanwhile, seems as cool and relaxed as ever – the sight of which makes Milly more tense. In fact, the sight of *anything* makes Milly more tense. Even closing her eyes makes Milly more tense. You get the picture. Milly Is Tense.

There is only one place in the office where Milly feels she can relax. In the Ladies, inside a cubicle, with the door locked. Sitting in her relaxation chamber one afternoon, she overhears Rachel talking to Kira. Milly's ears instantly prick up at the sound of her own name.

'I think Milly's on some kind of strike,' Rachel moans.

'She seems a bit weird today,' says Kira. 'Maybe she's got problems.'

'Anyone else, you could ask them what's wrong, but she's so uptight she'd never tell you.'

'Some people don't like talking about how they feel.'

'I don't know if she has any feelings,' says Rachel.

'Course she has.'

'Somewhere under all that Miss Perfect stuff.'

'She's just reserved, that's all,' Kira sighs.

'Repressed, you mean. Completely anal.'

Then the door clatters open, and squeaks shut. The room falls silent.

Milly sits still for a while, then creeps out of her cubicle, looking rather paler than usual. She runs her wrists under the tap, to cool her blood, and heads back to her desk.

So – chatty, ingratiating, flirtatious, pushy Rachel is now chatty, ingratiating, flirtatious, pushy, bitchy Rachel. Milly feels as if all her nerves, muscles, tendons and veins are being wound tighter and tighter. Her confusion is becoming muddled together with hatred for Rachel, resentment of both Egg and O'Donnell, and self-pity. She can no longer think clearly. She can no longer work. Even the toilet isn't a safe haven any more.

She needs a bath. Badly.

*　　*　　*

Francesca eventually persuades Miles to let her see his house. The moment he opens the door, his heart sinks. Egg and Ferdy are playing a noisy game of Subbuteo.

'Penalty! It's a fucking penalty!'

'Bollocks.'

'It's a penalty, you wanker.'

'Bollocks. He dived.'

'What do you mean, "dived"? How can he dive? He's a piece of fucking plastic!'

Clearly, the action in the sitting room is not going to

impress Francesca. 'Why don't we go upstairs and get some peace,' Miles says.

'Who's that?' she replies. 'Sounds interesting.'

He sighs, and shows her into the living room.

Egg and Ferdy look up, their curiosity aroused. It's the imaginary friend, made flesh. She's real! Miles glares at them, does a few swift introductions, and moves to the kitchen in order to open an uncharacteristically expensive bottle of wine.

'Err . . . I reckon if you can fix up that striker, your little brother can get some good use out of that,' says Ferdy, turning down the stereo.

'What?' says Egg. 'Oh, yeah. Right.'

The four of them sit down in the living room, and chat – Miles and Francesca drinking wine, Egg and Ferdy beer. Although everyone is on their best behaviour, Miles can't help wincing at everything Egg and Ferdy say. By comparison to Francesca, all his house-mates seem so young. It feels as if his house is full of children, and he hates the fact that Francesca has to stoop to their level. What is worse, she seems to enjoy it. Then, on top of everything, she asks for a game of Subbuteo. And just when it seems things can't get any worse, Anna comes home and talks about herself for half an hour.

Miles is mortified. He wonders if Francesca will ever forgive him.

*　　*　　*

O'Donnell calls Milly into his office. 'I want to ask if you're all right,' he says.

'I'm fine.'

'I get the impression you've been avoiding me lately.'

'No . . .' Milly blinks, and hooks her hair behind an ear.

'I wanted to reassure you there was no reason to. I wouldn't do anything to compromise you or your work here.'

'I know that.'

'Good,' he says, trying unsuccessfully to establish eye contact. 'So I'll be seeing you again as normal?'

'Of course,' she replies.

Head down, Milly walks back to her office. She stares at the pages on her desk, but they blur in front of her eyes. Leaving her briefcase behind, she picks up her coat and heads home.

*　　*　　*

Judging by the way they make love that night, Francesca has forgiven Miles. He has never been shagged like that before in his whole life. And certainly not for that long.

It's true what they say about mature women. It really is.

Miles is in love.

He insists on keeping her in bed until the others have all left, so they can have breakfast in peace. When Miles finally allows her downstairs, Francesca chides him gently. 'You act like you're ashamed of me.'

Miles laughs at the thought of it. 'I'm ashamed of *them*.'

'They're nice, Miles.'

'What, Anna, last night? That was nice?'

'She was just wound up about her work.'

'Drunk, more like.'

'She speaks her mind. You have to respect that. I thought she was interesting. And funny.'

Miles is physically incapable of taking in this comment. His auditory nerves have developed a long-standing immunity to any combination of sounds which serves to show Anna in a positive light.

He smiles at Francesca, his eyes slightly glazed over. 'What are you doing at lunch-time?' he says.

*   *   *

Ferdy, naked in his bedroom, with a towel over his shoulder, dials a number on his mobile phone.

'Hello? . . . Yeah . . . I've just noticed, the hot tap in the bathroom – it drips . . . Yeah . . .'

Chapter 26

Fluffy Miles

At yet another romantic restaurant dinner, Francesca tells Miles that she has to go to Italy on business for three weeks.

'That's nearly a month!' he says, puncturing the calm atmosphere.

'I know.'

'Why didn't you say so before?'

'They only asked me this afternoon.'

'And you said yes without telling me?'

Francesca is taken aback. This is her first clear sighting of Miles's emotionally retarded side. 'Of course I did. It's my job.'

'But we've only just got together.'

'Yes. And you're already telling me what I should do and where I should go.'

'No, I'm not. I just don't know where I stand, that's all.'

'Why are you being so demanding all of a sudden?'

'Because . . .' Miles has difficulty thinking of a reason, '. . . because you're backing off from me.'

'No, I'm not. I have to go away on buying trips. You'll have to get used to it.'

'Will I?'

'Yes. Be a bit self-reliant.' It's always the same with these public-school types. They'll keep you at arm's length for weeks, then as soon as they let you in it's like wrestling with cling film. You have to be firm, or you'll be suffocated.

Seeing Miles's stung reaction, Francesca instantly feels guilty – and apologizes, reaching out a hand.

'No – I'm sorry,' he says, cupping his hand over hers. 'I can't help it.'

They stare at each other dreamily, holding hands across the table, with neither of them speaking.

If Anna could see this side of Miles – the cutesy fluffy love-bunny Miles – she'd piss herself, and would probably vomit.

Outside the restaurant Francesca waves down a cab, which hovers expectantly while they talk.

'Are you sure about this?' Miles says.

'Definitely. You do understand, don't you?'

'Course.'

'It just takes a bit of getting used to,' says Francesca, apologetically.

'Sure.'

'This isn't what you expected, is it?' she says.

'I don't know what to expect. I've never been in this situation before.'

She smiles. 'Glad to hear it.'

'What if you change your mind?' he says.

'What if you do?'

'I won't.'

They kiss deeply, but with an unusual lack of passion, and Francesca climbs into the cab.

Miles watches her drive away, rather shell-shocked, and heads for the tube.

He arrives home to find Milly, Egg and Anna sitting at the dining table, gossiping about Ferdy's sex life. They all feel a strange vibe coming from Miles, and stop talking when he walks in.

'You're back early,' says Milly.

'Where's Francesca?' says Anna.

'She went home.'

Anna smirks. 'I knew it. She's dumped you.'

'I've asked her to marry me,' Miles says.

Three faces stare at Miles in dumbfounded silence. Miles holds their gaze, not giving anything away.

'No wonder she went home,' says Anna.

'She said yes.'

No one speaks. Miles pulls a beer from the fridge, and goes up to his room.

Chapter 27

The Plunge

Nicki comes off the phone, her face pale. Egg is rather more interested in the carrot he is chopping than in Nicki's shock, but she eventually gets the bad news through to him. Mrs Cochrane, their boss, isn't coming back from Ireland. She's selling the lease on the café, and estate agents will be visiting that afternoon.

'It'll be bought by some fast-food chain. We're going to lose our jobs,' she insists.

'Not necessarily.'

'We will.'

'We can make sure we don't.'

'How are we going to do that, then?'

Egg stops chopping, looks up, and grins. 'We'll have to buy the lease ourselves,' he says.

* * *

Anna always knew her relationship with Graham was bad, but only since being assigned to work with him on the Aylmore case has she discovered just how much worse it can get. Everything she says offends him. Every attempt at a joke is snubbed at. And the harder she works, the less impressed Graham seems to become.

It has finally dawned on her that one particular vein of humour – the Aylmore-must-be-guilty-because-he's-a-sad-lonely-old-bachelor vein – is particularly unfruitful. Graham – a bachelor, with no apparent social life, who no one would describe as happy – for some reason doesn't find it funny.

Anna tries to change tack, but however reverentially she discusses the greasy weirdo that is their client, it never seems to be enough for Graham. He always seems to suspect that Anna allows her personal feelings to come into play, and makes unprofessional snap judgements.

Anna's feelings towards Graham also remain pretty constant. She thinks he's a wanker.

*　　*　　*

Egg shows a copy of the lease to Milly, and explains his plan. Her instant reaction is that Egg, as usual, is full of grand ideas that amount to little more than fantasy. To say this, however, would be to hit Egg's rawest nerve.

'You'll need bank references and a guarantor,' she says.

'I'm looking for one.'

'Also, it's five years.'

'Yeah. It's a big step,' he says, with relish.

'You may find you're working night and day just to pay the lease off.'

Egg picks up a football from the bedroom floor and

squeezes it in his hands. 'Sometimes you've got to run a risk. Throw everyone forward.'

Milly is suddenly irritated by this analogy. It shows his utter lack of business sense in a nutshell. Egg is incapable of distinguishing between games and real life – of telling the difference between play risk, and real risk. He has no conception of what he is attempting. 'It's five years, Egg! Not ninety minutes!'

'Still – you've got to follow your instinct, haven't you?'

'You've got to think practically about it.'

'"Practical." What do you mean when you say that? It's just fear.'

'Fear?'

'Yeah – you're afraid . . .'

'Of what, exactly?'

'Of risk. Of the unexpected. You're afraid of anything that hasn't been planned down to the last detail.'

'Oh, am I?'

'It's a fear of life!'

'So you really think that?' she says, walking to the door. 'I'm boring.'

'I didn't say boring. Just safe –'

'Same thing!' she says, storming out of the room and locking herself in the bathroom.

Her mind is blank as she turns the taps and fills the tub. She does feel, however, a new resolve stirring within her. She's angry – but underneath her anger, she feels that the real tension which has been building up inside her has mysteriously slackened. Without having consciously done so, she realizes that she has made a decision. She is going to prove Egg, and everyone else, wrong.

Anna is working late in her room, when Milly walks in and sits on her bed.

'Everything all right?' Anna says, turning from her desk. Milly nods. She doesn't look as upset as Anna expected. You never usually hear Egg and Milly row. You never even hear them shag.

'That was a bit loud,' Anna says.

'Sorry.'

'Should I be worried?'

'Who for?' says Milly, enigmatically.

'Don't get a divorce. I'm already from a broken home.'

'Honestly,' says Milly. 'You always try to make me seem older than I am.'

'At least you're mature enough to be married – unlike Miles.'

'He's a romantic at heart.'

'Yeah – a serial romantic. Like his father.'

Milly gives Anna a piercing look, smiling slightly. 'It's a shame you never really gave each other a chance.'

'Is it?'

Milly turns to the mirror and plays with her hair. 'You'll never know if you missed something.'

'I'd never marry Miles.'

'No?'

'I hate Labradors.'

Milly frowns. Anna turns, and smiles at Milly's confusion

before explaining. 'That's where they'll wind up, you know. Plodding around Berkshire in green wellies, discussing bridge tactics.'

*   *   *

In a flash of inspiration, Anna suggests researching the social services' records of Katherine, the schoolgirl in the Aylmore case, and her family. Graham, who doesn't believe in flashes of inspiration, is instantly sceptical.

'It's worth checking,' Anna explains. 'Katherine told Aylmore that her father was abusive. Her mother hit the bottle –'

'He doesn't mention any of this in his statement,' Graham interrupts.

'He thought it was all fantasy.'

'Don't you?'

'No. Just because she comes across like a nice middle-class girl doesn't mean her home life isn't a mess.'

'You think the rape allegation is a way of drawing attention to it?'

'Yes.'

Graham looks at Anna, grudging respect seeping out of him. 'You may be right,' he says.

*   *   *

Suddenly, Milly isn't avoiding O'Donnell. She has been dithering for days over whether to take on a new, big case – on which she would have to work alongside O'Donnell – but her mind is now made up. The first thing she does in the morning is to walk into his office.

'I've thought about the Semple case,' she says, confidently.

'You'll take it on?'

'Yes. I've cleared aside the stuff I think Rachel can handle.'

'Excellent. Thank you. We need a very quick and detailed analysis of Mr Semple's finances.'

'I'll make a start tonight.'

'Great. I'll give you all the help you need.'

'I hoped you would,' says Milly, smiling, as she leaves his office.

* * *

There is a distinct boys-only feel emerging from Hooperman's office as the partners toast Miles's engagement. Hooperman spots Anna hovering in the corridor, however, and invites her in.

To her amazement, a pause emerges in the barristers' wife jokes, and Anna hears her work being praised by Graham, in front of everyone. She almost blushes. She also can't resist a quick glance at Miles, who is looking rather less green than she would have hoped. Still – love does that to you. You lose your edge.

* * *

Milly and O'Donnell are alone in the office, working late on the Semple accounts. When she suggests ringing for a pizza, he offers an alternative – that they use up some food sitting in the fridge at his flat.

With barely a moment's hesitation, she agrees.

* * *

On the way home from chambers, events take an even more bizarre turn for Anna. Miles trots after her as they emerge from the office, and asks if he can walk with her.

'Why?' Anna answers, suspiciously.

'So we can talk,' he says.

Anna isn't sure about this. It doesn't feel right.

They walk along in silence for a while, before he speaks. 'Look,' he says, 'what I did – voting against you – it was spiteful and stupid, and I really regret it. I was a complete shit.'

Anna stops walking and stares at him – looking for signs of any kind of medical condition that might explain Miles's change of heart.

'Is that it?' she says.

'No. I did it because I was jealous of you.'

'Jealous of me?'

'Well – you know – professionally. I know how good you are, and sometimes it makes me a bit insecure.'

Anna blinks with the shock. She feels as if someone has just thrown a bucket of cold water over her head.

'Shit!' she says.

'What?'

'I'm going to have to forgive you now, aren't I?'

Miles smiles, as they walk on, down some stairs, and into the underground.

*   *   *

Lying in O'Donnell's bed, Milly feels no guilt and no shame. For once in her life, she has done what she wanted without worrying about the consequences. And it feels great. It's a bizarre sensation having sex with someone other than Egg – all the bits are in slightly different places, and everything feels like it's at the wrong angle – but it's a good feeling. It's life. It's risk. For the first time ever, she has done something brave.

*   *   *

Arriving home with Miles, Anna instantly senses a tense atmosphere in the house. As she walks into the living room, Egg and Ferdy stare at her, blankly.

'Hi, guys,' she says. 'It's glum city in here.'

'There's been a call for you,' Egg says.

Anna walks to the fridge and peers in, paying Egg no attention.

'Anna – it's bad news,' he continues.

'Don't tell me you drunk all the voddie out of the fridge,' she says.

'A hospital in Glasgow . . . it's your mother.'

'Yeah?'

'She . . . she died about an hour ago.'

Anna pulls the empty vodka bottle out of the fridge, stares at it, and lets out a little chuckle.

'Shit,' she says. 'What a time to run out.'

Chapter 28

Two Beddings, No Funeral

With Miles turning into a gooey love monster, the post of Most Repressed Person In The House falls vacant. Anna, from the moment she hears of her mother's death, takes over the job with considerable enthusiasm.

If there's one thing Anna hates, it's sympathy. And when your mother has just died, you tend to get a lot hurled at you. The only way to avoid it, Anna decides, is to pretend the whole thing hasn't happened. If you do that, people get so confused they leave you alone.

The trouble is, everyone assumes she will immediately hop on a plane to Glasgow for the funeral, when in fact she has far too much work for her to leave London. Even Graham participates in the general sympathy drive and without asking Anna, rearranges her meetings so she can have time off to go to Scotland.

It rapidly dawns on Anna that missing the funeral involves more effort than simply caving in and going. The fact is – she hated and resented her mother, and hadn't spoken to her for four years. Anna wants as little to do with her death as she had with her life. But you can't go around explaining this to everyone who tries to make you weep on their shoulder, so she gives in, walks out of the office, and heads home.

*   *   *

Miles, after much procrastination, finally tells his father over a meal that he is engaged. Montgomery reacts with the kind of smug, self-satisfied approval that would be rather more appropriate to Miles explaining that he'd got a pay rise. Still, Miles doesn't dwell on the subject, and doesn't even bother to waste his energy being offended. If he is going to endure the agony of supper with his father, he decides that he might as well get something useful out of it, and as soon as he can change the subject, he moves on to solicit Montgomery on Egg's behalf.

Montgomery is eager, as ever, to show Miles that he is generous-spirited, and without even particularly realizing what he has done, he finds himself agreeing to act as a guarantor on some chap's loan for a lease on a café.

Miles makes all the right noises of appreciation, and Montgomery goes home feeling that he might have finally got somewhere with his son. Miles, meanwhile, dashes straight back to Benjamin Street to tell Egg that the old tosser coughed up.

Egg is happier than he has ever been before. He's never felt any comparable emotion in his life. If you took an orgasm, and multiplied it by the '93–'94 double-winning season, it still wouldn't come close. If this feeling was a person, he decides, it would be Claudia Schiffer crossed with Alex Ferguson. Perfection.

*　　*　　*

Milly, too, can't remember feeling happier. After work, she starts for home by tube, but suddenly finds herself hailing a cab, and heading in the opposite direction – to O'Donnell's flat.

He answers the door in his dressing-gown – surprised but obviously delighted to see her. They barely talk. Milly grabs him, kisses him, and tugs him to the bedroom.

Milly feels reinvented. If people knew what she was doing, no one would ever call her repressed or boring again.

*　　*　　*

On the day of the funeral, Anna sits at the dining table, smoking, and waiting for her cab. Everyone passes through on their way to work, each of them coming out with some drearily useless sympathetic comment. The last to leave is Miles.

'I hope you'll be all right,' he says.

'Thank you, Miles. I've packed my tissues and a warm coat . . .'

'Would you like me to come with you?' he says.

This is the first thing anyone has said to her that has actually got through. She looks up from her mug of coffee, genuinely touched.

'I've not much on today, anyway,' he adds.

Anna swallows and gives him a tight, closed-lipped smile. 'I don't need anyone to hold my hand,' she says.

'OK.'

Miles picks up his case and leaves for work. Anna quickly lights up another cigarette, fighting against the fresh confusion of emotions wriggling up inside her.

Five minutes later, the doorbell rings. Anna doesn't move. She listens to three or four rings, then to the sound of the retreating car.

She walks upstairs, slowly, and without even taking her clothes off climbs into bed.

Chapter 29

The Secret of my Excess

It's late, Anna's pissed, and she's lost her front-door key. The last thing she wants is more people nagging her, but the only thing she can do is ring the bell and endure the chorus of disapproval from everyone she has woken.

She rings, several times, before the door opens. It's Miles. She doesn't even want to hear what he thinks, and holds up her hand before he can speak. 'Lost my sodding keys,' she says, and immediately marches up the stairs. Miles is moaning; Egg is standing outside his bedroom, also moaning, but Anna doesn't hear a word of it. She just trudges up to her room and slams the door, wishing that more people could be like Ferdy.

Pulling a bottle of wine from her bag, she lies back on her bed, and rummages behind her alarm clock for the bottle opener.

She wakes at nine. *Shit!* She forgot to set the alarm. She also forgot to get undressed, which saves her a few valuable minutes as she takes a quick swig of wine dregs (hair of the dog) and heads straight for work.

She sneaks to her desk, hoping that no one spots her late arrival, but Graham, of course, has his beady eyes open and gives her a disapproving glance.

Staring at the paper on her desk, Anna can't make sense of anything. Her brain has turned to cotton wool. She decides that she needs something to get herself started, and heads, with her bag, for the Ladies.

Having checked that all the cubicles are empty, she takes a small wrap of coke from her purse, and lays a couple of pinches on the back of her hand. She sniffs sharply, checks her nostrils in the mirror, rubs the residue into her gums, and heads back to her desk.

Suddenly the day seems possible again.

In conference with Graham, it occurs to Anna that she is possibly the best barrister ever to grace the British legal system. Never before has she spoken with such clarity or incisiveness.

'It would be nice, it would be *very* nice,' she says, at top speed, 'in fact it would be positively brilliant if we found out she'd been on social services' records as a hooker since the age of ten. I mean, don't get me wrong, it would be terrible, a terrible *thing*, but brilliant for us. Terrible *and* brilliant all in one. But the fact is, Graham, and I've said this all along, I have no idea what's in those records, if anything, so we're talking about a long shot here, a hunch with a capital H and no mistake. Which means –'

'Anna –'

' – which means that if they open the book and all they

find are gold stars and brownie points, which God knows they might and, knowing my luck, probably will, it would be nice if we had some kind of fall-back position –'

'Anna –'

'– if only so that when I commit legal hara-kiri in five hours' time, there'll be something, God knows what, but something, to help drown out the sound of shit hitting the fan – not to mention my screams.'

Graham, Anna suddenly realizes, is giving her an odd look.

'What?' she says.

'Just calm down, will you? Don't let this get to you. There are other options, albeit limited. Would you like a drink?'

Anna decides that this is a trick. 'It's a bit early for me, actually,' she lies.

'Of water.'

'Oh. Right. Please.'

Graham is pacing up and down, itching to get to court, but there is no sign of Anna. 'She hasn't gone out, has she?' he says, exasperated, to Jo.

'Try the Ladies.'

Graham hesitates, glances at his watch, then nudges open the toilet door. He sees, reflected in the mirror, Anna snorting a line of coke off the back of her hand. Anna turns, hearing the door open, and they catch one another's eye.

'Can I have a word?' he says, letting the door close.

She follows him down the corridor to his office, her heart racing. She feels as if her life has ended.

Calmly, he closes the door behind her, then speaks, his voice filled with venom. 'Have you completely taken leave of your senses? Has it occurred to you what would have happened if it had been a client who'd walked in there instead of me?'

Anna looks at the floor. Graham checks his watch.

'Right now,' he continues, 'I haven't got the time or the patience to listen to any possible explanation you might have. All I know is that I don't want you near this case any more. I certainly don't want you near the court this afternoon and, if I get my way, you won't be anywhere near this chambers. I'll speak to you tomorrow.'

'I'm sorry,' she says.

'Oh, grow up.'

Jo reluctantly agrees to meet Anna for a drink after work. As usual, he knows exactly what has happened. Their evening together, however, doesn't work. He tries to offer her sharp career advice; she tries to seduce him. Neither of them succeeds.

Anna instead turns her attention to a rather dishy-looking guy at the bar. She walks up to him, stands close, and reaches her fingers out. 'I swear to God,' she says. 'Feel those hands. Go on.'

The man gingerly touches her on the knuckles.

'Shiatsu mainly,' she says. 'Same as Swedish only slower and harder.'

The man blinks with shock, and a girlfriend suddenly appears at his shoulder.

'And then there were three,' Anna smiles.

'You coming, or what?' says the girlfriend.

'Or what,' says Anna.

'Sorry?'

'Don't mention it.'

'*Mike.*'

The man picks his drinks hurriedly off the bar.

'He's coming, he's coming,' says Anna.

The girlfriend reaches out for a glass. 'I'll give you a hand.'

'There's no need,' says Anna. 'He's a big boy, now. Aren't you, Mike? At least, that's what he told me.'

'Why don't you piss off,' the girlfriend spits.

'Oh, dear. Its hackles are rising.'

'Yeah, it bites and all.'

'An out and out dog, in other words.'

The woman tosses her drink in Anna's face, grabs Mike by the arm, and marches him away.

'You should have warned me,' Anna calls after them, wiping her face. 'I'd have kept my mouth open.'

Miles is in bed with Francesca, both of them drifting post-coitally towards sleep, when the sound of breaking glass rings up the stairs.

'Miles?' she says. 'What was that?'

'What?'

'I heard breaking glass.'

'You sure?'

She nods, and Miles crawls from the bed, slips into a dressing-gown, and creeps downstairs. A few steps behind him, Francesca follows.

They both hear a strange noise emerging from the living room, and Miles gives the door a tentative poke. He sees Anna, on her knees, sobbing – a shattered wine bottle spread out in front of her.

'Anna? What's up?' says Miles, from the doorway.

She has her back to him, and speaks without turning. 'I smashed a bottle of wine.'

'Are you all right?'

She shakes her head, and half turns, showing him a distraught face, sodden with tears. 'What does it look like?'

Francesca appears in the doorway behind Miles. Miles enters the living room and gives a leave-this-to-me nod to Francesca, who stares at Anna for a second, then retreats upstairs.

Miles walks over to Anna and sits on the floor next to her. 'Come on,' he says. 'We don't need this.' He puts his arm round her shoulders, which triggers a fresh round of noisy sobbing.

Miles lifts her, and locked together, they hobble to the sofa, where Anna continues to cry, her face pressed against his chest.

'Anna? What's this all about?' he says, eventually.

Through her sobs, Anna forces herself to speak. 'I want . . . I want . . .'

'Take your time.'

'I want my mum.'

Miles holds her tight, rubbing her back. He utterly loses his sense of time as he clings on to her – anchoring her as she cries, shudders of pain and relief shaking her body.

When she sits up and looks at him, a bond of intimacy which Miles has never felt before seems to have formed between them.

'I'm sorry,' she says.

'Don't be silly.'

'It's crazy, isn't it? When she was alive I couldn't give a damn, now she's dead . . . and I didn't even have the guts to go to the funeral.'

'What?' Miles stares, unable to comprehend.

'I just couldn't.' Anna sobs again, this time fighting it – struggling to get words out. 'Now I know . . . why . . . It's typical . . . It must run in the genes.'

'What?'

'Being such a fuckwit.'

'You're not –'

'I am! I can't hold on to anything. Men, work, you name it . . . whatever I touch just slips through my fingers. And the worst thing is – I let it happen . . . I *make* it happen.'

'That's not true. You know that's not true. What are you doing at the moment? You're about to crack a really –'

'I got taken off it this morning.'

'Why?'

'Graham caught me snorting coke in the Ladies.'

'What?'

'I'll be lucky if I'm still at the chambers this time tomorrow. You see? I'm a Grade A fuckwit. The moment there's the merest whiff of happiness in my life, something in my brain goes into a blind panic and the next thing I know I'm sabotaging it, chucking hand-grenades at it, left, right and centre . . .'

Anna's voice cracks, as sobs take her over again. Miles hugs her, running his hands through her hair to try and calm her down.

'Listen. I'll talk to them tomorrow,' he says.

'Who?'

'Graham. Hoooperman. Whoever it takes.'

'Miles – you should save your breath.'

'Well, for what it's worth, I don't think you're a fuck-wit.'

'Yes you do.'

'All right, I do. But maybe that's why I like you.'

'Maybe. Not enough, though.'

'Not enough for what?'

'It doesn't matter.'

Miles is shocked at what she seems to be saying. He feels he can't react, though, until she has actually said it. He can feel his blood pumping faster.

'Not enough for what?' he repeats.

'Well, put it this way. Enough for a one-night stand, but not enough for anything more.'

'Said who?'

'Miles –'

'Said you –'

'Me? I'm not the one who's going off to get married, am I?'

Miles pauses, confused, and suddenly becomes acutely aware of Anna's hand, nestled in his. He squeezes her fingers, and touches her arm with his other hand.

'I thought after last time, you didn't want to know. Those were the signals I was getting,' he says.

'They weren't the signals I was giving. Not that it would have made any difference, would it?'

'Yes, it would actually.'

'That's easy to say.'

Miles moves his hand from her arm to her face, and the atmosphere instantly shifts. She smiles, sadly.

'You stupid bastard,' she says, leaning forward and kissing him deeply on the lips. Miles returns her kiss, and finds himself removing her top. Tenderly but passionately, they remove each other's clothes, kissing harder and faster, more urgently and with greater need, as they fall into one another's bodies – a tear-stained, unstoppable lust drawing them together.

Ferdy, creeping home late from Lenny's apartment, closes the front door quietly behind him. One foot on the stairs, he hears a noise in the living room. The door is slightly ajar, and Ferdy looks in. Anna looks back at him. She is flat on her back, naked. Miles is on top of her, thrusting enthusiastically, with his face pressed into her neck.

Ferdy freezes for a second, then turns away and walks up to his room.

Miles tiptoes back to bed, praying that Francesca will be asleep. She isn't, though, and gives him a fright with the volume of her voice.

'Is she all right?' Francesca asks.

'Yeah. I'll tell you about it in the morning.'

'She looked terrible. What was wrong?'

Miles sits on the edge of the bed, reluctant to get in, disturbed by what has just happened.

'She's just fucked up,' he says.

'Did you manage to unfuck her . . . as it were?'

'Sort of.'

Miles kisses Francesca on the forehead and climbs into bed, his mind racing.

Chapter 30

Stranger for Breakfast

Hooperman eyeballs Anna across his desk, allowing a tortuous silence to open up. Eventually, he speaks, even more portentously than usual, telling her that taking Class A drugs on the premises is extraordinarily foolish. The lecture continues, with Anna squirming in her chair, but it slowly dawns on her that if he was going to sack her, there would be no need for the lecture. He'd just sack her. So – as he talks and talks, Anna has to make an increasingly concerted effort to look contrite. In fact, by the time he has finished, her heart is singing. Her life has been saved. Hooperman even apologizes for not having insisted that she took a week's leave on her mother's death.

Anna, he says, can keep her job on one condition – that she attend Alcoholics Anonymous. The way he says this, handing over a card from the top drawer of his desk, explains to Anna the reason for his leniency. Hooperman – the mineral-water-and-press-up king – clearly has a skeleton in his closet. A skeleton rather similar to the one that Anna has just hung up in the middle of the office for everyone to see.

As she leaves his room, Anna wants to kiss him and thank him for being a fuck-up too, but she doesn't. She bows her head, looks repentant, and heads back to her desk.

*   *   *

Egg is so tense and distracted due to the impending opening of the café under his management, that he fails to notice how Milly has suddenly stopped being tense and distracted. After months of coolness, Milly is now loving and open towards Egg, but all her efforts are wasted. He doesn't even notice.

This doesn't bother Milly too much, however, since she now has a new and infinitely more exciting outlet for her emotional and physical desires. She feels annoyed with Egg, with his utter self-absorption, but she isn't really hurt by it. She can't even bring herself to care much. Egg is simply a blur of noise in the foreground of her life, while her emotional depths are stirred only by O'Donnell.

Egg's emotional depths, meanwhile, are stirred by a ladle. Or a menu. Or a flyer, or a two-line advert in the *South London Advertiser*. His mind is full to the brim with the minutiae of organizing the café reopening, and anything else – anything to do with Milly, for example – is an irrelevance to him.

*   *   *

With all the plumbing now in better condition than when the house was built, Ferdy no longer has a pretext for calling Lenny. This doesn't seem to get in the way, however, and the two of them start spending more and more time together. In fact, you could almost say they have fallen in love – which is a strange feeling for Ferdy, who falls in love about as eagerly as most people fall in debt.

Lenny, who is rather more familiar with the experience, is slowly reeling Ferdy in. His sister has just had a baby, and he drops a huge challenge on Ferdy by asking if he'd like to go along for a visit to see the nephew. Ferdy's natural instincts immediately start screaming in his head: *Quick – fuck off out of there – leave the room. He's talking about babies and family. It's all a trap.*

Ferdy blinks a couple of times, and swallows, with some difficulty. 'All right,' he says, with a slight catch in his voice. 'I'll come.'

* * *

Miles and Anna somehow escape the embarrassment that ought to have followed their sex. Neither of them refers to it but, somehow, they don't pretend it hasn't happened, either. For the first time ever, genuine warmth flows between them. Miles even passes some work over to her at chambers. And in the evening, he asks Anna to join him and Francesca for a meal he is cooking.

And while Miles stands in the kitchen, chopping onions with all the casual ease of a man amputating his own leg, Anna chats to Francesca.

'You don't mind me eating with you, do you?'

'No, no – of course not,' replies Francesca. 'I think it's a public-school thing. Miles can't eat unless he's sat at a table with at least seventeen other people. Either that or he's getting bored sick of me on my own, in which case we'll be lucky to make it through the honeymoon.'

'You don't mean that, do you?' says Anna.

'No. But I think he's going to miss you.'

'Me?' A flicker of panic flashes across Anna's face.

'All of you. He's afraid the moment he says "I do", it'll be like a spell and you're all going to disappear into thin air. So he's making the most of it. At least, I hope that's what it is.'

Anna smiles. *Shit*, she thinks, *I'm Camilla Parker-Bowles*.

* * *

Ferdy tries to act calmly, but he is utterly phased by the visit to Lenny's sister. She's charming, friendly, kind, genuinely interested in him – and the whole experience makes him feel as if he's drowning in treacle. He just isn't ready for it. He can't explain why – he just isn't. And he doesn't want to tie himself in knots trying to explain, either, so he tells them he's going to the toilet, picks up his crash helmet from the sideboard in the hall, and leaves.

* * *

After the disaster of the Tex-Mex night, Egg decides that his grand opening will take place without all his mates from the house filling up the restaurant and frightening away real customers. As a result, the opening isn't very grand. During the entire evening, he has only three customers. One of them pisses him off by abusing the all-you-can-eat-for-a-fiver offer and consuming thirty-quid's worth of food, and the other two piss him off because they come over all anorexic and barely eat anything.

By the time Milly turns up at about eleven o'clock, Egg is utterly dejected.

'How did it go?' she says.

'Disaster. It was an embarrassing disaster.'

'I'm sorry.'

'Maybe we're in the wrong place. Maybe we've got a crap menu, or the walls are the wrong colour. I don't know.'

Milly's heart sinks. More of this boring, juvenile rubbish. More indecision. Her eyes glaze over while Egg jabbers on relentlessly about the three customers he had that evening, and she thinks back, only half an hour or so, to the time she has just spent with Michael O'Donnell, screwing on the floor of his office.

*   *   *

Ferdy walks into a pub at random, just to escape the cloying family vibe that he can still feel clinging to his skin.

A pint in his hand, he prowls the room, looking for a woman. A girl by the pool table, wielding her cue with genuine skill, catches his eye. Ferdy moves in.

Miles is in the kitchen, eating his usual Weetabix. The kettle boils just as Ferdy enters the room.

'Cup of tea?' says Miles.

'Two, please.'

'Two! You had a good night, then?'

'Just pour it, will you?'

'You and Lenny'll get down the aisle before me at this rate.'

Miles turns from dropping the tea bags into the bin, and sees a woman walk into the kitchen. He's so surprised, he almost drops the tea.

'Hi,' she says.

'Hello,' Miles smirks, shoving a cup of tea into her hand.

'I was going to bring it up to you,' Ferdy says.

'It's all right.'

'Well, well, well. Just when you thought it was safe to go back in the kitchen,' says Miles, tucking into his cereal.

'Sorry?'

'So, how long have you known each other, then?'

'About twelve hours,' she says.

'Oh. You go back a bit.'

Ferdy, sensing disaster, stands between them and tries to nudge her towards the door. 'Just ignore him.'

'He's right,' Miles says. 'Ignore me. I can't keep up, that's all.'

Ferdy realizes that a quick exit is required to stop Miles fucking things up. 'I'll go upstairs and get a spare helmet,' he says, banking on this as the quickest way to get out of the house.

The girl, Gina, alone in the kitchen with Miles, examines him quizzically. 'This happens a lot, then, does it?'

'What – breakfast? Yeah – most mornings.'

'That you come down and find a strange girl in your kitchen.'

Miles chuckles. 'Er . . . now you're asking. Not exactly, no.'

'How often, then?'

'Don't worry – you're the first. This week.'

She laughs, insincerely, then presses on. 'So?'

'What?'

'How often?'

'Oh, I don't know. Hardly ever. Girls, that is.'

Gina twigs. 'You're having me on.'

'No.'

Gina grabs her coat, slung over a chair the previous evening, and heads for the door.

'What are you doing?' says Miles.

'I'm off.'

'Off where?'

'Sorry. Mistake. Just tell him I'm not into that, thanks very much.'

'You can't just walk out!'

She walks out.

Ferdy arrives in the kitchen with two crash-helmets, to find Miles laughing to himself, and no Gina.

'Where's Gina?' he demands.

Miles shrugs.

'Where is she?'

'Gone.'

Ferdy runs out of the house and sees Gina walking fast, disappearing around a corner. He walks back to the kitchen.

'She's legged it.'

'What! Why?' says Miles, still smirking.

'You tell me.'

'I didn't say anything.'

'You just couldn't keep your fat mouth shut, could you?'

'I didn't say anything! Why should I? It's very exciting not knowing who's going to be eating my Weetabix in the morning.'

'And that's what you told her?'

'Not in as many words, no –'

'But you told her.'

'As a matter of fact, she asked me.'

'I knew it.'

'There is a difference,' says Miles, smugly.

'You stupid prick!' Ferdy shouts.

Suddenly, Miles isn't amused. If there's one thing Miles hates, it's being verbally abused by the uneducated. 'Wait a minute,' he says. 'Don't call me a prick. I can't say I blame her as a matter of fact. There are health considerations, you know. If you're swinging it between Arthur and Martha every other night of the week, I think she's got a right to know.'

Ferdy doesn't answer back. He simply clenches his fist, and floors Miles with a single punch in the face.

Miles, sprawled on the kitchen floor, blood streaming from his nose, hears the front door slam. He groans, swears, and reaches for the kitchen towel. What an awful way to start the morning. He always knew Ferdy was mentally unhinged. It was just a matter of time before he did this. It's just lucky it happened to someone who can take it.

Dabbing at his face with kitchen towel is so painful that Miles decides his nose must be broken. He's ruined. He'll never be symmetrical again. His profile has been destroyed. With this thought swimming through his brain, the room dissolves into a blur, and Miles passes out.

Chapter 31

Milly Liar

As it turns out, Miles's nose isn't broken. It isn't even bruised very much. All he has to show for his suffering is a rather undignified purple blotch on the side of one nostril, which, with the bathroom door firmly locked, he attempts to hide under a thin dusting of Anna's face-powder.

Most annoying of all, everyone seems to assume that it's up to Miles to apologize. He's moaning to Anna about this – about how Ferdy has to develop a sense of humour over his sexuality – when Anna cuts him off with a sharp look.

'What?'

'He saw us, you know,' she says. 'On the sofa.'

'Oh, fuck!'

'Before you go into orbit, as far as I know he's kept it to himself. Despite ample provocation. I'd be grateful for a smack if I were you.'

Miles, in shock at the implications this has for his future life, stumbles from the room.

'And Miles!' Anna calls after him. 'Go easy on the Clinique. It costs.'

*   *   *

The second Milly enters the office, Kira bounces up to her brandishing a watch. 'This yours?' she says. 'Cleaner found it in O'Donnell's office.'

Milly glances at the watch, and instinctively grabs her wrist. It's hers. 'No. It's not,' she says, quickly.

'Oh. Right.'

Shit. Kira suspects. She recognizes my watch. 'Mine's being mended,' Milly says.

'I've asked everyone, now. This is really weird.'

'No it's not,' Milly snaps. 'The cleaner could have missed it before. It could have been lying there for days.'

'Right. Well I'll start ringing round the clients, then.'

'Haven't you got anything better to do?'

'You reckon I can just keep it, then?'

'Of course you can't.'

Kira stares at Milly, angrily. 'Well . . . ?'

'Whatever you want,' Milly says, walking away. 'Do whatever you want. It's nothing to do with me.'

*   *   *

Francesca asks Miles to sign a pre-nuptial agreement. The minute she mentions it, he becomes convinced that she's getting cold feet, and that her whole change of attitude has something to do with Ferdy. Ferdy must have told her, or at least hinted to her, or she wouldn't have suddenly changed her attitude.

At work, Miles can't keep out of Anna's office. However many times she reassures him that there's nothing wrong with a pre-nuptial agreement, and that Ferdy can keep a secret, he can't stop popping his head round her door and confronting her with a new paranoid theory as to why Francesca is wavering.

* * *

Kira, instead of wasting her time by ringing round the clients, has chosen to waste her time by organizing a lottery for the lost watch. Every female office worker has to choose a number, to be picked from a hat by O'Donnell, and the winner gets the watch.

To Milly's horror, Kira emerges from the prize draw in O'Donnell's office and walks directly towards Rachel. 'You slipped him a fiver, didn't you?' says Kira, placing the watch into Rachel's outstretched hands.

Rachel holds the watch up to the light. 'Do you really like it?' she says. 'It's nothing special.'

Milly stops work to listen.

'It's a bit boring,' Rachel continues.

Kira plucks the watch from her fingers. 'It's tasteful,' she says. 'All right – I wouldn't fork out for it . . .'

'Go on, then. Keep it,' says Rachel, waving away Kira and the watch. 'If a Rolex turns up, I want first refusal.'

Milly grinds her teeth, and presses on with her work.

* * *

Anna is sitting in the living room watching brain-death TV, when Francesca walks in, looking worried. Miles has vanished. He said he'd wait for her at chambers, but he left without her. And now he isn't at home, either.

Francesca sits on the sofa next to Anna, and looks at her with a nervous smile. 'Did he tell you I wanted a pre-nuptial agreement?' she asks, tentatively.

'No,' Anna lies, switching off the telly.

Francesca sighs. 'I've got a feeling it's muddied the waters. I'm not being unromantic, am I? I suppose it's the difference between twenty-something and thirty-something.'

'It's hardly the Grand Canyon. You don't remember the Beatles, do you?'

Francesca hesitates a moment, before deciding to confide. 'Actually, I do. I'm not thirty-one. I've been . . . I'm thirty-six, Anna. And ten years, I would say, qualifies as a modest canyon.'

'Are you going to tell him the truth?'

'I've left my passport lying around. I don't want to make an announcement. I don't want it to be a big thing.'

'Why did you lie in the first place?'

'I didn't know I was going to end up marrying him, did I? And if I tell him now, suddenly I'm this scheming harpy after his sperm.'

'How do you work that out?'

'I mention kids occasionally – with no particular sense of urgency – but if he thinks my eggs are getting past their sell-by date he's going to start wondering, isn't he? Am I

265

marrying him or am I marrying the father of my children?'

'As long as you're clear about it,' says Anna, feeling increasingly guilty as the conversation progresses. 'Tell him when you're ready.'

'I wonder if he knows. There's definitely an atmosphere.'

Anna reaches forward, and touches Francesca's hand, reassuringly. 'It's just good old-fashioned PMT. Pre-Marital Tension. Don't get paranoid.'

Francesca stares through Anna, her eyes unfocused. 'I hope so. This has to be it. Miles has to be it.'

Anna is relieved to hear the front door slam. Even if it isn't Miles, *anyone* will do to get her out of this excruciating conversation.

It isn't Miles. Ferdy walks in, rolling his eyes, closely followed by Kira, giving him a lengthy and, by the look of it, utterly unwelcome pep talk on his sexuality and what he should do about Lenny.

Anna does a double take, and stares at Kira's wrist. She's wearing Milly's watch.

Kira sees Anna's stare, and waves her watch so Anna can see it more clearly. 'What d'ya reckon? Nice innit?'

'Where did you get it?' Anna asks, trying to sound casual.

'Found it. O'Donnell's office. Don't worry. I asked around.'

Anna pulls deeply on her cigarette. *Milly has done it! She's fucked O'Donnell.*

A sour taste fills Anna's mouth. This is bad. This is very bad. Suddenly, compared to everyone else in the house,

Anna feels sorted. All around her, people's lives are turning to shit. And Anna's stuck in the middle.

Anna lies in bed, staring at the ceiling, too confused and angry to fall asleep. She gets up, creeps downstairs, and walks into Milly's room.

'Are you asleep?' she says, although it is obvious that both Milly and Egg are.

'Oh, *Anna*,' Milly moans.

'Can I have a word?' Anna says, loudly.

'Can't it wait till tomorrow?'

'It's about your watch.'

Suddenly, Milly is awake, sitting up.

Anna walks to her room, and Milly follows.

'You didn't tell Kira?' Milly asks anxiously, as soon as she has closed the door behind them.

'That you're fucking O'Donnell? No.'

Milly sits on the foot of Anna's bed, looking relieved. 'I didn't think anyone else would recognize it . . .'

Anna is horrified by Milly's utterly guilt-free reaction. 'Is that all you're worried about?'

'Thank God it's you. I don't know where to start –'

'Spare me the details,' Anna snaps. 'We've already been over this. You know what I think. You did it anyway. Right enough. You deal with it.'

'I did deal with it. I didn't run whinging to you, did I?'

'You needn't start now.'

'Why are you so angry?'

'In a word. Egg.'

Milly stares hard at Anna, unable to understand Anna's reaction. 'That's not the reason,' she says. 'You're transferring.'

'What? Who is *that*? I thought Warren was in Australia.'

'Oh, sorry. I forgot. You don't like dealing with things, do you, Anna? Not if you can brush them under the carpet. Well, I can't. I need help.'

Anna scowls. 'Make your mind up, Milly. Are you dealing with this or not?'

'Yes, I am,' Milly replies, her voice raised indignantly. 'I'm seeing a therapist. Warren's therapist, if you must know.'

Anna can't even be bothered to be stunned by this piece of news. She is suddenly disgusted by Milly and disinterested in her, all at once. She doesn't want to get dragged down into the deceitful details of her life. She honestly doesn't want to know any more about her. 'Good,' she says. 'Then you don't need my opinion, do you? Off you go.'

Anna points to the door. Milly doesn't move.

'Why do you think I'm paying someone to try and help me sort this out when my own best friend doesn't want to know!'

'Because you know your own best friend would answer back. Your own best friend wouldn't just parrot what you want to hear!'

The door creaks, and a bleary-eyed Egg shuffles into the room.

'What the fuck is going on?' he says.

Milly jumps up and, without looking at Egg, brushes

past him and out of the door. Egg looks at Anna, quizzically.

'Ask her,' she says, switching off her bedside light to
force Egg out of the room. She hears him close the door
as he leaves.

Anna is sitting at her desk, hard at work on a thrilling
TV-licence evasion case, when Francesca walks in.

'You know he's in court today?' Anna says, wanting to
be left alone.

'Aylmore. I know. I just wanted to say thanks for last
night. He came round after the case conference.'

'Oh, good. Panic over?'

'You could say that. He was amazing. It *was* just the
pre-nuptial. He just waded in then gave me this speech –
I can see why he's a barrister. We tore it up.'

'Fantastic.'

'I had no idea he was so committed. He just hated the
idea of it. I'm so glad you were there last night.'

'I really didn't do anything.'

'You did,' she insists.

The phone rings. 'Sorry,' Anna says, picking it up.
Francesca waves and retreats.

It's Milly on the line. 'Anna? I thought I'd better let
you know what I said to Egg.'

Anna sighs. She wants to join Warren in Australia. She is
desperate to escape everyone else's emotional battlefields.

'Are you there?' says Milly.

Anna lights a cigarette. 'Thrill me.'

'I'm sorry about this, but I had to come up with

269

something fast. I said I'd borrowed some clothes without asking, and it just flared up.'

Anna blows out a lungful of smoke, furious that she has been sucked in. 'Fine. And the articles in question? Just so I don't embarrass you under cross-examination.'

'Knickers,' Milly says, hesitantly.

'I see. So we're at daggers drawn over my last pair of smalls. Just so I know. I hope you never have to coach a witness.'

'It's the best I could do at short notice.'

'This from a woman who's been conducting an affair for how many weeks now?'

'You don't have to stick with it if you don't want to,' Milly barks. 'It's up to you.'

'Oh, please. The last thing I'd want is for you to be *embarrassed*.'

Milly's voice suddenly fills with aggression. 'I don't understand what you find so threatening about this. I'm doing what I want. Isn't that what you always do? When did you ever hold back?'

Anna slams the phone down – repulsed and shocked by the transformation of her best friend. Milly – mature, elegant, unflappable Milly – suddenly seems like a child. A selfish, ignorant child.

Chapter 32

Secrets and Wives

Anna isn't talking to Milly, which strikes Milly as utter hypocrisy. Initially, Egg finds it funny, and takes the piss out of Anna for getting uptight about her underwear, but as his jokes continue to fall flat, he becomes suspicious. Not suspicious of Milly – just curious as to what their argument was really about. It's obvious that they haven't told him the truth, but when Milly finally drops her original story about the subject of the argument, she simply refuses to come clean, insisting that it's about Anna, and it's personal.

Egg isn't convinced – and throughout the build-up to Miles's wedding, in the back of his mind Egg is dwelling on Milly and Anna's secret.

Under the influence of Anna's disapproval, Milly's feelings about her affair are slipping into confusion. Everything that felt daring and exciting now feels tinged with seediness. All the lies she has to tell Egg suddenly feel tacky and sordid. And a casual glimpse of O'Donnell's wife, turning up unannounced at the office, has torn away all her confidence in his feelings for her. Just the way he greeted his wife, with a kiss on the mouth, along with what looked like a casual happiness between them, suddenly made Milly feel like an irrelevance to his real emotional life. To his family life. What if he just thinks of her as a bit of fluff? A quick fling to relieve the boredom before returning to his wife.

In the two painful days since Anna learned of her affair, Milly's life gradually crumbles. Everything feels wrong, and she can't see a way out. She regrets what she has done, but she doesn't want to stop it continuing. She is stuck with her own inertia – passively allowing everything to descend into chaos around her.

All the tension is back in her body, and this time she can't pin it on Rachel. The only culprit now is herself – she has no one to blame and, with Anna's desertion, no allies. She is alone.

*   *   *

Miles, as is his new habit, appears sheepishly in the doorway of Anna's office. He smiles at her, clutching a sheet of paper in both hands.

'What?' she says.

He hands her the paper. 'It's a list of my solicitor contacts. I've been letting them know I'm going to be away for a few weeks.'

'It's called a honeymoon, Miles.'

'Right. Well, anyway, I've recommended that if any work comes up they should think about using you. They're blue chip, so you should get something.'

Anna stares at him, stunned. Delighted, but stunned. She can't even speak.

'Just don't fuck it up,' he says.

With that, she regains her faculty of speech. 'That's better. I didn't recognize you at first. Thank you.'

She smiles at him, genuinely touched by his generosity. He smiles back, and the conversation somehow grinds to a halt. Miles hovers over her desk, the pair of them grinning inanely at each other.

'I'd give them a call. Introduce yourself.'

'I will. Thanks.'

This is probably the first time in their entire relationship that Anna and Miles have ever run out of things to say.

After a little more gawping and awkward shuffling from Miles, he retreats, in silence, back to his office.

Five minutes later, he reappears.

'Anna?' he says. 'She's thirty-six. Did you know that?'

'Yeah, but only for a few days. I knew she'd tell you.'

'Is there anything else I should know?' he says, an edge of sarcasm in his voice.

'Like what?'

'I don't know. But if she hid that . . .'

'Does it make a difference, then?'

'No. Of course not. Why should it?'

'It shouldn't,' she says. 'She's been totally honest with you. I really admire that.'

Miles hovers, nods, smiles, and retreats again. Anna concludes that either Miles is suffering from advanced constipation, or he's got something on his mind that he can't bring himself to talk about. Judging by his general

diet of take-aways and lager, it could quite easily be constipation.

*   *   *

Her suspicions aroused by the presence of O'Donnell's
wife, and by his refusal to postpone a client meeting in
order to see her, Milly walks from work to O'Donnell's
flat. Seeing that the lights are on, she decides not to ring
the bell. Clearly, he isn't seeing a client. His car is parked
directly outside.

Then the lights snap off.

Milly watches intently as O'Donnell emerges, laughing,
from the building, with his wife next to him. They get in
the car, still smiling, and drive away.

*   *   *

Francesca invites Anna to her hen-night but, when the
evening arrives, Francesca rings to tell Anna that she's
stuck in Manchester, and that Anna should go ahead
without her.

She's just deciding what to do, when Miles clatters into
the living room, on the way to his stag-night. 'What's
wrong?' he says.

She explains the situation, and says that she's never met
any of Francesca's friends and suddenly doesn't feel like
going.

'Come with us, then,' Miles says.

'What?'

'To the pub. You can be an honorary bloke for the
night.'

She frowns, feeling insecure in her skimpy dress. 'Looking like this?'

'You look terrific. Please? It's my last night of freedom.'

She thinks, dragging on her cigarette, then stubs it out assertively. 'Fuck it. Why not?'

The stag-night starts well, with Anna downing a pint in one, and descends into a blur of crap jokes, noise and drinking games. Afterwards, Miles returns to his bedroom for the last time. It is now bare, containing only a bed, a few posters, and a collection of porn mags that Miles felt he ought to leave behind. Everything else has been carted over to Francesca's apartment.

He sits down heavily on the corner of his mattress just as Anna, on her way to bed, pops in to say good-night.

Seeing his slumped, defeated posture, she halts in the doorway and stares. 'You O K?' she whispers.

He takes a long time to answer. 'Don't go,' he says, eventually.

'I'm going to bed,' she replies.

He doesn't answer.

'Night, then.'

Miles looks up at her. 'Anna?' he pleads. 'Don't go.'

'What?'

'I don't want you to go. I want you to stay here. With me.'

Anna steps towards him tentatively, and crouches next to the bed. She stares into his eyes – looking for a pissed blur – but his eyes are clear. He is being sincere.

'I want what we had the other night,' he mumbles.

'No way,' she says, standing.

'No – not the sex. I'm not asking for that.'

'Then what?'

Anna crouches again, bringing her eyes level with his. Slowly, Miles meets her gaze.

'Do you love me?' he says.

'What?'

'Do you?'

'Miles –'

'I need to know. I can't do this without it.'

'Do what?'

'Call off the wedding.'

Anna's heart pounds. She can't speak or move.

'I'll do it,' he insists. 'Just say what you feel.'

Anna doesn't respond. Unable to take in what Miles is saying, her mind feels numb.

'Do you want me to go first?' he says.

Miles pauses, watching Anna, waiting for any kind of reaction, any clue to what she is thinking, before plunging in himself. 'I love you, Anna. I always have done and I always will.'

Anna stares at Miles. She doesn't want to believe what Miles has said. She takes a breath, and forces herself to ignore the urge to kiss him.

'Look,' she says, 'if you're getting cold feet –'

'It's got nothing to do with that.'

'– don't make me the excuse –'

'I'm not.' Miles places his hand on her arm. 'I need you to say it. "I love you."'

Miles's touch burns on Anna's skin. Her body is urging her to respond.

'And if I don't?' she says. 'What? You'll go ahead with it after all?'

'It's your choice.'

As these words sink in, Anna finds her resolve returning. This may be a gentler, more loving Miles, but it's the same person, with the same inability to take responsibility for his actions. Suddenly angry, Anna stands, breaking free of his touch.

'Whether you decide to get married is *not* my responsibility,' she says.

'I've told you what I feel. What I want.'

'What you want – yes, Miles – but it's what you *choose*. It's your decision. Don't try to make it mine.'

Before her will crumbles, Anna leaves the room. Closing the door behind her, she slumps against the wall, her legs trembling. As her head clears, a new certainty fills her mind. Miles is right. They love each other.

Chapter 33

Apocalypse Wow!

While everyone else was out at the stag-night, Milly sat at home, drinking her way through a bottle of vodka and quietly passing out on the sofa. She wakes the next day, having been put to bed by Egg, with a fizzing Alka-Seltzer by her bed, and a guerrilla war taking place behind her eyeballs.

She struggles to focus, and Egg's face appears out of the mist.

'Here you go,' he says, passing her the drink.

Milly isn't fully aware of the movements of her face, but something in her expression causes Egg to charge out of the room, shouting something about a bucket.

Milly wakes again and makes out a bucket on the floor next to her, an empty glass on her bedside table, and Anna standing at the foot of her bed.

'Look at you,' Anna sneers. 'It's pathetic. Don't tell me you're being wild and having a great time, because you're not. You're sad and lonely and fucked up and so is Egg. Sort it out. Decide one way or the other. Have some fucking self-respect and put us out of our misery, OK?'

Milly closes her eyes, and hears the door slam. She doesn't resent Anna's lecture, but it has come too late. She has already made a decision.

When Egg comes in to see how she is, Milly tries to tell him.

'It's finished now,' she says. 'This particular case. So it'll all calm down. Get back to how it was.'

'And that's why you got so pissed?'

'Yeah. Kind of celebration, really. All that stress. I just needed to . . . you know.'

Egg smiles at her, sympathetically – feeling slightly guilty that he has absolutely no idea what she has been working on.

'What was the case?'

'Oh, nothing special. Usual boring stuff.'

'You never talked to me about it,' he says, accusingly.

'There wasn't any point.'

Milly, desperate to apologize, feels a surge of warmth towards Egg – agonizingly tinged with shame at what she has done. 'I'm sorry. I've been really crap.'

Egg takes her hand. 'I'm not getting at you. I was just scared, that's all.'

Milly smiles.

'Fucking O'Donnell,' he says.

'What?'

'Well – working you like that. It's ridiculous. I mean, I know you want to impress him, but . . .'

Milly turns away, trying to hide the shock on her face. 'It was nothing to do with him,' she says.

'Just promise me you'll rest now?'

'Yes, I will.'

'I mean, really. Lie here, sleep, read a book, watch TV – anything but work. OK?'

'OK,' she says, pulling Egg into a tight hug. But she's lying. One final lie. She has to get to work. She has to speak to O'Donnell.

*   *   *

Anna avoids Miles at breakfast, and she avoids him at work. This isn't her problem, she keeps telling herself. It isn't her problem.

If he wants to break off his wedding he can break it off. If he really meant what he said, he'd break it off. It's up to him. Anna doesn't want to be responsible for breaking up someone else's marriage.

*   *   *

Milly marches straight into O'Donnell's office. 'Milly,' he says, smiling at her, 'I understood you were rather unwell.'

'I got better,' she barks.

He looks at her, confused. 'Is there something wrong?'

Milly stares at him, holding his discomfort for a few seconds, before answering in a sarcastically sweet tone. 'How was your meeting last night? With your client?'

'Um . . . fine. Thank you.'

'Good.'

'Milly – sit down.'

'You lied to me.'

'I'm sorry?'

'Are you? Well, I suppose that's something.'

O'Donnell, his face flushing, begins to lose his cool. 'What are you talking about?'

'I saw you. Last night. With your wife.'

'I see.' O'Donnell swallows. 'Spying?'

'I've done a lot worse, lately.'

O'Donnell, feeling intimidated by Milly's anger, looks through his blinds at the office outside and tries to compose himself. 'Could you at least sit down? People may be watching.'

Milly laughs, mirthlessly. 'Yes – keep up the public charade, shall we? For appearances' sake.'

Milly sits.

'Let's be clear about one thing,' O'Donnell says, quietly. 'I did have a meeting arranged, which I was forced to cancel. My wife insisted on staying down. She felt that there were things we needed to discuss.'

'Really?'

'Yes. Things are becoming rather awkward. She's . . . decided to attempt a reconciliation.'

'I'd say she's been pretty successful.'

'No. What you saw was –'

Milly cuts him off by standing up. 'Do we really have to do this?' she shouts. 'Is that all you think of me? Respect my intelligence, if nothing else.'

O'Donnell frowns, lifts his glasses, and rubs his face. 'You're right. I'm sorry,' he says, fumbling the glasses back on to his nose. 'Milly – I appreciate how you must feel, but . . . is it so bad? Things are at least more open now, surely? You have your relationship with Egg, which

I accept. I have mine with my wife, which you now know about.'

'You lied to me.'

'My emphasis may have been misleading.'

'Totally.'

'But that doesn't alter our situation.'

Milly, detecting a pleading tone in his voice, smiles falsely. 'You don't think?' she says.

'No. If anything, it's made it more honest. My feelings about you haven't changed. You know that, don't you?'

'So you're saying we should just carry on? Is that it?'

'Yes. Why not? There's no reason –'

'There's *every* reason.'

'Don't let your initial anger –'

'You used me.'

'No.'

'You don't give a damn about my feelings. All you're saying to me is that you're not tired of this yet. Well, I am.'

She turns, and leaves his office. Outside, she sees that Rachel's eyes are on her, staring curiously. Milly bows her head, hiding her face behind her hair, and walks with forced composure to her desk.

Milly stares at the papers spread out on her desk, unable to focus her mind. She stands, sending her chair spinning behind her, and heads for Anna's office.

Jo shows her in, and closes the door behind her. Anna and Milly look at each other, and Milly suddenly feels her insides collapse. She tries to say hello, but the second she opens her mouth, sobs emerge, quietly at first, then in a loud gush. Anna hesitates a moment, then reaches out and hugs Milly.

Without either of them speaking, Anna understands what has happened. The bitterness between them vanishes, and Anna finds herself almost joining Milly in tears. Milly may have created the situation, but that doesn't mean she hasn't suffered. Anna holds her tight, trying to compensate for her nastiness when Milly was in greatest need of help. Still, she doesn't regret it. The girl needed a kick up the arse.

Despite the enormous sense of relief surging through Milly's body, one lingering tension remains. It's only a suspicion, and she's not even sure where it comes from, but she can't help feeling that Rachel knows. Something in the way Rachel looked at her as she emerged from O'Donnell's office – not just with curiosity, but with a hint of understanding: as if something in her mind was slotting into place.

*   *   *

Egg decides to cook a final meal for the condemned man. Miles seems rather depressed to be leaving his house-mates behind, but Egg stops him becoming too maudlin by engaging him in a lively debate over whether or not he once stuck his knob in a trout. Miles insists that he was only pretending, and it was actually a haddock, but seems rather cheered up by the conversation. This choice of subject-matter doesn't have the same effect on Milly, however.

Noticing a strange vibe at the table between Anna and Miles, Milly insists on dragging Anna upstairs for a talk.

'Go on, then,' says Milly. 'What is it?'

Anna takes a deep breath, lights a cigarette, then answers. 'It's Miles.'

'I thought it might be.'

'Last night,' says Anna, exhaling a stream of smoke, 'when we got back from the pub . . . he said he'd call off the wedding.'

'You're joking?'

'No. He says he loves me, but it's up to me. All I've got to do is say I love him.'

'And do you?' asks Milly, stunned.

Anna looks at Milly, and her eyes fill with tears.

'Oh, Anna,' says Milly, crossing the room to cradle Anna's head as she cries.

Downstairs, the lads are engaged in an equally intimate conversation. Miles is trying to tell Egg about his doubts, and Egg is discoursing on the effect of doubt on his career path. The harder Miles tries, the more forcefully Egg insists on how impressed he is with Miles's lack of self-doubt. Miles eventually gives up.

*　　*　　*

It's the wedding day, and Miles still hasn't spoken to Anna since he declared his love for her. Bumping into her on the landing, a pang of regret and indecision hits him.

'You look fantastic,' he says.

'Thanks.'

They stare at each other – an awkward, emotionally intense silence filling the space between them.

'You look pretty good yourself,' Anna says, lamely, before walking away, silently willing Miles to call the whole thing off and run away with her.

By the time the Benjamin Street crowd arrive at the registry office, an array of Miles's family is already spread out on the front steps. Miles joins them, unwillingly, wanting to find a free moment to talk to Anna. When he eventually breaks free and goes over to her, he finds his mind blank. The instant he appears by her side, Milly retreats, leaving Anna and Miles alone together, but they just stare at each other, awkwardly.

'Well – this is it,' he says, eventually.

'Yeah. I think you'll be really happy together,' she says, forcing the words out.

'Wasn't quite the point, was it?' he replies, ambiguously. Then he looks at her, as if still waiting for her to do something that will make his decision for him.

Anna, seeing a car draw up behind him, points with her cigarette. 'She's here.'

Miles turns, and walks down the steps to the approaching limousine. Francesca gets out, dressed in a beautiful ivory-coloured wedding gown. She kisses Miles and, amid a swirl of people, they sweep into the civic hall. Anna, concentrating on composing her face into a smile, is unable to move as the crowd shuffles away from her.

Milly suddenly appears and grabs Anna's arm.

'I'm OK. Really. I'm OK,' Anna protests. They walk

up the steps together, but as they are about to enter the building, Anna stops dead. 'I can't,' she says.

'Well, I won't either, then,' Milly replies, squeezing her encouragingly.

Anna pulls her arm free of Milly's grip. 'No. You go.'

'I'll stay here with you,' Milly insists.

The crowd is now some way ahead, inside the building, and Egg is calling for Milly.

'Go on. I'll be O K,' Anna says.

'Are you sure?'

'Milly – just go. I'll wait outside, all right?'

Milly is dragged away by Egg. Anna turns and sits on the steps, lighting up. Thank Christ for nicotine.

She watches the traffic, her mind numbly absorbed in the world passing by on the street, suppressing the deep sense of regret exploding silently in her chest.

As the group emerges, Egg looks so ecstatic that you would think he was the bridegroom. He is the official wedding photographer, and he snaps away at Miles, Francesca and the assembled families, before suddenly abandoning his duties and bounding over to Milly.

'Hey! Why don't we do it next?' he says.

She looks at him askance, only half grasping his meaning. 'What?'

'Get married.'

Milly stares at Egg, aghast.

'I'm serious,' he says, grinning.

'Egg?' Miles calls. 'Come on. Friends of the bride and groom.'

Egg ignores him. 'I want to marry you, Milly,' he says.

Milly puts a hand on Egg's shoulder, and leans forward to whisper in his ear. 'Yes,' she says. 'The answer's yes.'

'Yeeeeeaaaaahhhhh!' Egg replies, romantically.

Miles's wedding reception, as you would expect, is the genuine article. Open bar and a sit-down meal for more than two hundred people. And, through Anna's eyes, everyone there seems to be in a couple. Egg and Milly, Jo and Kira, even Ferdy and Lenny. Anna, as she drinks, finds herself having a Jane Austen moment – worrying that she's on the shelf. A few more drinks, however, and it passes swiftly enough. So what if she's on the shelf – she can put herself on special offer.

Milly is ecstatic – walking round the room, telling everyone her news. Egg, meanwhile, paces up and down in the corridor outside the hall, stressing about his best-man speech. And while Miles's dad pins Hooperman to the wall, boring him back towards alcoholism with a series of golfing anecdotes, Ferdy and Lenny shag in the Gents.

Rachel sidles up to Milly, who instantly realizes that she can't ever remember being so happy, because even simpering slimeball Colleague From Hell can't puncture her mood.

Rachel smiles; Milly smirks.

'Great outfit,' says Rachel. 'Where d'you get it?'

'I can't remember.'

'It's good.'

Milly nods, doing her best to help the conversation towards a standstill.

'I suppose you'll be needing someone else, now? For the house, I mean.'

Milly almost bursts out laughing. Rachel's *still* after a room in Benjamin Street. Buoyed up by a surge of self-confidence, Milly decides to be honest. Telling Rachel what she really thinks will be the perfect way to signify that she has left Milly Liar behind her, and has entered a new, untainted era in her life.

'Rachel,' she says, 'why don't we stop pretending and admit the truth?'

'Sorry?'

'We don't like each other.'

'Yes we do.'

'No,' Milly insists, 'we don't. We never have. I mean, I'm sure you're a really nice person, but I'm sorry – there's something about you that I just can't stand.'

'What?'

'So let's not talk about the house. I don't get on with you. Why on earth would I want you to move in? I wouldn't. And you won't. Sorry.'

Rachel stares at Milly, stunned. 'I don't want to move in.'

'Well that's all right, then,' says Milly, smiling sweetly, before turning on her heel and swanning away.

Rachel watches her go, blinking with shock. A blush rises to her cheeks, and a frown descends: one thin vertical crease between her eyebrows on the otherwise smooth skin of her forehead. She scans the room, looking for something – or someone – and walks off, purposefully.

Egg is sitting on a bench in the lobby, working on his speech, when Rachel appears and sits down next to him.

'Hi. What are you doing?' she says.

'Working on my speech. Are they sitting down for dinner yet?'

'About five minutes. Milly sent me to try and find you.'

'Right.'

Egg, feeling slightly uncomfortable, turns back to his notes for the speech, and shuffles through his prompt cards.

'How does she seem to you? Milly?' says Rachel. 'All right?'

'Yeah, great. Why?'

'She's been really odd at work lately.'

Suddenly, Rachel has Egg's attention. 'Odd? How d'you mean, odd?'

'I don't know. Odd. Touchy.'

'She's been under a lot of pressure,' insists Egg, defensively.

'I know. She's never out of that office.' Rachel gives him a deep, concerned stare. 'But she's been all right, yeah?'

'Well – she fell out with Anna over something. D'you know what that was about?'

'No. I'm sorry – I shouldn't have mentioned it. I'm just worried about her, that's all. I mean, yesterday she had this huge row with O'Donnell.'

'What about?'

'I don't know, but something's happened between them. They're usually as close as anything.'

Egg's face darkens. 'How d'you mean? Close.'

'Well, you know. Working late together, meetings . . . you feel like you're intruding half the time.'

Egg puts his cards down beside him. 'What are you getting at?' he says, aggressively. 'If you've got something to say, then say it. Don't piss about.'

'Sorry?'

'Working late together – so what? It happens all the time. There's nothing wrong with that.'

Rachel, rising to his aggression, barks back. 'It's pretty common, you know. Your boss asks you to work late – you do – you get on really well, so he makes a pass.'

'She wouldn't do that.'

'I'm not saying she responded. Jesus! I'm saying maybe he tried it on – not that they've had an affair. What's the matter with you? I'm just trying to look out for her, Egg. That's all. Maybe you should start doing the same.'

Rachel, looking offended, stands and walks away, leaving Egg brooding.

Anna, on her way to the loo, sees Egg sitting alone, staring ominously into space. He catches her eye, and instantly rushes towards her.

'Anna!'

'There you are!' says Anna. 'Milly's looking for you.'

'She's been sleeping with O'Donnell, hasn't she? That's why you two fell out.'

A second's hesitation flickers across Anna's face before she can answer. 'No,' she says. But Egg, by now, has had his suspicions confirmed. He knows the truth.

Egg is at top table, with Miles and Francesca's families, and he eats his meal in silence, not talking to anyone or catching anyone's eye – not even looking at Milly, who is sitting at a table just out of earshot. The blur around him breaks only when Miles taps him on the arm, and tells him to make a start on his speech.

Egg stands, coughs, and taps his glass with a knife.

'Ladies and gentlemen. Could I have your attention, please? Thank you.'

He looks around the room, and seeing everyone's eyes on him, realizes that he's going to have to make it up as he goes along.

'As the best man,' he says, 'I've been called upon to say a few words and . . . I had a speech . . . it's right here, but . . . I don't think it's . . . really what I want to say.'

He stops, and looks directly at Milly. Anxiety is etched on her face.

He takes a breath, and continues. 'I want to wish Miles and Francesca all the best. They've got something that's . . . well . . . more than most. There's no lies . . . no pretence . . .'

He looks at Milly, and seeing the guilt on her face, he feels himself cracking. Fighting tears, he presses on.

'I realize now why people cry at weddings. It's because days like this make them wish for all the things they once hoped for themselves. And in Miles and Francesca, we see what true love really is. Two great people, a great future. I wish them all the happiness in the world.'

He raises his glass in a toast, and feels the other guests responding uncertainly, thrown by his strange, short speech. Egg sits down, and as Miles stands to introduce another speaker, Egg decides that he can't contain his anger and misery any longer. He rushes to the exit at the back of the hall. Milly stands and follows, catching up with him in the foyer.

'Egg!'

He turns to her – his face red with fury and pain. 'You fucked him, didn't you? Didn't you?'

Milly bows her head and recoils, frightened by his rage – a pitch of anger she has never seen from him before.

'If you sleep with someone else when you're going out with me, it's over!' he shouts. 'I told you that.'

'Egg –'

She reaches out to touch him, but he yanks his arm away, and runs off.

While Anna and Milly search the building for him, Egg sits in the Gents, sobbing deeply, unaware of the dribble of semen on the wall of his cubicle.

Anna, finding Milly at the exit to the building, touches her sympathetically on the arm. 'I can't find him,' she says. 'D'you think he's gone?'

Milly doesn't respond to Anna's question. Her fear and hurt suddenly seem to have transformed themselves into something else. Pure anger. She turns to Anna, her eyes blazing. 'It was Rachel, wasn't it? She told him.'

'I don't know.'

'I do.'

Milly turns back into the building and stamps up the stairs to the hall, where dance music is now playing. Anna follows.

Milly scans the dance floor, and instantly picks out Rachel. As she marches towards her quarry, Rachel sees her and flinches. 'It wasn't me,' she says, backing off.

Milly piles in, punching Rachel in the face, and following up with a thick scratch on the neck. Rachel instantly fights back, pulling Milly's hair, and plunging a nail into her cheek.

As various guests join the fracas, trying to pull them apart, Rachel's dress tears, but not before she has taken a fistful of Milly's hair. Milly screams and spits at Rachel.

In the doorway, a tanned, ill-shaven man in a Hawaiian shirt appears. He smiles, admiring the cat-fight taking place in front of him. Plucking a full glass from a nearby tray, he raises it, and toasts the brawlers.

'Outstanding,' he says, his Welsh accent ever so slightly tinged with a faint Australian twang.

A SELECTION OF BOOKS
FROM BBC/PENGUIN

Absolutely Fabulous   Jennifer Saunders

Wicked and funny, *Absolutely Fabulous* is the hit television comedy series that blows the lid off the fashion industry. The cast includes PR mogul Edina, slave to every media-induced fad from designer diets to flotation tanks; her alcoholic and sponging best friend Patsy, addicted to everything that's harmful (and probably illegal); and Saffron, Edina's long-suffering, sensible daughter who struggles to stay sane in the midst of the chaos which erupts around her.

A brilliant send-up of all the trends and neuroses that afflict life in the nineties, *Absolutely Fabulous* contains all the episodes from the first series including some scenes and dialogue not eventually transmitted. Written by Jennifer Saunders in her uniquely acerbic style, this book of scripts demonstrates just how fabulous *Absolutely Fabulous* really is!

Absolutely Fabulous 2   Jennifer Saunders

Edina and Patsy, television's most outrageous duo, offer a riotous second helping of the award-winning *Absolutely Fabulous*.

Blazing their way through the world of fashion PR, all their adventures from the second series can be found in this explosive collection of scripts, including the photo-shoot in Marrakesh where Saffy is exchanged for a small amount of dirhams, and disturbing revelations about Patsy in *Hello!* magazine.

A SELECTION OF BOOKS FROM BBC/PENGUIN

EastEnders: A Celebration   Colin Brake

The full, inside story of the BBC's most popular programme.

No television serial has ever offered viewers as much drama, excitement and gritty realism as *EastEnders*. From its first episode over ten years ago it gripped the nation, and it has kept us enthralled with some of the most compelling storylines and controversial issues – from kidnapping to teenage pregnancies – yet seen on prime-time television. This is the real story – including the tenth anniversary and beyond – of Britain's favourite soap, and it gives the low-down on the who, what, where and when of more than a decade of *EastEnders*.

Casualty: The Inside Story   Hilary Kingsley

Casualty is the BBC's most successful, most gripping medical drama serial ever.

A compelling mixture of soap opera and documentary, it is both hard-hitting and human. Powerful enough to annoy politicians and upset health workers, the inside story of Holby City Hospital's Accident and Emergency Department is always controversial and attracts praise and criticism in almost equal measure. Now you can peek behind the screen and find out all the *Casualty* low-down. Award-winning journalist Hilary Kingsley talks to the creators, the advisers, the cast and crew, gives a resumé of the story, and tells how the make-up and special effects are created and what to expect from the next series. Discover for yourself the true life behind the scenes in *Casualty*.

A SELECTION OF BOOKS FROM BBC/PENGUIN

Island Race John McCarthy and Sandi Toksvig

As a hostage in Beirut, John McCarthy had a dream of sailing on the bow of a classic yacht: to him it was a powerful vision of freedom. In *Island Race* he teams up with his old friend, comedian Sandi Toksvig, to fulfil the dream by sailing around the coast of Britain. In the beautiful *Hirta*, an eighty-year-old wooden cutter, they call in at nearly fifty ports and harbours, and encounter an enormous range of communities – from Buddhist monks on Holy Island in the north to the busy seaside resorts of England's south coast. In this warm-hearted book, by turns thoughtful and hilarious, the gutsy duo make a great many entertaining discoveries and offer two sometimes conflicting but complementary views of Britain from the sea.

The Making of Pride and Prejudice Sue Birtwistle and Susie Conklin

Filmed on location in Wiltshire and Derbyshire, *Pride and Prejudice*, with its lavish sets and distinguished cast, was watched and enjoyed by millions. Chronicling eighteen months of work – from the original concept to the first broadcast – *The Making of Pride and Prejudice* brings vividly to life the challenges and triumphs involved in every stage of production of this sumptuous television series.

Follow a typical day's filming, including the wholesale transformation of Lacock village into the minutely detailed setting of Jane Austen's Meryton. Discover how an actor approaches the character, how costumes and wigs are designed, and how the roles of casting directors, researchers, and even experts in period cookery and gardening, contribute to the series. Including many full-colour photographs, interviews and lavish illustrations, *The Making of Pride and Prejudice* is a fascinating insight into all aspects of a major television enterprise.

A SELECTION OF BOOKS FROM BBC/PENGUIN

The Complete BBC Diet Dr Barry Lynch

If you enjoy food and dread the thought of dieting, think again. Now you can lose weight without the misery of hunger with *The Complete BBC Diet*. By reducing fat and sugar and increasing fibre you can transform your diet – and your figure – and keep weight off for good. Medically approved, easy to follow and tremendously successful, this book has helped hundreds of thousands of people become fitter and slimmer.

Body in Action Sarah Key
The Complete Self-Help Programme for Stiff Joints

Many people suffer from joint pain or stiffness at some time in their lives, whether it is tennis elbow or chronic arthritis. Much discomfort is preventable, however, and some conditions reversible, if we know how. This remarkable book demonstrates how to keep the back and limbs supple, what to do for particular joint problems, how to spot warning signs, which exercises to do to maintain suppleness and improve flexibility, and provides a general programme of preventative exercise.

With clearly illustrated instructions, *Body in Action* is a professional approach to improving your health and to looking and feeling younger every day.